Love in Cripple Creek

CRIPPLE CREEK SERIES, BOOK 4

SARA TURNQUIST

MOUNTAIN
SUMMIT PRESS

If you would like to stay up-to-date on this and other series from Sara and receive a free ebook, sign up for her newsletter:

https://saraturnquist.com/list

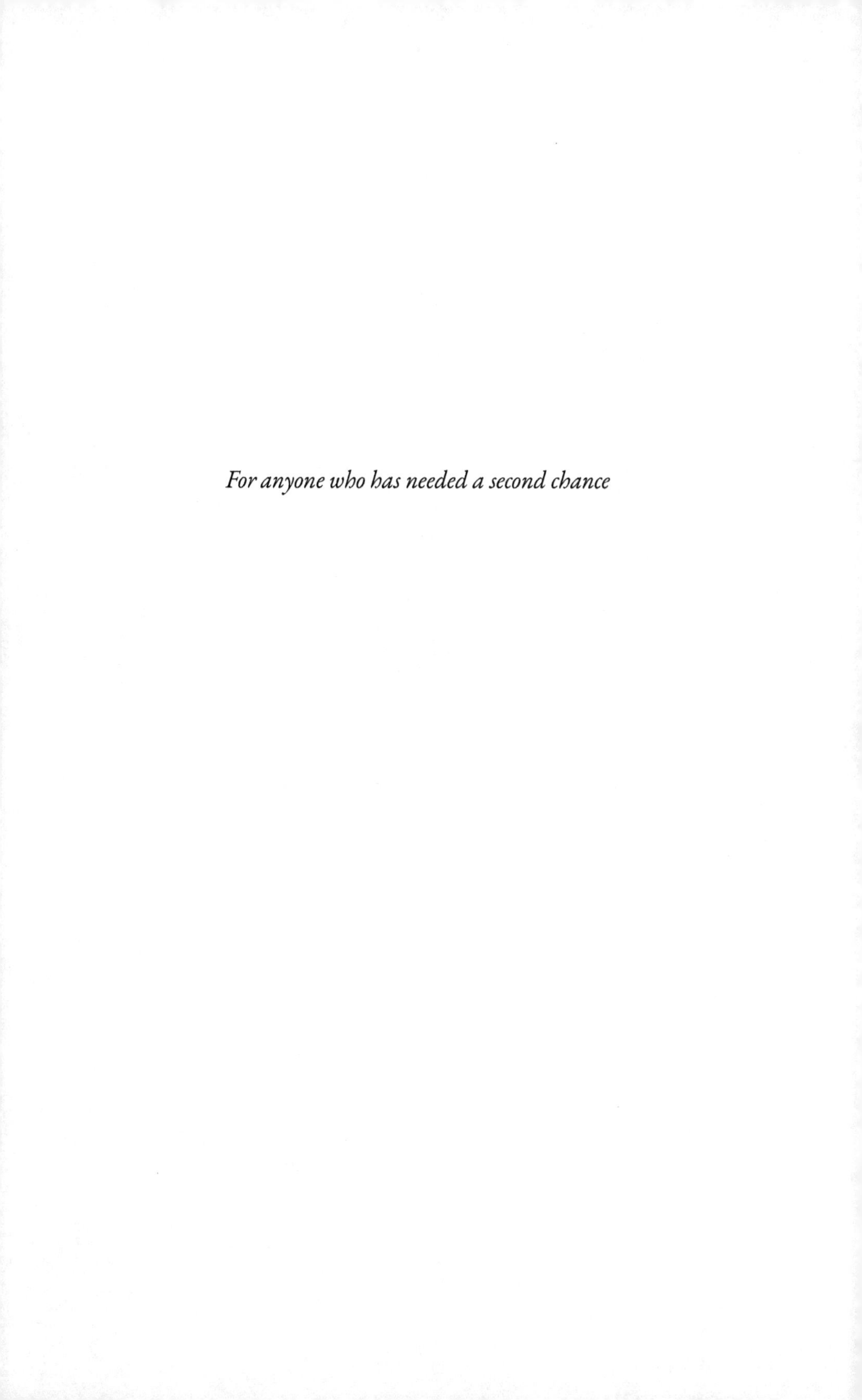

For anyone who has needed a second chance

First of all...

Betsy Callaway had never been so humiliated in her entire life. She was quite certain this was so. What could she do but duck and run? So, she held her breath, kept her head down, and bolted for the nearest exit. Had he seen her?

She was mortified. As much as anyone could be. After all, she was Betsy Callaway, the darling of Cripple Creek. And now, nothing more than a governess. How far she had fallen. From having every hope in the world for a fine match, to...hired help. It was too much.

As she rushed for the door that would bring her some form of escape, she heard a voice call out. "Miss Callaway?"

She could just die.

But she turned toward the telegrapher.

"You left your ticket."

She glanced around then slinked toward the counter. There were so many eyes on her. Too many. Didn't these people have anything better to do? Dare she glance in his direction and see if he had noticed?

If he had, he gave no indication. Nick Hammond was talking adamantly with another man. She prayed his attention on the conversation would hold. As the son of Cripple Creek's banker, a man who had grown up with much privilege, he could not know how she struggled.

"Miss Callaway," the telegrapher called out even louder. He seemed irritated. Well, so was she.

She hurried the remaining distance to the window and grabbed for her ticket.

The telegrapher all but rolled his eyes. Who cared if he was bothered? She certainly didn't. All she cared about was not being spotted by...

She spun and smacked into a wall. Or what she hoped was a wall. But as she glanced up, she renewed her prayers for death to come swiftly. For the young Mr. Hammond stood, broad and tall...and he was looking down at her.

Maybe he wouldn't recognize her. *If only.*

"Betsy?" There was a twinge of amusement in his voice.

"Why, I didn't see you there, Nick." She stepped back and pulled out her fan, attempting to wave away the red that likely rose in her face. Maybe he would think it due to the heat.

"That much is clear." He grinned.

She could just smack that smug smile off his face. Longed to. But that wouldn't relieve her from this predicament.

"What brings you to Colorado Springs?" His eyes danced, proving that his carefree attitude from childhood had not changed. As schoolmates, she had continually been frustrated by his tendency to make everything and anything a farce for his own amusement.

Unfortunately, some of their classmates had enjoyed his wit. The lack of a larger group to laugh with him was her only saving grace.

"I am..." She fanned herself faster, her gaze darting about. But no one paid them any mind. Then she returned her focus to him. "It's not really any of your concern." Her words took a sharper turn than she'd meant.

Nick jerked back as if her tone bit at him.

Just as well. It wasn't as if she wanted to renew their childhood acquaintance. She had not seen him in Cripple Creek for near on five years. So, there was little point in ingratiating herself to him now.

"I only wondered," he muttered.

"What was that?" She firmed her expression, determined to not let anything give.

"I only wanted to express how good it is to see you." His smile—a grin that had always been a little too charming—spread across his features. "You are looking good...I mean, well. You are looking well."

She frowned and stuck her nose in the air. "I did not invite you to look."

His grin fell. Quickly. "Same old Betsy." He sidestepped and started for the door.

"And what is that supposed to mean?" She should let him go. And be thankful he did so without a further word. But she couldn't help herself. Why give him the satisfaction?

He spun, appearing just as surprised at her words as she. He scanned the small office. Was he looking for reinforcements? More friends to join him in laughing at her? At length, he shrugged. "You always did have a way with words."

Her fan halted and her look became a glare. There was no way she would let him know how his words pinched at her. It wasn't as if he looked any better off. In fact, his dusty trousers and wrinkled plaid shirt told a different story than the suits his father wore. Perhaps he, too, had fallen from grace.

Her lips parted, but she stopped her comment before it was uttered. They were not the same. They had nothing in common except some rather unfortunate schoolyard memories. That was all.

"If you'll excuse me, I have a stage to catch." With that, she grabbed for her skirts, whirled away from him, and stomped outside.

A rush of wind and dust assaulted her senses. She cringed, wishing she was anywhere but here. But she refused to let Nick Hammond tell her what was and what should be. His judgment stung, but she wouldn't have it. Not today. Not with what she faced.

Another woman, perhaps the same age as Betsy, bedraggled and slumped, made her way to the platform, a small girl at her heel. The child's blonde ringlets and pink bows reminded Betsy of herself at that age.

"Mama, when will the stage be here?"

"Soon, dear," came the woman's tired response. Indeed, everything about her looked haggard. Perhaps that just came with mothering. She'd seen many a mother who seemed thusly fatigued.

Not that Betsy's mother ever had a hair out of place. From the look of this woman, she had hastily pulled her hair up. And even now, pieces fell from her pins here and there. The woman had clearly spent more time on the child's appearance. Was this a glimpse at what Betsy would be like in a few months? The two children she had been hired to mind and teach were young. Their mother had described them as being 'full of life.' Betsy was no dunce. She knew that meant 'difficult.' But she hadn't many other options.

She'd become an old maid. Done for, before her time had come.

The small child bounced on the balls of her feet as if she could spot the stage better that way. Her gaze caught on Betsy, and she smiled widely. How innocent. How naïve.

Her mother glanced about as well. Only she appeared to be concerned about something.

"Excuse me, miss." The woman's warm, worn voice called to Betsy.

These two would likely be on the stage with her. Dare she ignore the woman and face an even more uncomfortable ride to Denver?

"Yes?" Betsy tried to put a kindness she didn't feel into her words.

"Do you know...has the stage come?"

"Not yet. But it's due any minute."

The woman nodded and thanked Betsy.

"I'm Diana," the small girl announced.

Who was she talking to? Betsy chanced a glance and found a pair of dark blue eyes staring up at her. Could she just ignore the child? Maybe if she didn't look at her more than necessary...

"What's your name?" The girl was unfazed.

"Leave the nice lady alone," her mother admonished.

Betsy nodded at the young mother, relieved she wouldn't have to play nice. That thought struck her. How was she to manage two 'lively' children if she couldn't even answer this girl's simple question? She fought back the sting of moisture in her eyes. This was not how she had planned her life. It was not what she wanted.

But none of that mattered. It was what she faced just the same.

Movement at the door drew her attention. But it was only Nick Hammond and the other man exiting the establishment.

She jerked away, but not before Nick tipped his hat in her direction with another too-wide grin. Again, would it be terribly rude to smack it from his face?

Then a thought hit her...was he on this stage too? She shut her eyes and decided the Lord could not be so cruel... But He had been—landing her in a situation she loathed and then topped it with this uncomfortable interaction.

But Nick and his companion moved off farther into town.

Maybe God had heard her. Maybe.

But she doubted it. Why would He start now?

Rumbling in the air told that something large approached. Sure enough, the stagecoach rounded the strip of buildings on the edge of town and barreled toward the small group.

Destiny had come for her in a dust-covered and mud-marred coach. A far cry from Cinderella's grand carriage. And this one would not bear her to a prince, but to a family in Denver. She sighed as she looked at Nick's retreating form. At least it would take her far from that ogre.

And that, she was truly grateful for.

Nick Hammond checked his wares at the mercantile counter. His and Elias's journey would not last much longer, but they would need some provisions. Just in case. Anything could happen on the trail.

A quick glance at what Elias had gathered had Nick shaking his head. While Nick's pile consisted of jerky and a few other foodstuffs, the man-child had mostly candy. What good would that do?

Nick opened his mouth to encourage the younger man to think more of his purchases but stopped himself. He wasn't Elias's father...or even his overseer. There was really only one way the pup would learn. Besides, Nick had plenty of sustenance for the two of them during this stint of their journey.

The General Store owner tallied their wares and gave each their total.

Nick pulled out a few coins and set them on the counter.

"Who was that lady you spoke with?"

Nick jerked toward his companion. "What?"

"That pretty blonde. Who was she?"

"Just someone I knew. Not very well."

"That's not how it seemed. Wish I had a beautiful blonde that I didn't know all that well."

Nick wanted to shove Elias or do something to make him shut his trap. But he simply gathered his few things and moved out of the store. Maybe that would communicate he didn't wish to speak of it any further.

All in all, he had not been prepared to see anyone from Cripple Creek, much less Betsy Callaway. The girl had always put on airs and had always been a bit much in that regard. She always walked around like she owned the place. Her and her perfect blonde hair and magnetic laugh. He stopped that train of thought.

How was she not married by now? He fully anticipated that, with the way she'd always thrown herself at Wyatt Sullivan—even during their school years—she would have been able to convince him to get to the altar by now.

Such was apparently not the case. What, in fact, was she doing in Colorado Springs? And about to board a coach for Denver? Did she have business there? Or a beau? Not that it was any of his concern. The woman was barely tolerable at best.

He shifted, noticing that Elias still watched him.

"What?" Why would he give Nick such a look? The younger man fairly stared him down. Was Nick's distraction so obvious? It was merely due to the surprise of the interaction from the past, not about Betsy. True, she was a pretty picture. But sometimes those were the riskiest.

"Ready?" Elias smiled far too broadly.

Nick tipped his hat brim downward before mounting his horse. "You bet."

Soon enough, the two men urged their horses out of Colorado Springs. Nick could not help a glance back at the stagecoach.

Betsy slipped within, making a show of how carefully she did so. Did she not want to soil her dress? That was for naught. With the amount of dirt those wheels would kick up, she wasted her time.

That made him grin. Perhaps a little too much.

Then he turned his attention forward and pressed his horse into a trot.

Elias did the same and they set Colorado Springs, and Betsy Callaway in their past.

The younger man had never been much for conversation on the trail. In the end, it was a blessing as the speed of the horses eliminated any possibility of exchange. But that gave him time to think, time to mull. Too much time.

Nick hadn't considered Cripple Creek, the town he had left behind, for many years. Not that he never thought of his family there, but he could not allow himself to dwell on it. Did his father know he wrote home? Did Pa care? Probably not. His father had likely never given Nick another thought but to regret his son's choices.

Choices that Nick had to make. For himself.

He couldn't follow in his father's footsteps. It would have been too stifling. Nick would have suffocated if he'd tried. Leave that to Karl—the perfect son, the son that Pa always wanted, the son that Nick couldn't be.

His heart ached at that truth. But he couldn't deny who he was. He needed to work with his hands. A life of numbers and people was just not for him. Why couldn't Pa understand that? And more, why couldn't Pa let him be who he was born to be? Not try to force him into a mold he could never fit?

This line of thinking was nonsense. Not only had he puzzled on it far too long this day, he had a history of doing so. It just wasn't what God intended for him. And it had been a long road getting to this place where God's plan was enough—more than enough—to bring Nick joy and worth.

Suddenly, Elias dropped back. Was something amiss?

Nick slowed his horse and turned. "You all right?"

Elias had brought his horse to a halt and swung one leg over to dismount. "Not sure."

Nick eased his mare around to backtrack a few paces to where Elias examined his animal. When the man lifted one of the back hooves, he frowned.

"Threw a shoe." Elias grimaced. "That's going to cause a delay."

Nick nodded and pointed to the east. "There's a small town a half mile that way. Think we can make it?" Looking in that direction, Nick examined the terrain. It wasn't as rough as it might be. That may be their saving grace.

Elias shrugged. "Guess we'll have to see." He walked to the side of the horse, patting the animal to offer what comfort he could. Stroking the mare's neck, he made soothing noises.

"You sure?" Nick frowned. It would be quite the trip for a horse missing a shoe.

"We can give it a try." Elias grabbed for the reins and started walking the horse. It would take longer that way, but it was not worth injuring the animal more by riding.

The horse jerked a bit at Elias's urging, shifting back and forth, definitely favoring the un-shod hoof.

Sheriff Brandt wouldn't be happy about the delay, but it couldn't be helped. And the man wasn't terribly unreasonable.

Nick nodded and urged his horse into a slow walk. How long would this half mile journey take? It would be drudgery for certain. But necessary.

All things considered, today was definitely not going well.

CHAPTER 2

Disaster

If Betsy had thought things were bad before, she had been sorely mistaken. For the bumping of the stagecoach, the dirt and mud being slung within, the smells of the horses...all made for a less than comfortable trip.

And Betsy could do no more than look out the window as the mountainous scenery passed. How long until they would arrive? Who would the family have sent to collect her? And how was she going to withstand the looks of derision and pity from the townsfolk in Denver?

That may be the hardest part of all this. So lofty her goals in life had been, so little had she accomplished.

She just knew she was meant to be the wife of someone of import. Someone who would take care of her...

At least that's what her mother had always preached. There had never been a second Betsy thought otherwise...until now.

Sensing eyes on her, she shifted her focus to find Diana staring. Rather boldly. Did her mother not keep her more reined in?

Where did the mother-daughter pair travel from? Was Denver their destination? Or somewhere beyond? Did they intend to meet a husband and father at the station? Or would they be received by relatives taking them in?

There was no way to know. And no reason she should care.

Still, she offered the nosey child a slight smile.

The girl returned it, her lips spreading across her face.

Please don't let her see this as a chance to chat.

"What's your name?" The child's innocence was not an excuse for such intrusion. Still, something in Betsy found it endearing. A small something.

The mother's gaze fell on her daughter and, while she did set a hand to the girl's clutched fingers, she did not attempt to dissuade her.

So permissive.

But Betsy couldn't find it in herself to be rude. "Miss Betsy Callaway." Why had she given her full name? She wasn't certain. Perhaps in hopes to distance herself from those wide blue eyes that seemed to look through her.

Diana nodded. "I'm going on an adventure."

Betsy looked again to the mother, hoping that a sharp glare would cause the woman to distract her child. No such luck.

The woman sniffed and looked out the window.

And Betsy knew. They were not meeting a husband and father. Because he did not exist. From their apparel, it seemed that they had been well cared for, but the man doing the providing was no more.

Betsy cleared her throat. "What kind of adventure?"

Diana's eyes gleamed. "We are going to Denver to see my grandmother and grandfather."

"How nice." Betsy opened her mouth again, intending to ask for how long. But as the mother swiped at her eyes, Betsy backed away from her comment. For there was likely no answer to come. Because they didn't know.

"Dear God in heaven," the mother gasped.

That was a bit over-dramatic.

The woman reached an arm around the girl and pulled her close. "Lord, save us!"

Betsy looked out the window on the far side and saw what had disturbed the woman so—three men on horseback neared, their horses pounding the ground with a fury, and their weapons raised.

She was not so daft as to not realize their purpose.

Her gaze flitted to the girl and mother. Would the coachman be able to resist the bandits? Would he be able to protect them in some way?

"Mama, you're squeezing me too tight," Diana squealed as she squirmed.

The woman's widened eyes fell on Betsy. What did she expect Betsy to do? She would be no match for three bandits with weapons...if she even cared to help these two.

Betsy was helpless but to watch as the bandits closed in, surrounding the coach, and hemming them in.

The stage bounced to the side. And Betsy, not normally given to prayer, petitioned God to spare her...well, them. And she continued praying until the coach stuttered to a halt.

They were doomed.

Betsy tore her gaze from the window and settled it on the mother and daughter. The girl continued trying to squirm free, while her mother's face paled and her breaths came in gasps.

This was unthinkable...and more, that Betsy would be stuck with these two vulnerable souls. What was she supposed to do? How could she keep them safe? Not that it should be her concern.

She glanced out the window again and saw that two of thieves had dismounted. How much longer until they forced the women from the stage? What might they do when they found three defenseless females within?

If she ever got out of this, Betsy was determined she would only travel if a man came along. This would not do.

Even if she wanted to try, there was nothing she could do to stop the meanest looking of the ruffians from stepping near the coach.

One remained on horseback, his gun drawn on the driver. Only then did Betsy realize that no one had ridden shotgun on this drive. No one sat by the driver with measures to guard the lockbox.

Who had made such an egregious oversight? She would certainly find that person and make sure they paid for it.

Diana's mother pressed the two as far into the back of the seat and into the corner farthest from the door as possible. As if that would save them.

"Mama," the girl squealed.

"Hush," came her mother's harsh voice. No doubt the woman was scared thoughtless. Her fingers fairly claw-shaped as she grappled for something solid. Not that anything in the coach would suit.

One of the bandits on foot moved closer to the driver's bench, and the sound of a skirmish ensued. A loud thud and flash of fabric beyond the window told that the driver had been unseated and forced to the ground.

The other bandit drew closer to the coach. Soon enough, the door jerked open.

Betsy drew back and shrieked.

"Well, what have we here?" The dark-haired, filthy man let out a laugh. He reached in and grabbed Betsy's arm, hauling her out.

Betsy clamped her jaw, allowing her outrage to soak through to her bones. That would give her strength.

He poked his gun into the small space.

Diana and her mother's soft cries were discernible.

"How dare you," Betsy seethed.

"Excuse me?" The man whirled toward her.

She wanted to shrink back, but her anger wouldn't allow it. "How dare you threaten two defenseless women and an innocent child!"

The man looked her up and down, a leer upon his face. "Is that all?"

Betsy jerked her chin up. "I demand that you leave us be and go about your way."

The man's nearly black, greasy hair shook as he laughed. "You demand it?"

She kept her jaw firmly in place. "Leave us be. Take whatever you want, but you will not harass us."

He stepped closer.

Betsy wanted to move away, but she forced herself to plant her feet.

Now he loomed over her. "And just who do you think you are?"

She swallowed. "It doesn't matter. At least not as much as it matters what you aren't."

His eyebrows rose. "And what is that?"

"A decent man. A man capable of taking care of himself. A man with a conscience."

His eyes bore into her.

She worried that his stare would pierce a hole clean through her.

He grabbed her arm. "See here," he said with a growl. "No two-bit hussy is going to tell me what's what."

"Leave her be, Claude," the man on horseback called. "Get their valuables so we can get out of here."

The man named Claude grimaced but pulled back. "Where's your coin purse?" His hot breath nearly made her gag.

She turned away, unable to stand the stench.

"I'm guessing the purse is full of your pa's money."

She narrowed her glare. It irked that he would insinuate she lived off her father. And hated even more that it was true.

"You know I'm going to take it. One way," he pressed out as his eyes wandered her person again, "Or another."

She held his gaze as she jerked off the small pouch and threw it in the opposite direction as the coach. "If you want it, go get it."

His teeth clenched and his grip on her arm tightened.

She refused to show how it hurt, letting a smile tip her lips instead.

Claude spun her and threw her to the ground beside the purse.

She bit her lip to keep from crying out.

Then Claude came around, gun at the ready and pointed straight at her head. "Get it."

She wanted to fight him further. But she was beaten, and she knew it. Reaching for the soft bag that carried far more coin than the man deserved, she grabbed for it.

A boot came down on her wrist. "Don't even think about trying something cute."

She couldn't stifle the whimper that came as he put more pressure on her hand. Thwarted, she could do nothing but pray for relief.

He bent down and plucked the bag from her fingers. Only then did he remove his foot.

Betsy let out a gasp and, rolling to her side, cradled her injured limb close to her chest. All the fight left her. She was only somewhat aware as Claude and the other bandit on foot pulled Diana and her mother out, took their meager purse amid tears, and pulled down the few trunks that had been settled atop the stage.

In the next moments, Betsy watched as the men rifled through their things, throwing them about. Her few possessions now shared the same dirt stains as her current dress.

When the men had satisfied themselves that they'd taken all of value, they approached the women again.

The stage driver was still being held at gunpoint by the bandit that remained atop his horse.

"It's been nice doing business with you, ladies," Claude said, tipping his hat in their direction. "Such a shame that—"

Gunfire split the air.

The two bandits on foot jerked around to see two riders bearing down on them at the fastest gallop she'd ever seen. It was like something out of a novel—fearless lawmen riding to the aid of a fair maiden.

The horses hitched to the stage began shifting. Would they take off? The driver turned and grabbed the bit of the closest animal.

As grand as it all seemed, it was for naught. Claude and the other bandit on foot lifted themselves into their saddles and fired a couple of shots in the direction of the would-be rescuers. They rode off at a pace too fast for those coming upon the scene to possibly overtake them.

What did it matter? Her wrist throbbed, and her hand ached sharply. Maybe broken. And she had lost everything of value. Including her pride.

Nick rushed toward the men that had clearly intercepted the stage. And though his blood boiled at the thought of the criminals getting away, he knew a lost cause when he saw one. There was no real chance he and Elias might reach them. Not even if they pushed their horses as hard as possible.

He would have liked to have gotten closer before giving their position away, but Elias's trigger-happy finger had not allowed it.

As he indicated to Elias that they should head toward the stage and its passengers, Elias frowned.

Did the young man wish to pursue the bandits even considering it was moot?

Nick did not suffer the youth's defiance but shifted his mare's direction.

If Elias wanted to continue, let him.

Now focused on the area surrounding the stage, Nick attempted to take in what he could about the state of things. And frowned. Though there was movement about the space, one dress-clad body lay in the dirt. Had the ruffians taken a life?

A rush of emotion—equal parts fear and anger—spread through his body. No matter how many times he'd encountered a dead body, it never eased his ability to withstand it.

Soon enough, he neared the small group and dropped from his horse.

He first made eye contact with the driver, who nodded. The man was certainly grateful.

But Nick had already moved on to the passengers.

A woman and child, perhaps a mother and daughter, clung to one another near the stagecoach's door. He would deal with them in a moment.

Striding quickly to the fallen woman, he knelt.

She lay on her side, but her eyes were closed and there was no sign of movement. Until he leaned over her. Then she came to life.

She screamed and, sitting up, pressed her legs into the ground, as if attempting to push away from him.

He held up a hand to soothe her, but her screeching continued.

"What in the world did you do?" Elias's voice cut through the sharp noise. He circled the area on his horse.

Nick glared at him.

The younger man's chest heaved as if he'd spent himself in the vain pursuit. And the horse's coat glistened with sweat from the ill-fated chase.

The woman in the dirt looked to Elias and then back at Nick. Her widened eyes softened. And then narrowed. "A little late, aren't you?"

He balked. What did that mean?

She blinked at him as if curious about his lack of comprehension.

That's when he recognized the fair skin, soft jawline, pointed nose, and bright green eyes. Though dirt covered as he had never known her to be, it was Betsy Callaway. And she was spitting mad.

"I beg your pardon, miss," he managed to press out. "But we did not expect to come upon a stage hold up."

She grimaced and bit at her lip.

And then he saw how she held her right hand. Was she injured? Guilt for his harsh response slammed into him. It was his duty to keep calm and handle this situation—*any* situation—with understanding and care.

She worked herself into a seated position, still nestling her right hand close.

"Are you hurt?" He reached out, seeking only to examine the injured limb.

She jerked away, causing herself to lose her balance and fall over.

If he wasn't so concerned, he might have laughed at her antics. But, as a fact, he *was* worried. Very worried.

"Please..." He forced his tone to be gentle, though something about her reaction irritated him. Still, he had to remember that she was a victim, even as much as she did not wish to play one. That touched something in him. Perhaps her barbs were no different from a porcupine's quills...meant to protect her vulnerable state.

She stared him down, her chest rising and falling in a steady motion, but somewhat exaggerated. Was she so stubborn that she would not betray her fear? Not even to her rescuers?

"I need to see your arm." He felt Elias's regard. Whatever the man may think, Nick didn't care...he had a responsibility to Betsy. No matter how infuriating she could be.

Her eyes narrowed and her jaw clenched. She wasn't going to give one inch.

He shifted to look at Elias. "Check on the other passengers."

Betsy followed Elias's movements as he dismounted and walked to the coach.

"Betsy," Nick said as he exhaled, "I'm not going to hurt you."

The way she watched him gave him pause. Had they hurt her beyond whatever damage to her hand?

His patience had become stretched to its limits.

After some moments, she looked down and eased her arm forward, still supporting it with her left hand.

Not taking her surrender lightly, he leaned toward her and felt along her forearm and wrist.

She seethed.

"What hurts more—when I press or when I move it?"

She looked up at him, her green eyes a torrent of emotion, like the anger of tinted sea water. "All of it."

He frowned and then looked back to her hand, grazing her palm and fingers.

She hollered but quickly captured her lower lip with her teeth. Goodness, she was brave.

He let out a long breath. "Is this..." He kept his gaze glued to her hand, not able to look at her directly. "Is this the only injury?"

"It's quite enough, don't you think?" Her words bit at him.

He closed his eyes and tried to still his own rising ire. This was the reaction of a wounded animal. And he did not want to kick at the snake, so to speak. But he needed to know.

"I meant, did they..." How could he say it? "Did they take advantage of the...?" He couldn't put words to the horrid thought.

"Oh," Betsy said, then took in a breath sharply.

He peered at her, though his face remained pointed at the ground.

"No." The word was so quiet, he almost missed it.

But relief poured into him all the same. "Good."

He looked to where Elias chatted with the remaining passengers and the driver. And suddenly, he wanted to get Betsy far from this place.

"Do you think you can ride for a few miles in the stagecoach?" His heart thumped. For whatever reason, he quite nearly offered to have her ride with him. But if the hand or wrist were broken, that would be more jarring.

She breathed out a punctuated exhale. "Well, I suppose I have to do something, don't I?"

He grimaced at her tone but remembered it was just the barb of a quill. "Yes."

"I can." Her chin lifted in a defiant way. She was strong.

"May I...help you up?" He shifted to steady his feet.

She appeared to wrestle with the question that had an obvious answer. Then she relented and nodded. Just how stubborn could she be?

He gripped her upper arms and steadied her, lifting her as he stood, and bringing her with him.

That drew her closer to his chest. The shortened distance between them unnerved him in an odd way.

She pulled out of his grasp, though her stare lingered. Then she cleared her throat. "I will need to speak with the sheriff in Denver."

"Of course." He pressed a hand to her upper back and urged her toward the stage.

"Don't placate me. I mean it."

"I'm sure you do." He shot back. "But maybe you'll consent to seeing him while the doctor tends to you."

She inhaled as if preparing another shot at him. But jerked her head in a nod. "That would be most efficient."

But as she stepped in front of him, he caught a glimpse of her features scrunching. She was in pain. How much, she would never show. But it had to be excruciating.

He assisted her into the coach as much as she allowed and then Elias directed the mother and daughter to do the same. The driver as well hopped back onto his bench.

"We'll make sure you make it to Denver safely," he said, more to Betsy than to the others. For whatever reason, something in him wanted to reassure her.

"We are going all the way to Denver?" Betsy called out. "Surely you mean we will go to the closest town." There was a hint of fear in her words, though hard.

"That *is* the closest town, miss."

She leaned back into the coach's bench, a frown splitting her features.

There. Hopefully that would be the last of her digging comments until Denver.

Though as he turned away to mount, another came.

"You intend to just ride off now?" Betsy screeched.

"I will be with you every step of the way." He looked away quickly as his face heated. He had meant to say, 'We will be with the stage every step of the way.'

And as he whirled away and mounted, he knew that it was more than a slip of the tongue. He would stick with her until she was passed into another's capable care. Whatever that may mean for him. So be it.

Betsy strove to calm her racing heart. What was this? How could the man's concern move her so? No, she had simply been rattled by the holdup. There was nothing more to it. Though the image of him riding up to save her, upon his steed that may as well have been white, chasing away the men that intended harm...it was difficult to think on anything else. When she tried, her fear overcame her. What if Nick hadn't come? What if the bandits...? She couldn't let that line of thought continue. He *had* come. And he *had* saved her.

The whimpering of the mother and daughter across the coach brought her back to reality. A harsh reality. How could she stay in Denver? How could she resist the urge to go home? That was what she wanted. But no one there wanted her.

Hadn't her mother decided Betsy would take this position? Had not her father arranged it? She was bound by her word—and that of her parents—to attend the Clement children for as long as they desired.

She blew out a breath. Yes, she had resigned herself to this fate. She would not back down now.

Straightening her spine, she settled into herself that it would be so.

Then the pace of the horses changed.

Diana and her mother glanced out the window even as the woman continued to cling to her child. Such a sweet picture. It made Betsy's stomach turn just a bit. Had her mother ever doted on her like that? For certain, her father had. But Mother had always been no-nonsense.

The stage slowed to a stop as Diana pointed out a few of the buildings in the area.

Betsy kept her gaze within the coach. No need to face her fate too soon. She was grateful the vibrations and bumbling of the vehicle had stopped.

Diana wiggled free of her mother's loosening hold and reached for the door.

Her mother jerked her back. "We wait."

Betsy forced out another breath before the door was flung open from the outside.

"Ladies, we are in Denver." The stage driver spoke more gently than he had previously. "I think the sheriff and the doctor will want to see you."

Diana's mother nodded.

But Betsy wasn't so certain she needed to speak with the lawman anymore. Or that she wanted to. However, she still held a throbbing hand and wrist, made even more so by the constant bumping along. A visit with the physician was a must.

Soon enough, Nick appeared behind the driver, all but shoving the man aside. As he came to the forefront, his gaze found Betsy's. His blue eyes were vibrant, alive with concern. Why did he have to be so kind?

"Are you well?" His voice was little more than a verbal caress.

She felt the eyes of the other two in the coach.

Why did he have to be so tender?

She watched him, wanting to give in to her more vulnerable emotions, but held back. This would not do. There was no way she would open any part of herself up to hurt again. Anger was much easier to deal with.

"I am not. This confounded oversized box nearly rattled the sense out of me."

Diana shrank back. At Betsy's sharp tone? But there wasn't time to regret her words as Nick reached in, taking her good arm, and helping her out.

"Then, for heaven's sake, let's get you to the doctor."

She didn't have to be adept at reading him to catch the edge of sarcasm in his voice. And she didn't appreciate it in the least.

Resisting his warm touch, she pulled away. Or tried to.

His grip firmed and he leaned closer. "Don't do this. Not here."

She flung her arm up...no man would tell her what to do. No man. Pain tore through her wounded hand, but she was free of his hold. "Do *not* presume to—"

"Miss Callaway?" A masculine voice, not as deep as Nick's, called to her.

She whirled, grabbing her injured arm to herself. A man, his wife, and two small children stood on the platform. Were these the Clements? Had they all come to collect her?

They stared at her wide-eyed, and the man had a gruff look about himself.

"Mr. and Mrs. Clement?" She softened her voice, but the look in the eyes of the pair told her it was too late. They had witnessed her outburst. And they didn't approve.

The couple exchanged a look.

Mrs. Clement's mouth became a thin line and she reached for her children, who were clearly agitated, stirring and restless, by the whole thing.

"I..." Betsy wet her lips with her tongue. How to explain? But she must try.

Nick's hand was on her elbow again. Did he dare offer her support? She didn't need it.

Pulling away again, she shifted toward him. "Give me a moment."

He balked. Where were her manners?

She ground her teeth. "Please."

He nodded but said, "I will need to get you to the clinic soon."

She offered a nod but wasn't certain that she could.

When she turned back to the Clements, Mrs. Clement was tugging the children toward the far end of the platform. Only Mr. Clement remained.

His gaze moved to her injury and back to her. "Are you hurt?" Though his words were well enough, the dismissive undertone chafed.

"I...was...ah...wounded on the trip here. Our coach was held up."

He raised a hand. "That is truly tragic."

"Yes," she said, testing the waters.

He glanced in the direction his wife had gone. And then toward Nick, who spoke with the other man—Elias—not far away.

Betsy swallowed. How to unravel this mess? Best to face it head-on. "Is there a problem, Mr. Clement?"

He straightened his necktie. "I'm afraid there is."

Why was he so hesitant? Would he chastise her right here in public? This may not be a good match. Not that she ever expected it would be. But to be sent home, unacceptable yet again...she just couldn't.

"Mr. Clement," she said before clearing her throat, trying to put force to her words and erase all semblance of painful expression. "I came all this way...with, some delay. But I have come and am ready to take on your children."

He looked to the people moving by on the street. "I understand all of that, but I don't know that you will be a suitable fit for my family."

"What?" The word had slipped out...borne of her tortured wrist or of her frustration, she didn't know, but there it was. She swallowed and lowered her volume. "I mean, I am not dissuaded by this horrid event. I just need to visit the physician and the sheriff. Then I will be ready to—"

"Where shall we put your trunk, ma'am?" A porter rudely interrupted their conversation.

Two workers bore her trunk, damaged and no doubt lightened by the bandits' rough treatment.

The porter looked between Betsy and Mr. Clement. "Shall I load it in your wagon, sir?"

Mr. Clement shook his head. "Leave it at the stage office. Miss Callaway will be heading back to Cripple Creek."

A quizzical look came over the porter's face, but he obeyed and directed the workers to the office.

Betsy forced herself to meet Mr. Clement's eyes. "I don't understand. I may not appear my best, but I assure you, I am a fine—"

Mr. Clement held up a hand. "I am certain. But I will not have my children exposed to, much less raised by a simpering, hysterical woman."

"Simpering?" Betsy muttered. "Hysterical?"

The man jerked his jacket into place. "I will not explain myself further. We will, of course, pay for your passage back to Cripple Creek."

"But I—" Her voice rose.

The man cut her off. "It is but our apologies for this...misunderstanding."

She stammered for words, but none came. Her eyes stung, but she would *not* give in to tears. Not here, not now.

"Good day, Miss Callaway." Then Mr. Clement spun and walked off.

Betsy watched him go. And, as he passed Nick, the deputy's gaze followed him before turning back to Betsy, a question in his eyes.

She shifted so her back was to him. This could not be happening.

CHAPTER 3

Distressed

etsy blinked at Sheriff Brandt, whose kind words had steel under them.

She bit back. "What do you mean you won't chase them down? Do you understand what they took from me?"

Sheriff Brandt's eyebrows rose.

Too late, she realized the error of her words. "I mean...us?"

She saw Nick grimace off to the side.

Not that it bothered her. Why should she care if he labeled her a hysterical female? She was mad. And...she had every right to be. He had seen what she'd been through.

She seethed as the physician moved her arm. Biting at her lip to keep from screaming, she gripped the edge of the exam table with her good hand so she wouldn't slap him.

"You are upset." The sheriff spoke slowly as if he were explaining something to a child. It chafed. "That is understandable. How much money did you have in your reticule?"

Betsy closed her eyes against the pain of the doctor's movements and the grating of Sheriff Brandt's lack of concern. "Does it matter?" Then she leveled her gaze on the sheriff again. "Whether a small fortune or a poor sum, does it make a difference?"

Sheriff Brandt looked at Nick and shook his head. "Perhaps if there were more details of these bandits—"

"More details? I told you everything I know." She lost control of herself for a moment and let her words fly in a cutting manner. Then she took a slow breath and spoke, her tone much more calmed. "Are you blaming me?"

"Certainly not," Nick interjected, earning a steely glare from Sheriff Brandt.

"What we mean to say is that the bandits could have come from anywhere. And they could have gone anywhere."

She frowned as the doctor finished splinting her arm.

"Please understand, Miss Callaway, as of right now, there is little we have to go on. What more would you have us do?" The sheriff said it simply, as if that were enough.

Betsy widened her eyes and flared her nostrils as the doctor stepped back. "Your *job*. Is that too much to ask?"

Nick ducked his head. Did she also see his shoulders shake? Was this amusing to him? *The cad.*

"We have every intention of keeping the peace...to the extent we are able."

She could not tamp her anger any longer. "Tear this town apart! And all the towns around it. Everywhere. Until you find the dirty thieves."

Sheriff Brandt exchanged a look with the doctor before meeting Betsy's gaze again. And again, she wondered if he but attempted to appease her into silence.

The sheriff sighed. "I wish we could. Believe me, I do. But I don't have the resources to—"

She snorted.

Sheriff Brandt's gaze hardened. "Miss Callaway," he said with dwindling patience. He had nerve. "I have explained the situation to you with as much patience as I can. And we will do all that we *reasonably* can."

The doctor stepped away and Betsy laid the weight of her arm into the sling. And grunted at the sharp ache.

Sheriff Brandt waved for Nick to follow him, and he turned toward the door.

"So that's it?" Betsy called after them. They wouldn't get away that easily. She refused to be dismissed. "And what am I supposed to do?"

The sheriff halted and took another breath. "Go about your merry way. Surely you had business in Denver. Or family."

She dropped her eyes to her lap. "Not anymore."

The sheriff's tone became even more unsympathetic. "Then I will get you on the next stagecoach back to Cripple Creek."

She shot up then. "On my own? After what I've endured? How cold and heartless can you be?"

Sheriff Brandt exchanged a look with Nick yet again. "On the contrary, I am doing everything I can to help you. Deputy Hammond will make sure you have proper arrangements for the night and for the stage." Then the sheriff stepped to the door.

Betsy moved to cross her arms in front of her chest, but a sharp pain reminded her of her injury. Regardless, she straightened as much as possible. "I demand an escort."

"You...what?" Sheriff Brandt turned; the movement slow.

"You can't expect me to travel alone. Not only have I been ruthlessly attacked, I am injured. And...helpless." That last word was more difficult to get out. Why?

The lines of the sheriff's face softened. Did he think more of her choked-out word?

She opened her mouth with every intention of retracting that last statement.

But Sheriff Brandt interrupted her before she could speak. "I wish I could help you. I really do. But, as I said, my resources are limited."

"What if I were to accompany her?" Nick's statement cut through the tension.

What did he say? Did he think she needed him? Well, she *had* said as much. But she refused to be pitied.

The sheriff again spoke before she could. "I will not make you. And you would have to take a short leave, you understand."

Nick nodded and shuffled his feet. "I do. It's not a problem. I've been...meaning to make my way back to see my family."

Sheriff Brandt watched Nick. As did Betsy. Was he making an excuse? She would not have it.

"Will that suffice?" The sheriff whirled on Betsy, a hardness about his features.

They were supplying her with what she requested. Was she so stubborn that she would now turn down the escort? And the safety it afforded her?

She schooled her face to tighten. How else might she cover her relief and stay in control? "That will be satisfactory."

Nick's mouth tilted upward. So brazen. Did he think he had her in a corner? He would soon learn otherwise.

"You finished here, doctor?" Sheriff Brandt called to the back of the room.

"Yes, sir." Then the doctor focused on Betsy. "Be easy with your arm and stop in to see your local doctor when you get back home."

She jerked a nod out.

Sheriff Brandt turned to Nick. "Would you see Miss Callaway to her accommodations for the evening?"

"I am quite certain I can manage..." As she spoke, she remembered... she had no money. No matter how stiff she kept her back, that fact would not change. "That is, I appreciate the assistance."

Nick nodded at the sheriff, who threw one more glance at Betsy before exiting. That man had nerve.

Betsy dropped off the exam table, losing her footing for a moment. She had not accounted for how off balance the splinted arm would make her.

Nick reached out a hand to steady her.

As she regained her composure, she jerked away from his touch. Nearly upending herself again. "Do lead the way. I am quite tired."

Nick's mouth widened into a smile. What was that for? She wished again that she might wipe that smirk off his face.

"Certainly," he said, holding the door open for her. "Right this way."

She wanted to retort that there was no other obvious exit but held back. This would be a long evening.

Nick threw Betsy a sideways glance as they walked away from the clinic. But if she could sense his gaze, she pretended she did not, keeping her eyes trained on the walkway in front of them.

He cleared his throat. "Pardon me, Miss Callaway, but I wondered to where I might be escorting you?"

She paused, her eyes on something in the distance. And let out a long breath.

"Miss Callaway?"

"Drop the formalities, Nick. It isn't as if you haven't called me by my Christian name before." Then she peered at him.

She looked vulnerable for once. What had happened to her? What brought her so far from Cripple Creek? And what had she intended coming to Denver?

"My apologies. I only wanted to show respect."

Her gaze became hard, as if she merely tolerated him.

He glanced around then took her by the arm and gently steered her from the middle of the boardwalk and closer to the line of buildings.

She resisted at first but relented. Was he breaking through that iron exterior?

"Miss Cal—," he started, but stopped himself. "Betsy," he said, watching as she shifted uncomfortably under his scrutiny. "Where do you plan to lodge for the night?"

She closed her eyes. "I have none."

"What?" Had he misheard? How could she not have a plan?

She spun to face him. "I don't have any accommodations for the night." Then she looked to the boards under their feet as if shamed by her admission.

Dare he prod? But he couldn't stop himself. "You must have had plans. Even if you are just passing through. Are you en route to see family?"

"No." The word was edged with a tightness. "I...my plans fell through."

He couldn't make heads or tails of what she meant. But he couldn't move on from it either. "What were your plans?"

She jerked her arm from his grasp and balled her good hand into a fist. "They certainly didn't include an interrogation from the likes of you!"

He frowned. "I apologize. You've been through a lot. I shouldn't have pried."

Then he looked up and down the street. Where would he take her for the night? There was no chance he would let her wander the streets. And even less likely he could take her to his small shack of a house. It wouldn't be proper...nor would she consent to his modest home as a reasonable place to lay her head.

"Look, I don't want to put undue responsibility on you. I can work out my own stay."

Before he could stop her, she strode onward at a clipped pace.

He made short work of catching up and, with a gentle grip on her arm, halted her progress. "You can't be serious. I will figure something out. Perhaps Sheriff Brandt—"

"I will not be beholden to that man." Her eyes flashed.

He held up his hands in surrender. "All right."

Laying a hand on her shoulder, he steered her toward the boarding house. It wouldn't be as fine as the hotels, but it would suit her needs... and his wallet. Mrs. Scottsman was fond of him. Maybe he could make some sort of arrangement.

Betsy made a show of holding back but trudged forward alongside him all the same. "Where are you taking me?"

"There is a boarding house on this side of town. I trust the owner. She is an upstanding woman."

"Who will take pity on me?" Betsy's lower lip protruded. Was she pouting?

"No. Not at all. I can call in a favor. It's no trouble."

"I insist on paying you back when you return me to Cripple Creek." Her eyes narrowed. She meant it.

He would prefer they not have this conversation, but she would likely not let it die. So, he nodded. "Of course."

They walked in silence to the outskirts of the town's main stretch.

"How far away is this boarding house?" Her words had a forceful brokenness about them as if she gasped for breath.

He pounded the walkway with a long stride, completely unaware that her gait wasn't as lengthy...and she was injured to top it off. He slowed and shortened his steps. "It's just up ahead," he said, pointing to the white boarded house in the distance.

She sucked in a breath. Yes, the house was a bit more run down than he'd have liked. Mrs. Scottsman had her hands full cooking and cleaning for her tenants. And with her husband having passed, she had little help with the upkeep of the exterior.

"Trust me," Nick said, leaning closer. "She keeps a fine house. It just needs some work on the outside."

Betsy tsked but said nothing. Was she resigned to her situation—falling on the mercy of what help may come?

They slowed as they approached.

Nick moved onto the path leading to the front door, but Betsy held back.

He turned. "Come on, it will be all right. I promise."

She looked off toward the barren field to the right of the house. Now what was with her?

He took a step in her direction. "Are you well?"

She faced him then, the lines of her face betraying her emotions a little too well. Certainly, in light of how tightly she had held them in thus far. "I...owe you an explanation."

He took another step, now standing directly in front of her. "You don't."

She sniffled, looking up at him. "Yes, I do. You've been so kind and I..."

He waited, counting his breaths.

"I truly am grateful."

Little else could have shocked him more. This wasn't quite what he expected. Not from Betsy Callaway. "I understand that you—"

"I came to Denver for a job," she blurted. Then her hand flew to her lips, as if the words had escaped a carefully guarded vault. Her shoulders sagged, and her hand dropped to her side. "I was to be a governess."

His eyebrows rose, even as much as he tried to school his features to remain placid. A governess? He wanted to ask what had happened, but he could guess...she had decided she couldn't stoop so low. And, after her ordeal, she just wanted to run back home.

"They...saw what a mess I was and rescinded their offer." Her lower lip trembled.

No, not tears. He could handle a row with three men better than a woman's tears.

"And they..." She stared at her good hand, fidgeting with the edge of the sling. "Called me hysterical."

A tear made its way down the side of her face. She brushed it away.

He pulled out a handkerchief that was far from the fine lacy ones she likely carried. But it was all he could offer.

She sniffed and all indication in her face of her troubles was erased. Looking in his direction, she frowned at the proffered handkerchief and turned her nose up. And then stomped toward the front door.

CHAPTER 4

Dismissive

Betsy looked out the boarding house's small, dusty window. What was she to do...just wait here until Nick decided to retrieve her? That was ridiculous. She needed to get out of this horrid place and back home where she was treated in the way she deserved. At least by her parents. And with her father's money, no one in Cripple Creek dared look down at her. No one.

Her father had become one of the wealthiest and most revered men in the area. And he doted on her.

But her thoughts whispered to her. Why had her parents insisted she seek employment? Had they given up on her ability to catch a fine husband? Was she no longer, then, their precious princess?

She shook her head and lifted the cracked mug to her lips. The tea had grown cold. Rubbing offended lips together, she set the cup down. Was there no respite for her? Would nothing go her way?

"Miss?"

Betsy closed her eyes and pulled in a steadying breath before turning to Mrs. Scottsman. Could the woman read Betsy's irritation? If the thickness of her spectacles weren't telling enough of the woman's weak eyesight, then the drips of poorly poured tea about the table would be.

"Might I warm your tea?" The woman's kind voice wavered with age as she leaned toward Betsy, a teapot in her hands.

Betsy glanced at the pot and then at Mrs. Scottsman. Dare Betsy risk being likewise a victim of the woman's bad aim?

"No." Her voice was perhaps a little sharper than she'd intended. So, she added a quick, "Thank you."

The woman nodded and moved off toward the kitchen.

Any other tenants had already left on their sightseeing or errands. Only she remained to be visited upon by the ancient woman. Why would she keep accepting boarders in her condition? It was beyond reason.

But Betsy couldn't help the pang that shot through her. The woman had not the option to return to a beloved father and mother. This was her livelihood.

Turning her attention back outside, Betsy tried to force her thoughts somewhere else. Like what she would say to Nick Hammond when he decided to come. If he ever did.

The floorboards behind her creaked. Had Mrs. Scottsman forgotten something? Returned to attend to Betsy in some way?

"I am quite well, Mrs. Scottsman," she said slowly, trying to keep her voice even. "There is no need to hover."

No response.

Had her words come too sharply? Guilt flittered on the edge of her thoughts.

"I am quite certain no one intends to hover over you. And I am absolutely sure you have me mistaken." It was a masculine voice.

Betsy jerked around, nearly knocking the cup of chilled tea.

Nick stood in the doorway to the dining room. His eyes bored into her while his lips turned down. Was he cross with her?

Regret for her quick and harsh words filled her, but she would not give in to it. What reason did he have to scold *her* when she had spent half the day waiting on him?

She cleared her throat and threw her napkin on the table. "I'm relieved you decided to show up." Wishing she could suck the frustrated words back in, she made a show of smoothing the folds of her skirt.

"Decided to show up?"

Was that a question or an exclamation? It was difficult to discern. But she couldn't hold back the ire that rose as she stood. "Yes. I have sat by this window for who knows how long while you..." She let her words trail. Then she straightened her blouse. "Never mind. You have come, and I am eager to get out of here."

A dark cloud fell over Nick's expression. As if his irritation had given way to anger.

What did it matter? She cared not for his good opinion. "Shall we, then, depart before the second half of the day is spent?"

"Before the what?"

She straightened her shoulders. "Is your hearing somehow affected? You keep repeating my words."

Nick shook his head and his lips thinned. "Unbelievable."

"We'll, there is that." She pretended to not catch his true meaning. "A girl does what she can."

He scanned her top to bottom, but there was no lightening of his expression.

She was used to having a very different effect on men. Not exasperation.

No matter. Lifting her eyebrows, she pressed out. "Let's not tarry."

He jerked his head down, then turned and retreated.

Betsy let out a breath, releasing pent up air, and forced herself to follow the man who clearly found her tiresome.

As she stepped into the hall, however, she did not see him at the front door. Where had he gone?

Voices filtered into the hall from the direction of the kitchen.

"That is too kind. I cannot let you overpay for her stay." It was Mrs. Scottsman.

Then Nick's deeper voice resounded. "I won't have it. Miss Callaway engaged your hospitality. You should be paid."

The silence that followed was deafening.

Betsy's face heated. Yes, Nick had paid for her night's stay and apparently added on quite a sum for her incidentals. Being a source of his charity left a foul taste in her mouth and a twisted stomach. It wasn't right. Yet as she prepared to march into the kitchen and set him straight, she remembered...she had no money, nor anything with which to barter. *Curses!*

"You are a generous man, Nick Hammond. God bless you."

Though difficult to discern, Betsy imagined she heard a rustle of clothes as the older woman perhaps embraced Nick.

"Have a safe journey. And be mindful." The woman's words were sweet though serious.

What could Mrs. Scottsman mean by that? Did the older woman not trust Betsy to behave herself? Of all the...

Betsy straightened, forcing a pride she wasn't sure she felt.

Apparently, the woman would have rather Betsy not tangled Nick in her mess. And Betsy had to admit, she wished that too.

Boots clapped upon the wooden floorboards and Betsy barely had time to pull in her emotions before Nick stepped into the small hallway.

She prayed he hadn't seen her vulnerable moment. It would be better if Betsy kept the dangers of that in mind. Much advantage was given to those who witnessed her weaknesses. And she would not permit it. Not now, not ever again.

"Are you ready?" Nick's gaze sought hers.

She lifted her chin and sighed. "I have been ready."

He shrugged and then strolled toward the door. As he did so, he had to pass her in the narrow space. His shoulder grazed hers.

Heat filled her face once more. Was she so embarrassed? For certain, she didn't care enough to feel such. She had to shake free of this.

"Your trunks are already at the station." Nick opened the front door.

Betsy gripped her skirt in her good hand to keep herself from tripping on the hem as she stepped onto to the front porch. That was the last thing she needed—to fall and damage her other hand.

Almost as an afterthought, Betsy called, "Mrs. Scottsman, I thank you for the evening's rest. And the breakfast."

There was no answer.

Had the woman heard her? Or was she just so ready to be free of Betsy, whom she perceived as a manipulator?

Refusing to show Nick how that possibility pinched at her, she turned opposite and navigated the stairs.

The door closed behind her, and Nick's steps followed. The trip to Cripple Creek would be lengthy...and tiresome.

Nick couldn't understand it. Betsy was plenty capable of being pleasant. He had seen it.

Why, then, did she insist on being so intolerable?

He watched her from his seat in the stagecoach. But she did not look at him. Did she avoid him purposefully?

Nick sat beside an older, gray-haired woman who talked about the son she planned to visit. He listened and attempted to respond appropriately, but his mind churned with how it could be that Betsy Callaway's behavior had not matured one bit since they were younger.

Betsy, for her part, gazed out the window.

Though, the man beside her likely had something to offer she might find tempting. He was well-dressed with all the appearance of having money. And he seemed rather interested in her.

"My boy will be so glad to see me. We've exchanged letters, but it's been months since I laid eyes on him," the woman next to Nick continued.

The gentleman beside Betsy leaned toward her and spoke.

Nick couldn't hear whatever he said, but Betsy shifted and moved impossibly farther from him. And was now pressed against the window. Any closer and she might very well fall out.

Despite his mixed feelings toward Betsy, Nick bristled. The man's words may not have been audible from this distance, but the leering look that passed over Betsy made the man's intentions rather clear.

"You all right, Mr. Hammond? You don't seem well." The elderly woman beside him put a gentle hand on his arm.

But he remained focused on the pair on the bench across the coach.

The man scooted closer to Betsy and muttered something indiscernible.

"Has the lady not made herself clear?" Nick blurted. The rise of anger within his gut was unstoppable. His hands curled into fists and his body tightened, prepared to leap forward. What that man might hope to accomplish with his advances in such a small space was perplexing.

The man stared at Nick. Then sneered. "I will thank you to mind your own conversation. Let the young lady speak for herself."

Nick wanted to teach the man some manners.

But before he could, Betsy's voice cut through the space. "I would like to be left alone." Her eyes flashed as she moved her gaze between Nick and the man.

The man in the suit balked. "I only wished to extend a sort of kindness to you. After all, you are out here all alone."

Something about the way he said it came out as a threat.

The older woman's grip tensed more than Nick thought possible.

He ignored her unspoken warning, and pressed out, "She's not alone. I have been charged with escorting her."

As the man's eyes widened, then narrowed, the gray-haired woman spoke up. "Mr. Hammond, would you mind terribly if you trade places with Miss Callaway? I have a mind that she might enjoy chatting with another woman."

Though the simple woman's smile lit her features, there was no mistaking the wisdom behind those eyes. She saw. She knew. Perhaps far more keenly than he did.

Catching Betsy's gaze, he said, "I would be happy to."

Betsy reached out a hand that trembled. What, in fact, had the man said for her ears only? Her reaction raised the heat of Nick's indignant ire.

Nick gripped her shaking hand and made surprisingly short work of swapping places in the cramped space.

As Betsy sat beside the gentle woman, she visibly relaxed into the bench.

Nick settled back as well, crossing his arms, and letting his muscles flex a bit. If the man knew what was best, he would not speak to Betsy again. Ever.

CHAPTER 5

Frustration

The up-and-coming town of Black Forest was anything but inviting. That did not surprise Nick. Though it had become a good source of lumber to the region, he had found the people to be similarly closed off the last time he'd traveled through the area. The main dirt road into town had all but emptied and the heat of the day bore down. Once again, Nick thanked the Lord for the small shade offered by the telegrapher office's overhang. The dirt roads and rugged few buildings did not make one want to linger.

Nick averted his gaze and focused on Betsy who sat board straight, staring into the nothingness that surrounded them. They had waited in silence for the last hour. How much more could he take? A barren landscape and alarmingly quiet companion—not quite the stuff dreams were made of.

His mind turned back to the stagecoach ride. What exactly had happened en route? In the moment the man spoke to her, Betsy had held none of the pretense she usually carried. None of the quills. She had been afraid. Very much so.

The exchange had given rise to something in Nick. Something primal. Something protective.

And the whole encounter left him wondering if something was amiss in Betsy. Perhaps her response to the man had been nothing more than an over-reaction due to the hold-up she had lived through. All her airs and harshness may have been her first reaction, but everyone who went through what she had would have to deal with their fear and anxiety eventually. Didn't she?

Did he prefer this Betsy—quiet and somewhat subdued? Or the one with fire about her?

He leaned against the wall on the opposite side of the small porch from where Betsy sat. What did it matter? He got what he got from her. There was no need to linger in that moment...or dwell on thoughts of her. It just wouldn't do.

Motion to the right drew his attention. Betsy had dropped her regard to her lap. And a glisten of moisture became evident. That, he could not abide.

Pulled by her distress, he stepped toward her.

As he approached, she jerked away and looked up in his direction. Then released a long sigh. Had he startled her? What filled her thoughts such that his simple movement would surprise her?

"What do you want?" Her voice grated, coming out rough and harsh. More so than the foreboding of this town. Yet there was a hint of resigned sadness as well. And for some reason, he missed the bite her tone typically contained.

He crouched until he had lowered to her eye level. That was a mistake. Her green eyes drew him in even more. They were brilliantly pigmented and lush, just like the color of a meadow. As well, the shimmer of unshed tears pooling within offered a flash of vulnerability.

She blinked and he was pushed out.

He resisted the urge to shake free of the moment and remember why he had come to her.

"Are you all right?" He kept his voice low...perhaps unnecessarily so. There hadn't been another soul pass this way in the last thirty minutes at least.

Her eyebrows rose then came together as her eyes narrowed. "I am perfectly well, thank you."

Then came that bored rejection he'd always associated with her. As she turned away, a small smile tipped the corners of his mouth. But quickly fell.

She hid something from him. Perhaps from everyone.

He set a hand on the bench inches away from where she sat, more to balance his awkward positioning than anything else.

Her gaze shot to his hand and then to his features. "What?" There was that bite again.

"I just wanted to help you." The stirring of sympathy and concern within him surprised.

"Help me?" Her gaze bore into his as if issuing a challenge.

He looked to the open field beyond the stage office. "I only wanted to help you learn to protect yourself if anything..." Turning his regard back, his gaze collided with hers.

Sorrow and indignation were raw there.

She bit at her lip then fairly shoved out, "If what?"

He cleared his throat. "If you were ever to be the victim of another bandit."

Even as he said the words, he prayed it would never be so. And that this thing he feared to have been was not so. How could he not have sought more explanation? Not questioned her more deeply?

He had done her a disservice. Both he and the sheriff had not followed through. True, he had been certain no further trespass had occurred...as had Sheriff Brandt.

The sheriff had seemed eager to be done with her unpleasant insistence and dramatic overtones. But that did not excuse such a lack in procedure.

"What exactly are you saying?" Her tone was more subdued than before. As if she fought a wave of emotion even then.

He looked to the ground. His knees ached from retaining this crouched position for so long. While he preferred to give her space, he could not. So he eased onto the bench, feeling her glare the whole time.

When his gaze sought hers again, he found her glancing at the space between them. Almost as if she wasn't certain it should be so small.

"Please, Betsy." Her name was soft on his tongue. Why should that be? Perhaps it was nothing more than this brotherly protectiveness that had been stoked in him. That must be it.

Her gaze met his. "What?" The word was strangled as it emerged, broken and lacking firmness.

He swallowed against his growing concern for her. How dare it make him feel weaker? And that would not serve either of them. "I can show you ways to defend yourself."

She stared then. Did she weigh his words? Or consider how best to bring an end to this line of reasoning? Though after some moments, she nodded.

A warmth spread through his chest. What that involved, he wasn't sure. Nor did he wish to dissect it.

He stood and held out a hand to assist her to her feet.

She ignored his proffered hand and rose without assistance, pushing up with her uninjured arm. Goodness, she was determined. But that only brought a smile to his face again. Did he like her brazenness?

That thought was best left alone.

How was he to go about this training moment? His thoughts churned through his knowledge base and what she might be capable of with the sling and a smaller frame.

"Now then," he said as he took a step toward her.

She twitched as if wanting to move away, but she held her stance.

So he continued, "There are a few vulnerable places that would make anyone think twice about attacking."

Her brows cinched.

Was he jumping in too fast? He dismissed that; it would be best if he didn't think too much on it.

"But you must be quick." He firmed his footing. "A hard punch to the stomach may work. Stomping on a foot. But the best would be a kick to a...um...more sensitive area."

Her face colored, but she nodded.

"If the attacker is close enough to grab you, though, that might not be best. The reaction may be to grip you tighter even if pained. In the case that your assailant is within arm's reach, you may want to punch at the throat or poke an eye."

She cringed.

"Yes, I know it can be a bit difficult. But if your life or your...well-being...depends on it, I believe you can."

She nodded. It was only a slight movement.

"But let's say the attacker grabs you from behind." He circled around until she stood in front of him. There was still some distance between them, and he hesitated to pull her closer. But he refused to give her less than his best lesson. So he tugged her back a step, narrowing the space between them.

She let out a puff of air. Because she was startled again? Or because he'd overstepped his bounds?

He waited a moment, but there was no further resistance. "You could try an elbow to his midsection or stomping on a foot behind you." He turned her to face him once more, and the space between their bodies had closed more than he'd thought. His heart beat harder.

Focus! He must focus. For her sake.

And he commenced his teaching. "If you can, turn while your attacker is distracted and go for the throat or eyes."

The blank expression on her face gave him cause to worry. Did she not understand?

"Let's try that." He stepped back a couple of paces. "I will come at you."

He moved in her direction with his hands raised as if to grab her.

Her eyes widened and she dropped.

Halting mid-step, he crouched and set a hand to her shoulder. "I'm sorry. Was that too much?"

She pushed out a breath and shook her head. "I don't know what made me do that."

He helped her to her feet, careful not to tug at her wounded arm. How could he push her in this condition? "Maybe this is too much."

"No," she insisted. "I want to try again."

He watched her. She was quite serious. So, he sighed and firmed his expression. "Perhaps it would be best if we start from the other direction, then." He came around her and pulled her back to his chest as if he had grabbed her from behind.

The moment her body settled against his, he knew he had erred. His thoughts were not on the task, but on the sensations that coursed through him.

Ridiculous. He had to keep his mind on what they were trying to accomplish. That required focus.

"Try to..." His voice was surprisingly hoarse. "Try to fight me off."

She thrust her good elbow back, into his stomach.

He gasped and his hands flew to his midsection. Stepping backward, he bent over and attempted to catch his breath.

"Nick," she cried as she turned. "Did I hurt you?"

He held up a hand to keep her at a distance as he sucked air in and pushed it out steadily. "No. That was..." He grimaced. "...that was very good. Very...realistic."

She leaned down, resting her unencumbered hand on his shoulder. "Did you not intend for me to do that?"

He shook his head. "It's okay." Indeed, he had not expressed that she should not actually try to injure him. The fault lay with him.

As he was able, he stood up. "Don't worry." He settled his gaze on her...and found that she was within arm's length and looking up at him, a sense of regret about her features. Eyebrows were turned up in the center and her perfect lips were pushed out in a pouted frown.

"Truly, it is all right." He attempted to smile. It was difficult.

She dropped her hand.

He caught it in his. "I am not upset. It was my mistake. I should have been prepared." Why were his words so gentle? And why did her nearness affect him so?

She scanned his face and the harsher lines of her expression eased. Her beauty shone as she relaxed. She was more becoming than he remembered. More than what he had seen on this journey.

"Betsy..."

Her eyes lit from within, as if she welcomed him speaking her name so softly. She leaned toward him.

"Stagecoach should be here in the next ten minutes." The voice cut through the thickness of the moment between them.

Nick stepped back and looked over Betsy's shoulder at the telegrapher, who had come out of the small structure.

The man did not look favorably on them.

"Something wrong, Deputy Hammond?" The man's curt words judged Nick.

"Nothing at all." Nick tried to catch hold of his wayward emotions. "I but assisted the lady with something."

The telegrapher grunted and retreated to his office.

But when Nick turned once more to Betsy, he found that she had shifted away from him, her back to him and her posture as stiff as ever. Why must she be so guarded?

"Betsy?" He tried. "I didn't mean to trespass."

She shook her head, a jerking motion. Then she whirled toward him. "Do not worry. I am well."

Once again, her quills were out.

And something deep within him ached.

Betsy stared at the mountains in the distance. They were magnificent, glorious even. Though they reached into the heavens, they were grounded and solid upon the earth. What a mystery. What a struggle that must be. To reach among the clouds while being anchored. Did she know either in her life? For it seemed more than not that she wandered about, aimless and floating along...no place to connect to with any security.

Such nonsense. It was time to put all of this behind her and rejoin her parents. They would open their arms and embrace her. Her mother would be so pleased to have Betsy home, and her father would smile in that way he always did. There, that was her protection, her security.

Shifting her focus from the inspiring vistas to the interior of the stagecoach brought her back to earth. The sweat-stained benches certainly smelled as if they had seen better days. As well, the smell of the horses was pungent. But she was thankful the car only held her and Nick.

She glanced across the space to find Nick somewhat reclined with his head back and his breathing heavy. Had he fallen asleep? How was that possible with the way the wheels on the rough terrain juggled them about? Yet there he was...perfectly at rest.

Sighing, Betsy eased back into the well-worn bench...or tried to. It was lumpy and stiff. She would never be able to rest with any amount of success. In fact, she didn't want to. Yes, it was best if at least one of them stayed alert. What was Nick thinking? Wasn't he supposed to see her home safely? And yet there he was...sleeping on the job. Ridiculous.

What if they were attacked? Would he be easy to rouse? Protect her, indeed.

Her hand ached and she moved it as much as possible until the pain subsided a little. She'd had no peace from it the entirety of the trip. And this jostling did her no favors.

Fighting a rising trepidation within that she refused to put words to, she decided she found nothing redeeming about the stagecoach. So she turned her attention back to the window. Wide valleys and fields portended a freedom on the range. Freedom that she would never know. Her sole focus in life had been on making a good match. Until her parents decided she needed to find some form of employment. She prayed they had since seen the error of their ways. Her? Work? Preposterous.

Her gaze flitted to Nick once again. Could she possibly still make a fine match? Not with him, of course. He was a deputy. She needed something more...substantial to support her. But all hope was not lost. Even if things hadn't gone well with her pursuit of the doctor, there may be a chance for a happily ever after. One that would grant her a good lifestyle.

As she watched Nick in his respite, she thought on his kindnesses. She'd never admit it to him, but his care had moved her. He'd taken on the burden of paying for her stay at the boarding house, offered to escort her to Cripple Creek, and even tried to ensure she had some ability to defend herself. While she doubted she could ever poke someone's eye out or hit their throat, it was a good thought.

And there had been that moment when he'd pulled her against him, when her back had met his solid chest. It had caused her skin to prickle as if chilled even as it was warmed by his touch. There had been a somewhat pleasant sensation as his arms wrapped around her. Something with a force she hadn't experienced.

She shook her head. Nonsense. A match between them would never work.

Looking again out the window, a field of lilacs and lavender appeared. Just breathtaking. It almost seemed as if she might reach out and touch them, feel the soft petals, and the—

Ow!

She jerked her regard to her hand which now radiated a sharp pain... and a prick of blood. What had happened? Pulling it away from her travel dress as best she could, she scanned for what had offended. There, on the window frame...a portion had a rough edge to the wood. That was likely to blame.

Seething, she struggled to find a cloth to press against the wound.

A warm hand wrapped around her wrist and a handkerchief covered the cut.

She looked up to find her face just inches from Nick's. When had he awakened? What had stirred him? Surely not her quiet gasp.

"Hold this on your hand. Firmly." His instruction took her by surprise.

She started to nod, then something rose in her—a desperation for some distance. She frowned and ground out, "How am I to do that with this thing?" Then she tipped her head toward the splint.

He grimaced. "Of course." Shifting, he moved beside her on the bench and kept pressure on her hand.

A rush of heat filled her at his closeness. Ludicrous. She was not about to let Nick's nearness affect her.

"Let me see it," she insisted as she tried to tug her hand back to herself. Something...anything to create the needed space.

He held her hand with a firm grip. "Hold still." Then his eyes met hers.

The intensity of the blue made her want to shrink back. Only...that wasn't possible with his hold so tight.

She attempted to pull away again.

His brow lowered. "You're going to make it worse."

Biting at her lower lip, she stilled. She wanted to tear her gaze away from his. The lock of his eyes was too much. It stirred something in her chest. Something she hadn't felt a hint of since her ill-fated interactions with Dr. Wyatt Sullivan. The very memory of it crushed her. Yet, this was more...intense.

His gaze altered. No longer did it bore into her with irritation. Rather, his regard softened. Why? Did he feel bad for her? Wish to merely indulge her?

It was not to be borne.

As tears welled in her eyes, she found the strength to turn away. It didn't matter. Neither his presence nor what he might say.

But he said nothing, merely held her hand.

Even as the temptation to look at him again filled her, tears rolling down her cheeks stopped her. She wouldn't let him see.

"Are you in a lot of pain?" His words were gentle. So much so that her chest ached. Why was he being so kind?

She shook her head, not trusting her voice.

The pressure of his hand eased.

She jerked back toward him. "What—?"

Their gazes collided again, only he had managed to create a little more distance between them.

"I need to see how deep the cut is." Again, his tone was almost tender. Could he sense the war within her?

She nodded, a small, quick movement. And she forced herself to remain still as he slowly lifted the cloth.

The sting of air hitting her cut brought a hiss through clenched teeth.

He rubbed his thumb in circles on her wrist. Did he even know he did so? Did he sense how that affected her?

Tingles shot up her arm. She had to stop this. Now.

Shaking her head, she braced herself and said, "Is it bad?"

Her changed tone did not seem to affect him. He turned her hand this way and that as he did his exam. It was too much—the feel of his warm touch, but also the memory of Wyatt and similar assistance from him. Only that had felt completely chaste. Nothing like this. Still, she had lost much in her pursuit of the town doctor. And she may never reclaim all she'd lost in the eyes of the townsfolk.

Nick looked at her again with those dark blue eyes that seemed to see more than she wished him to. "I don't think it will require stitching."

She nodded, wishing herself more numbed to his ministrations.

"But I'd like to keep the handkerchief tied on it for good measure."

What could she do but assent with a jerked nod? The quicker it was done, the quicker he could return to his own bench.

True to his word, he tied the cloth to her hand. And paused.

What now?

She was tempted to pull her hand free, but his hands enclosed it. What was he doing?

Nick's gaze landed on her face once more. Then the blue darkened as if a storm settled on the sea. "Are you all right?"

She opened her mouth but found herself unable to respond. This would not do. Pulling her hand free of his now lighter grip, she tried to scoot away only to find she was already pressed to the side.

He still watched her. What was in his head? Had he seen the trails her tears made? Did he pity her?

She cleared her throat. "I am." Firming her jaw and lifting her chin, she wanted to create separation any way she could. "I only wished to see you return to your bench...and your *rest*." The last word was sliced out.

His expression fell. Her barb had hit its mark.

Although, it did not bring freedom, it brought guilt. That she jabbed at him with her words? Or that she hadn't done it sooner?

"Of course." He moved to the opposite bench and stretched out his legs as much as he could, folded his arms over his chest, and turned toward the window.

There was quiet then, save the creaking of the stagecoach wheels and the pound of hooves.

Only, now the silence stirred something else—regret.

CHAPTER 6

Returning

When the stagecoach pulled into Cripple Creek, Nick decided it was none too soon. Could he stand one more minute of this strained silence? He had become far too soft where Betsy was concerned. It was best they went their separate ways. He straightened his shoulders. Because of the fatigue of some muscles on the trip? Or because he wanted to pretend his resolve was firm? He wasn't certain.

He glanced at Betsy across the interior of the moving coach. How could a woman possess such beauty and yet be so hard-edged and pretentious? Her fair skin, silken blonde waves, and petite frame was certainly something that would draw a man. But the way her words would lash out...it didn't seem as if the two matched.

As she had been most of the trip, she stared out the window. Was she as eager to be rid of him as he was to put her in his past once more? He watched as her head tipped in his direction and her eyes met his.

He should turn away, but the sorrow in her affect pulled at him. Nonsense. Had she not expressed over and over in word and deed that she was perfectly fine without him? He'd best give her that very wish. There was little sense in him getting entangled further.

Her eyes widened. And he realized he stared.

Tearing his gaze from hers, he shifted to focus outside just as the stagecoach slowed. The driver directed the horses to turn and slow their rapid pace. Indeed, Nick saw that they drove through the outskirts of town.

His chest expanded. He would see his mother soon. There hadn't been time to wire her. Even as he considered the words, he recognized it for what it was—an excuse. He hadn't wanted her to know and tell Pa. Would Nick's father have forbidden Ma to let him stay?

This was best. Ma would welcome him, and his father would not have the opportunity to turn him away. Would Anya be home when he arrived? An image of his younger sister filled his mind and he grinned. She had a smile that could warm any heart.

But then, there was Karl. How would his brother react? Likely the same as Pa. Was Nick ready for that? The words that the two men would throw at him and the accusations? At least Betsy's barbs had only irritated. He wasn't certain he was ready for words that would wound.

The stagecoach slowed even further then came to a stop. He could not help but steal a glance at Betsy.

Her eyes were closed, and she drew in a long breath, as if she steadied herself. But for what? Her parents doted on her. Tirelessly. Everyone in Cripple Creek knew that.

And her father had the ability to do so. Mr. Callaway owned the largest hotel in the area. For the most part, anyone who wanted accommodations that were more than the boarding house went to the hotel. And there were many people who sought to patronize that establishment.

Yet something nagged at him about the way Betsy set a hand to her midsection as she blew out the breath.

Then her eyes were on him again. He had been caught staring once more.

Guilt spilled through him. But why, then, did he not tear his gaze away?

"What?" Betsy's words bit at him—harsh and demanding.

He shook his head and glanced out the window. "I suppose this is where we part ways."

Her eyebrows shot up. "You don't intend to escort me any longer?"

He furrowed his brow as confusion took hold. She expected him to get her home? Had he not brought her far enough?

A retort filled his throat, but he stopped it. That was only his tired, aching body speaking. He had a job, and he would do it. "Of course not."

"But you said—"

"It was my mistake." His response was sharper than he'd intended. Wasn't she due some of that after all she dished out? But he knew better. Her abrasive nature was a protection. His was borne of his own sinful flesh.

He cleared his throat. "Forgive me, I only considered that your parents might be at the stage office to collect you. And I did not want to intrude."

Her features smoothed as she watched him. Did she consider his words? At length, all she offered was a quick nod before shifting her focus.

The door flew open, the stage driver appearing on the other side. "Cripple Creek." His words came without ceremony. In fact, he seemed fed up with the entire ordeal.

That was neither Nick nor Betsy's problem though. Still, Nick offered him a small smile and a quick, "Thank you." Then Nick moved for the opened door.

And collided with Betsy.

She let out a grunt and fell back.

He jerked around. "Are you all right?"

She had landed on the bench a bit askew and struggled to sit up. A grimace took over her fine features. "What is the matter with you?"

It was awkward for him to stand half in and half out of the coach, but he didn't want to exit until he was certain she didn't need assistance. He reached back in toward her, his hand extended.

She jerked away, losing her balance, and toppling to the floor of the stage.

Having seen her irate, he prepared himself for the worst to come out.

Only it didn't.

She dropped her regard downward and her shoulders shook. Was she laughing? Or crying? Which was more likely?

"Is there a problem?" the stage driver muttered. "I got places to be."

Nick ignored the man and leaned in.

Betsy turned to the side, the back of her hand to her mouth, a tear trailing down her cheek.

Why did that pull at him? Was he so weak at the sight of a weeping woman? "Let me help you."

He pushed down his rising sympathy. And when he reached for her again, she did not pull away. Nor did she take his hand. Or look at him.

"Please, Betsy."

As her name fell from his lips, she lifted her eyes to his. Moving her gaze upward from his hand to his face, she seemed caught in a moment of indecision. Would her pride never take a break?

She sniffled. And after taking another breath, she slid her handkerchief-bandaged hand into his.

With careful movements, he assisted her out of the stage as he himself exited backward.

He offered her a smile once they were on solid ground.

"'Bout time," the stage driver shot out. Then he whirled. "Can I get some help with these bags?"

Nick would have helped, but all his awareness homed in on Betsy— the way she pushed her curls back from her face and tilted her chin up as if that might preserve her dignity caught him. And gave his heart reason to stutter. Yes, she was a beautiful woman. Always had been. That wasn't the problem. It was those barbs.

The more tender parts of his heart eased at her struggle to recapture her pride, and he realized he kept a firm hold on her hand. And that she did not pull free. Did she not notice?

They were nearly to the planked sidewalk.

The intensity of her gaze landed on him moments before she released him and pushed his hand away.

He opened his mouth as she strutted past him but closed it. This ordeal was almost over. Almost.

The bumping of the rugged wagon was quite unwelcome. Betsy had long since become sore with the many hours spent aboard the stage-coach. And now this. It would be a good while before she agreed to ride on any infernal wheeled contraption again.

She took a breath. All would be well. Soon enough, she would be home. Her mother and father would surely see that she wasn't cut out for being a governess. After all, how many people were released from their employment before it even started? Mother and Father wouldn't ask her to go back...they couldn't. *She* couldn't.

She released a rather guttural moan and grabbed for her splinted arm when the wagon hit a rut.

Nick's gaze was on her then. "You all right?" Concern etched his eyes. More than she liked. More than she'd permit.

"Must you hit every single bump in the road?" she seethed. But the tiniest bit of guilt skirted on the edge of her mind. Why should she care? She didn't.

He frowned. "That is not my intention." Then he let out a long sigh as he turned back to the path ahead. "We're almost there."

"Thank heavens," she pressed the statement out in a harsh way. Yet her heart dropped at the thought. Because of her parents and their possible reactions? Or because she would part ways with Nick?

Now that was complete and utter nonsense. She hadn't given him a second thought when they were children. And he hadn't earned one now either.

She scooted farther away. Well, as much as possible. And then looked to the side as she gripped the bench once more with her good hand, though still bandaged with the handkerchief.

Why was it necessary to be so sharp with him? He had taken care of her after the robbery, had paid for her accommodations, and then had taken off from his duties to escort her home.

Regret gave way to a tenderness, and she glanced in his direction.

He'd grown into a rather good looking man. Not the most hand-some man of her acquaintance. Still, his square jaw covered in stubble, his long straight nose, and blue eyes bespoke of a strength beyond the surface. Especially when his jawline clenched.

Then his eyes were on hers.

What? Had she let her gaze linger too long? What did that matter? He'd spent much of the stage ride either sleeping or staring at her.

Still, as his eyes gentled, she became self-conscious and looked away. Her heart pattered in her chest. She scolded herself for such a reaction. Hadn't she been in this predicament before—letting her feelings for a man drive her actions? And all for naught.

For all her trying, Wyatt remained married to Katherine. It just burned her up. And not because the townsfolk found her to be over-reaching where a married man was concerned. She contended then—and still did—that this particular marriage was a sham. Nothing more than an attempt to help those pitiful orphans.

Betsy bit at her lip. Though she still told herself this, it sounded less reasonable as Katherine and Wyatt added to their family and paraded about town, the very picture of love and loyalty.

It made her sick. If she were honest, that was partly due to her own actions.

But what did that have to do with her life now? With Nick?

Nothing.

This wasn't the same. Betsy and Wyatt had been a good match, since their school years. Nick had never been more than a bother and had never looked at her but to find a fault...or two.

The horses slowed.

Betsy turned, prepared to give Nick an earful, but she noticed that her parents' home was just beyond the field they'd moved into.

She gripped her hands, wringing them. Because she feared what her father would say? Or how her mother would react? Perhaps the latter. Betsy was Father's little princess. For always.

Mother was the one who'd pushed her out, who'd wanted her to make a good match. And then sent her to Denver for the governess posi-tion. So that was who she had to convince.

Working a trade was not for Betsy. She had never dirtied her hands, and she had no intention of doing so now.

She set her jaw and clenched her teeth, determined.

A warm hand set on hers as she gripped the seat.

She jerked her regard in that direction as Nick's fingers rubbed along hers.

Of all the—

What made him think he had the right? The gall of that man!

Still, she couldn't make herself pull away. She watched as his long fingers trailed along the back of her hand and then covered her fingers.

He had nerve.

His hand curved around hers and his fingers pried at hers.

What did he think he was doing? She fumed as she lifted her gaze, glaring at his profile.

His attention remained forward even as he worked to loosen her fingers.

She would *not* let him hold her hand. No matter what he had done for her. Though the rush of her pulse as her heartbeat thudded a bit harder did catch her off guard.

"You'll surely get a splinter." Nick finally looked at her. "Or at the very least scrape yourself."

She pulled her hand away from his.

His eyes widened as his now unoccupied hand felt for the reins. "Just trying to help."

"You could've just said something." She moved her hand as if trying to erase his touch. Why was she being so petty?

"I did." His words were gentle but held a weight to them.

It was her turn to be surprised.

"You were in your own little world."

Another bump in the road jerked her body and she reached for the bench again. But this time, when the cart's movements evened out, she released that grip.

Nick looked to the dirt-packed way again and tugged on the reins.

The horse responded immediately by altering its gait.

Betsy lifted her gaze. Her parents' homestead loomed. It was, as a fact, one of the finer houses in this area.

The wagon came to a stop in the next moment.

Nick set the brake and hopped down.

Betsy took the moment to steel herself against what awaited her.

The front door opened, and her mother stepped out. Her eyes were wide, and her mouth curved into a frown. This would not be pleasant.

There was one thing she might do to stave off her mother's ire.

Nick was on her side of the driver's bench now, arms up to assist her.

Betsy sucked in a breath and turned, putting her good hand on his shoulder. She let her gaze linger on him as he helped. She even batted her eyelashes and smiled.

As her feet touched the ground, she slid her hand down to his chest.

His surprised expression filled her vision.

"Why, thank you kindly." She did not disengage her hand but fingered his lapel.

"Are you all right?" His question had the sound of incredulity about it.

"I am...now." She leaned into him, tipping her face up to his.

His hands, which had been loosening from her waist now settled on her upper arms. "I'm not sure what's going on here."

"Sure you do, silly." She pursed her lips and gave him her most innocent look. As much as she wanted to sneak a peek at Mother, she dared not.

Nick's warm hands on her arms shot a thrill through her, giving her cause to wonder what it would be like to be held by him. Really held.

The lines of his face softened as did his eyes. His gaze flitted to her lips.

Suddenly, the air between them thickened and sparked. What had she invited? Would he kiss her? Did she want him to take such liberty?

Lifting on her tiptoes, she pressed a kiss to the side of his face. But as she pulled back found she couldn't bear to look at him. What if he scowled? What if he resented her action?

"Betsy?" Her mother's distinctive voice called across the space.

She whirled away from Nick and toward the porch. "Mother!"

Crunching in the dirt told that Nick shuffled his feet. Did he trail her? Or simply reel from their nearness? One thing was certain—his gaze bore into her back. It made her rather uncomfortable.

She shook her shoulders and then straightened them. That might give her the appearance of a bit more strength than she had.

"Betsy?" Mother repeated, though she didn't move closer. "What in the world are you doing here?"

Betsy pushed aside her trepidation and, reaching back, looped her uninjured arm through Nick's. "I've come home."

Mother's gaze moved between Nick and Betsy. "Home? What about your job in Denver?"

Betsy put on a frown that would communicate her indifference. "Never mind that." Tugging on Nick, she moved to the porch.

Mother squinted. "Is that...Michael Hammond's boy?"

Nick still seemed confused.

Betsy jerked her elbow into his side.

"Yes, ma'am," he pushed out.

"He was kind enough to escort me." Betsy looked up at him with what she hoped was an expression soaked in adoration. "Please do get my things for me." Her words dripped with sugar and were spoken loudly enough for Mother to hear.

Nick nodded and disentangled himself before moving to the back of the wagon.

Betsy stepped onto the porch. "It is good to be home."

Mother arched a brow and tightened her lips. "Is it?"

"Of course." Betsy pressed on her best smile before turning and calling back to Nick, "Bring my trunk into the house, please." She almost added an endearment such as 'darling,' but stopped herself. Why she wouldn't play this to the fullest was beyond her. After all, she had already started. This wasn't about Nick's feelings.

Now in front of Mother, Betsy wrapped her arms around the woman.

Mother's body stiffened. This was not going well.

Betsy worked to shift her mother's attention into the house. "Might we offer Mr. Hammond a glass of lemonade? It is fearful hot outside."

She strolled into the great room, not looking behind herself to see what Mother did.

"I suppose." Mother's response was tight.

How was she to work this out? And what part would Nick play in this? With her mother in the kitchen area, Betsy gulped and sucked in a breath. What kind of mess had she created?

CHAPTER 7

Stuck

What was going on with Betsy? He wasn't ignorant...nor was he blind. She attempted to cozy up to him. What he didn't understand was why. Did she always feel the need to pull an unassuming fly into her web?

Beyond that, what of her mother? The woman was clearly not pleased to see her daughter. That perhaps surprised more. Betsy had given him every indication that she would be a welcomed sight to her parents. He was still a little unclear about why she had left in the first place. For an opportunity in Denver? One that she shirked as soon as she arrived? It couldn't be more obvious that she had her preferences. And Cripple Creek was one of them.

Betsy sidled up to him and handed him a glass of lemonade. One that he appreciated. He sipped when he wanted to gulp, but Mrs. Callaway watched him. It unnerved him.

"I'm sure you are eager to get home and see your parents." Betsy's statement was bland and blunt despite the hand she set on his bare forearm.

He looked down at the unnecessary touch. Why hadn't he rolled his sleeves back down as soon as he finished? For the softness of her skin on his mesmerized him, though he didn't want it to. Should he jerk his arm away from her? He didn't want to give her room to play this game, nor did he wish to embarrass her in front of her mother. Whatever went on there.

"Nikolai, is it? Do you mind if I call you Nick?" Mrs. Callaway spoke up.

"Yes, ma'am. I'd prefer it if you did."

She looked away and waved a hand as if she couldn't care less what he thought. "How are your parents? They are in good health?"

"As far as I know." He squirmed, causing Betsy's hand to loosen its hold. The fact was he didn't really know much of his parents' current state. Letters from Anya had come less and less frequently over the last months. So, he could only guess.

"As far as you know?" Mrs. Callaway's hawk-like gaze found his.

It was rather disconcerting.

"Do you mean that you don't correspond with your mother?"

Betsy stepped forward. "Of course not, Mother. Nick is the picture of loyalty. He's a deputy in Denver. So he couldn't—"

Mrs. Callaway's eyes narrowed. "Is that so?"

"Yes, ma'am." He straightened his shoulders, hoping to firm his stance, but feared he appeared shifty. Then he stopped. What did it matter? It wasn't as if he courted Betsy. Or owed *her* anything. "In fact, I am on a charge to escort Betsy home."

Betsy laid her head into her hand. Had he said too much?

"Oh?" Mrs. Callaway now leveled her gaze on Betsy, then on her daughter's wrapped hand and slung arm. Had she just now noticed?

Betsy shrugged but wouldn't look at her mother.

"Yes, although..." How was he to fix this? And why did he feel as if he needed to? "...Betsy held her own during a stagecoach robbery."

Mrs. Callaway's eyes widened. "A stage robbery? What kind of lawlessness does your sheriff permit in Denver?"

Now it was Nick's turn to be sheepish. "That's not what I—"

"And was it under your care that she was injured?" Now the woman's hard steely glare was on him again.

"That wasn't...that is, no...well, yes. But it's not what you think." Sucking in air became rather difficult. He struggled both for breath and the right words.

"And you know what I'm thinking?" Mrs. Callaway challenged.

"No." He rubbed a hand along his brow. Was he sweating? This was unbearable. "That is, she was injured by one of the bandits. And then on the stage ride to Cripple Creek, she got a small cut on her hand."

"I see." Mrs. Callaway looked back to Betsy. "And what happened with the Clement family? Were they not capable enough to care for these...minor injuries?"

Betsy drew in a breath. He wished it had been that easy for him. His chest tightened as he worked for each inhale.

"They...were no longer in need of a governess." At last, she looked at her mother, her jaw tight and her own gaze steady. Truly she was made of iron under those quills.

Mrs. Callaway put a hand to her chest as she pulled in an exaggerated breath. One that Nick envied. "Well, that is unseemly. They commissioned you and had you travel all that way...just to decide they no longer needed you? Your father will have something to say about that when he gets home."

The way the woman bit at Betsy with her words was unnerving. Nick wished he had the fortitude to rescue her in some way. But he'd rather dive in front of a racing herd of horses than jump between Betsy and her mother.

"It wasn't just that." Betsy's words were quiet, almost lost in the shuffle of her feet on the floorboards.

"What?" Mrs. Callaway crossed her arms. "Did you say something?"

Betsy looked up. "They...were not pleased with how I presented."

"You had just been robbed and probably traumatized out of fear for your life. Surely they can't—"

"That's not quite what I meant." Betsy turned the side.

Nick watched the exchange, uncertain what he should do. But it became increasingly apparent that Betsy wanted for his absence. He set the cup on the counter behind her, his forearm grazing the fabric at the back of her dress. It warmed him more than the lemonade had cooled. "I think I need to—"

Mrs. Callaway held up a hand in his direction while holding her glare on Betsy. "What *did* you mean?"

Betsy glanced at Nick, her eyes sad. That he remained? That he was hearing this interchange? What was behind that look?

"They thought I was..." Betsy chewed on her lower lip.

"For the love of all, Betsy Callaway, spit it out." Her mother's words were icy.

Nick wanted to shield her somehow from the bitterness and harshness of her mother's words. But he couldn't move.

"They thought I was...hysterical." Betsy pressed it out, but her voice wavered.

Mrs. Callaway drew back. "Hysterical?"

"...and unfit." Betsy looked to the floorboards.

What she had been through was horrid. And, while her reaction to the robbery had been a bit extreme, he couldn't fathom that she deserved that kind of judgment.

That thought struck him. Had he judged her as well? For this quieter, more timid Betsy was a side he'd not seen.

Mrs. Callaway stood watching them for several seconds...very long seconds. Uncrossing her arms, she set fisted hands on her hips. Then she focused on Nick again. "I think you'd best go. I'm sure your mother is aching to see you."

Nick looked to Betsy. It took another long moment for her to lift her gaze to his. Sorrow pooled in her eyes, but she simply nodded before turning away.

As much as his heart pulled at him to stay, to make sure Betsy was all right, he also felt that he was the awkward outsider. And there was no connection between him and Betsy that would reasonably permit him to remain.

So, he nodded and turned toward the door. The silence was uncomfortably thick. All conversation paused as he reached for the wooden barrier's latch.

The pause became a stunned intake of breath when the door opened and revealed Mr. Callaway standing on the other side. If he'd thought Mrs. Callaway's gaze had been difficult to bear, Nick discovered that Mr. Callaway's hard stare held the weight of an anchor.

"What is going on here?" the man barked at Nick.

Betsy wanted nothing more than to sink into the floor. But she couldn't. Her father's angry face, not something she was accustomed to, settled on Nick. What did he fear was happening here?

Gathering what courage she could muster, she stepped to him. "Father, this is Nick Hammond, Michael Hammond's son."

"Ah..." Father did not divert his hard stare from Nick. The lines of his face were evident as his whole being tensed. Almost as an afterthought, Father jerked his regard to Betsy. "And just what are *you* doing here? I thought you were in Denver."

Betsy swallowed, a difficult thing with the lump in her throat.

"I was, ah, just leaving," Nick said in a rush. Then he attempted to step around Father.

Her father moved into his path once more. "No, you're not. I need some answers."

"Nick came to ensure I made it home safely." Betsy prayed her father's ire would be quelled by that simple explanation.

Father's eyebrows lowered, creasing the skin between them. "Is that so?"

Betsy nodded, not able to fight against the thickness in her throat anymore. This was every bit the nightmare she had hoped against. Why did life always find a way to kick her when she was down?

Father glanced at Mother, who shrugged as her features mirrored his —both uncertain and stern.

As much as Betsy didn't want to endure on her own what would surely follow, neither did she care for Nick to be put in the middle of it. She had erred terribly in her actions earlier and had now trapped Nick here.

Father stepped to the side and waved a hand as if to shoo Nick out.

Nick glanced back at Betsy, his gaze lingering. What was that softening about those blue eyes? She didn't need that. Nor did she want it. Turning her focus away, she stared in the direction of the kitchen. She found that she couldn't watch him leave. No matter how much he infuriated her. There had been a comfort there. And that, she would not abide.

Footsteps told that Nick made his exit. She closed her eyes against the pang in her chest.

Soon enough, the door firmly shut. Only then did she look in that direction.

Father set his hat on its peg just inside the room. And then worked to discard his jacket.

Betsy knew better than to move. Between Mother's glare and Father's frustration, it was best she wait.

But Father moved at a painstakingly slow pace. Did he revel in her discomfort? That wasn't like him. At length, he stepped closer. "I'd like an answer, young lady."

Betsy opened her mouth, but Mother cut her off. "She was dismissed from the governess position."

"Dismissed?" Confusion made the lines around Father's eyes deepen.

"Yes, Father. I was dismissed." Time for a little encouragement. She stepped to him and took his arm while she pushed her lower lip out in a pout. "They didn't think I was a good fit."

Father watched her for a moment. Then his features eased and the spark she customarily saw in his eyes returned. "They rejected my girl?"

She nodded, letting her eyelids and lashes lower a bit in an expression she knew from experience was easy to pity.

He looked down at her sling and bandaged hand. "Whatever happened to you, darling?"

Darling. Yes, this was much better. She widened her eyes and let tears come. "The stagecoach to Denver was robbed. I was injured trying to help a mother and her small child."

Father picked up her bandaged hand. "That's my girl. Taking care of others."

Mother threw up her hands and walked toward the kitchen.

Betsy offered her father a sweet smile. "It was so scary. And the Clements thought I overreacted. I was ready to go with them." Then she frowned. "But they wouldn't have me."

Father glowered. "That is their loss." He patted her cheek. "Shall we call on Dr. Sullivan to have a look at you?"

"No." Her response shot out. A little too abruptly, she realized too late.

Father's brow furrowed.

"That is, the doctor in Denver took good care of my injuries. I am already feeling much better. It's just some deep bruising in my wrist and a cut on my hand. It will only be a little while before I can use my arm again."

He laid a hand on her bandaged one. "That's good to hear. I am glad you came home."

Betsy kissed his cheek. "Thank you, Father. I knew you'd understand." She jerked her head as subtly as possible to glance at Mother.

The woman's back was to them, but she shook her head as she cut vegetables.

It didn't matter. Father was there for her. Always had been, and always would be. She was his princess. That wouldn't change.

"Why don't you sit down and rest your arm. I'm sure you've had a long, hard trip." Father led her to the settee.

She nodded as she batted her eyes. "I did. It was just horrid."

"I'm sure it was." Father assisted her to settle on the piece of furniture. Then he looked toward Mother, who refused to turn around. "I'll go freshen up for dinner."

He moved toward his and Mother's bedroom at the back of the house.

Betsy kept her focus on the pattern of the settee. But she felt Mother's steely stare. What did it matter? Father was on Betsy's side. Something tugged at the back of her mind. If that was completely true, why had she been sent to Denver in the first place?

As she felt Mother's regard shift back to dinner preparations, Betsy looked at her. What if Mother had more pull with Father? If it happened once, could it happen again?

CHAPTER 8

Discouraged

Nick tried not to think about Betsy as he drove the wagon and horse back to the livery from whence he rented it. He tried not to see her face in his mind as he pulled into town. And he fought against a softening in his heart as he walked toward the outskirts of town after returning the cart and animal. Was it hopeless? How had her visage come to assault his senses so? Their interactions were not so tender, nor so prolonged that he should care about what happened to her. That was her due.

And this was his.

He sighed as he gazed up at the house that had once been home.

Pulling in a long breath, he let it out slowly. What would be waiting on him, he did not know. And that concerned him. He could fairly guess that Ma would be pleased to see him. As well as Anya. But Karl and Pa...there was no evidence that would give him any optimism. Would Pa yell? Would he throw Nick out of the house? Could Nick stand for that to happen?

Perhaps he should just find a place in the boarding house. Would that simplify things? If he did that, he could stop by and see his mother during banking hours when Pa would be out.

He paused and looked back toward the center of town, hoping to find a beam of light shining down on the boarding house...a sure sign that would be the best option.

The house's door flung open, clattering against the outer wall. He jerked his head, training his gaze on the movement.

Anya was on the porch and racing down the few stairs to the ground. Was she hurt?

He braced himself, prepared to rise to the occasion.

"Nick!"

Her eyes were wide and, after navigating the stairs, she picked up speed.

Concern sliced through him, but as she ran into his arms, he found he wasn't as fully braced as he'd thought. He stepped back to keep himself upright. But breathing became difficult as the air was pressed from his lungs by her slamming into him.

"Is it really you?" Anya held him tightly. So much so he wondered if she would squeeze out what breath remained.

His arms came around her. "Yes." He closed his eyes and swallowed back rising emotions. "It's me."

"I thought..." She sniffled and hiccupped. "I thought I might never see you again."

He smoothed a hand down her braid. "That's silly."

Even as he said it, he knew it wasn't. He'd never indicated in any of his many letters that a return home would be a possibility. And she had been well aware of his situation with Pa.

"Why didn't you tell me?" She pulled back.

He was thankful for the chance to refill his lungs. After some deep breaths, he said, "I didn't know myself."

Her eyebrows pinched. "You...what?"

"Nikolai?" A shaky voice said from the direction of the house.

He looked over his sister's head.

Ma stood on the porch, leaning on the railing. "How...?"

He held up a hand toward Anya and released her. "I will explain everything, but let's go inside. No need to have the neighbors wagging their tongues."

Anya wrapped her hands around his arm. "Let them talk. My brother is home, and all is well."

A pang went through his chest. How could he tell her that he would only be here for a couple of days? But he had to. He had duties to return to in Denver. This wasn't a vacation; it was a simple task to bring a wayward woman home. And he had.

Nick and Anya climbed the few stairs and stepped toward the door.

But Ma hadn't moved. She reached out both hands and framed Nick's face. "It is good you are home."

He just smiled and offered her a one arm embrace during which she kissed his cheek.

"Come, let's talk." The Russian accent that she could never fully get rid of tinged her words and soothed his worn heart.

Nick held out a hand for his mother and sister to precede him into the house. Once within, the aroma of stewing beef and potatoes anchored him. Yes, Ma's cooking—hearty and deeply warming.

"So..." Ma said as she indicated a seat at the dining table. "Tell us the news. And of how we should thank God for bringing you home. Safely."

Nick smiled as he sat.

Anya settled into the chair beside him, but Ma moved to the stove-top, lifting the pot's lid, and stirring the contents. All the best smells in the world wafted through the house. He closed his eyes and just breathed it in.

"What brings you home?" Ma's voice was edged with concern. He wondered what could have done that, but then realized he had been caught up in the scent of the meal that he'd not answered.

"I am actually on an assignment. Official business."

Ma turned to the stewing pot and Anya frowned.

"But I volunteered because I wanted to come home." He'd not intended to bring discouragement on his mother and sister. Here he was, giving them cause to think he hadn't wanted to see them. "I *needed* to come home."

It struck him just how true those words were. He had missed his family. And his home. But as that tugged at his heart, he remembered why he'd had to leave. And why he'd stayed away.

"What assignment could bring you to Cripple Creek?" Anya spoke up, pressing a small smile on her features which displayed her very deep dismay.

"Betsy Callaway needed an escort home."

Ma turned toward them, and Anya exchanged a look with her.

"Betsy Callaway?" Ma set the lid on the pot and the spoon to the side.

"Yes. She had come to Denver for..." Dare he betray Betsy's embarrassing loss of her governess position? Not only might it bring some amount of shame on her, it wasn't his to tell. "...something. But her stage *en route* to Denver was held up."

"Oh my!" Anya pressed a hand to her chest. "Is she okay?"

Not that there had been any love lost between Anya and Betsy, but his sister's good heart was ever caring for others.

"She is. Some injury to a wrist, but she will be fine."

Ma stalked to the table and took her seat across from Nick. "What would make her need an escort?"

"She was...intimidated and perhaps a little afraid after the encounter. And, as I longed for a reason to come home, I volunteered to see her back safely."

Ma's eyes darkened just slightly, and her voice softened as she patted his hand. "You don't need a reason to come home. You are always welcome."

He wanted to kick himself. Everything had come out wrong. "That's not what I meant." Even to him, his words sounded timid.

Ma took a deep breath and let it out. "It is no matter. You are home and that is what matters."

"How long will you stay?" Anya's voice wavered almost imperceptibly.

Ma might be ready to put his tripped-up words to the side, but they had pained his sister's tender heart.

He rubbed his hands together and licked his lips. As if those things could delay his answer. They did little to put his sister off. Her wide eyes pled with him to give her a better answer than the one he had.

"Two days."

Anya leaned back, her shoulders steady as her torso caved slightly. She was not happy. And he had known she wouldn't be. Still her reaction wounded him. Yet he refused to sugarcoat the truth. Even as much as he wanted to.

In the thick silence of the moment, footfalls outside the door were audible. Nick looked at the case clock. That would be Pa.

There was little time to prepare himself—as if any preparation would ward off his fears—before the door opened.

Pa's tall, bulky frame filled the doorway, his silhouette illuminated in the setting sun.

Nick held his breath. But the awareness that he did so didn't cause him to draw breath.

Pa stepped within, his gaze taking in the scene. Landing on Nick. His mouth stiffened and his eyes clouded. Then, without taking his regard from Nick, he said, "Tatiana, what is this?"

Nick rose, wishing he could make his words come.

Ma also stood, moving around the table to intercept Pa. She took his arm and waved with her other. "Our son is home."

Pa glanced at Ma before moving farther into the house. And though he came closer to the table, he did not look in Nick's direction. "My son is closing up the bank. I have no other."

Ma gasped.

Anya grabbed for Nick's hand, which now hung at his side. But he only barely noticed her touch.

Pa stepped around the dining table toward the back of the house. "And I will not abide a stranger in my house."

Betsy could not be happier to lie down in her own bed. After all she had been through, it was solace to her worn nerves. How wonderful—her own room, her own space. Why did her parents ever think sending her away had been a good idea?

For certain, it was Mother's idea. Perhaps a way to punish her for not securing a good marriage. Not that she hadn't tried. For goodness sakes...she had breached the line of acceptable with her pursuit of Wyatt.

Just thinking of him made her stomach churn. As had been the case for some time. Was that because of what she had become to chase him after his marriage of convenience to Katherine? The sham that had perhaps...well, maybe apparently...become real. But her heart didn't jump or flutter. Had it always been about making him a prize? Not about any real feelings of love?

She frowned. Her mother had engrained in her the advantages of a good marriage. That meant advantageous. Betsy had known that much. And so, the boy that started as a schoolyard affection became the town doctor. Was there anyone more secure to seek after?

But the churning...it gave her cause to worry that the contents of her stomach would not remain settled. She rolled to her side and curled her legs closer. What was this? Was God chastening her? Glancing at the ceiling, she couldn't find the words to pray. Nothing new there. Perhaps she did deserve every bit of hardship He wished to deal out.

She closed her eyes and tried to settle again. The night was still and every bit as calm as she should be. Still, she found the silence deafening. As if the random creatures roaming about found cause to judge her.

Jerking upright, she flung the covers off. This would not do!

Maybe her stomach would settle if she put something bland in it. There had been some bread left from dinner. That would be just what she needed.

Sliding out of bed, she slipped from her room, down the short hallway that was thick with darkness, and crept below stairs. Why had she not brought a lantern or candle? It would serve her right if she tripped on her own feet with no ability to see where she went.

Nonetheless, she muddled her way to the lower level and then turned toward the kitchen.

But as she glanced at her parents' bedroom, she noted light seeping from the edges of the door. What could be keeping them awake?

Even as her body demanded the promised morsel of bread, she tiptoed closer to the barrier. The voices within became more discernible as she neared.

Of course, it was Mother and Father. But their words were louder than she would have expected. It was doubtful they would have heard her on the stairs if she had fallen, such a disagreement raged between them.

"I tell you, she has to stand on her own feet." It was Mother.

Betsy cringed at the angry voice. They discussed *her*. Her heart thumped harder and her determination to catch their words intensified.

"She is but a girl." Father's voice sounded more even toned. "Let her have a few days before we seek out another position."

"A girl? Hardly. She is nearly four and twenty. I was married and carrying a child by the time I was that age."

Silence from Father. Would he not speak for her again?

"We must help her. She needs to find an agreeable occupation or she will be an old maid that we will care for rather than the other way around."

A long pause filled the space. It was heavy.

Then came Father's voice, sounding somewhat resigned. To Mother? Or to giving up on Betsy? "What about your aunt? Could Betsy be a companion for her?"

Betsy shut her eyes. Death would be preferable. The woman was difficult and terse. About everything. Nothing had ever pleased great-aunt Hilda. Not even her very comfortable living situation in Virginia. Married to a wealthy man, surrounded by sons—all married and out in the world. Had Father given up all hope of Betsy finding a suitable match?

An anchor weighed in her midsection and a tear slid down the side of her face. She couldn't listen to anymore. Nothing they could say would assuage a heart that had been jolted with such a dose of reality. Was she no more than a problem to be solved?

Backing away from the door, she rushed up the steps, uncaring as they creaked. She didn't stop until she fell upon her bed. What had her life become? What *would* it become?

More tears came. Though she didn't care to wipe them away. Let her emotions rain on her features. It didn't matter. Nothing mattered. Not anymore.

CHAPTER 9

In the Light of Day

Sunlight filtered into the bedroom that felt as if it entombed Betsy. Therein, the light was welcome. Wasn't it? Or did it portend but another day in which she couldn't win? She jerked around to face opposite. What could she do? How could she escape her mother's plan?

Betsy had removed her splint for sleep and noted the gained strength in her arm. Perhaps she didn't need the sling anymore. As well, the makeshift bandage had come off her other hand. The relatively small injury had healed well enough; it likewise didn't need any more attention. Then her thoughts turned to her plight once more.

If only Father could see, could understand the harm of what Mother intended. Betsy ran a hand down her face. No doubt her eyes were puffy from her spent emotion the night before. All of it was utter nonsense. All was lost.

Unless...

An idea ricocheted about in her brain. And it was nothing short of genius. It gave way to her lips curling up. Yes, she could do this. Her father would then see the ridiculousness of her request and of her being forced to work, practically groveling for everything she received. *Perfect.*

Jumping out of the bed that had served as her refuge last night, she dressed quickly and pulled her hair back, choosing a large pink ribbon.

Her father couldn't—wouldn't—resign his darling princess to any such thing.

She glanced in the vanity mirror and silently wished herself luck. Then shook her head. She didn't need luck. Her plan was sound. Twirling briefly, she needed a moment to reorient herself. Now, to the dining room.

As she made her way, bounding down the stairs, she smelled bacon and eggs Mother must have prepared for Father's breakfast. Her mouth watered and her stomach cinched. She had lost track of that altogether and neglected to feed it last night. All too soon...she would sit down as the victor. But for now, she needed to remove her smirk and become the picture of contriteness.

The corner at the bottom of the stairs was the last obstruction between Betsy and her parents. She paused there, snatched a quick breath, and lowered her chin.

Her feet hit the floorboards and she turned in the direction of the dining table.

"Glad to see you up and about." Mother stood and moved to the stove. No emotion leaked into her voice. She then turned to their maid-servant and issued instructions.

But Betsy's gaze was on Father.

He shoved a forkful of eggs into his mouth as he read the papers in front of him.

Betsy cleared her throat.

Nothing.

Mother scooped eggs onto a fresh plate and Father continued his perusal of the documents.

Betsy cleared her throat even louder.

Mother looked in Betsy's direction as Maria walked Betsy's plate to the table.

Father set down his papers, eyebrows raised. "What is the matter?"

She pushed out her bottom lip. "I know I have disappointed you... with my inability to keep the governess position."

Mother strode to stand beside Father.

He waved a hand. "I wouldn't say that you—"

Mother grabbed his arm, silencing him.

Perfect.

Mother waved Maria off, and the maid moved off into another room.

Betsy lowered her voice and her gaze. "And I don't expect you to look after me forever." Then she peered up to see the effect of her playacting.

Mother's brows rose. "Oh?"

Lifting her chin to be level, Betsy continued, "Of course not." She took an exaggerated breath. "So, until we can make an acceptable match for me, I will work in the hotel."

Mother and Father looked at each other.

It went just as she'd hoped.

Then Father shifted his focus to Betsy again. "That seems sound."

What? Father was well with this?

"Betsy?" Mother moved toward her. "Are you well?"

Too late, Betsy realized her mouth was agape. She shut it and swallowed hard. "A-are you certain I wouldn't be in the way?"

"It's a brilliant plan." Father glanced at her again, a smile about his features.

Betsy forced herself to breathe. This couldn't be happening.

Mother stepped to her and set an arm around her shoulders. "Come, let's get you a full breakfast. You will need it for a hard day's work."

Betsy gulped and let her mother lead her to the table. As she sat, she forced herself to not slam her hands on the table. "I suppose I'm going to work."

Father offered another smile before going back to his reading.

How had this gone so horribly wrong?

Nick rubbed his left shoulder. It had been quite some time since he'd slept in a barn. How was it that his body was so sore? He'd slept on the trail many times in the last year. This shouldn't have affected him so much.

Then again...

There had been much tension in his muscles last evening...continuing into the morning. He'd had little sleep and none of it had been restful. Perhaps he should make his way back to Denver this afternoon. But a memory of his mother's pleading eyes was before him. She had been so torn last night after speaking with Pa.

The stubborn man had refused to let Nick stay. She had worked on him to relent to letting Nick stay in the barn, as the boarding house and hotel were likely already closed for incoming guests. But that had been the only thing she could convince him to give on.

Pa was just as upset at Nick as the first day he'd walked away. Why could Pa never understand what was in Nick's heart? He didn't want to be a banker—wear a stuffy suit and be confined to those four walls. He needed space to breathe, to be.

Leaving home to pursue his own dreams had been difficult. But it had perhaps been the best decision he'd made. With the exception of leaving Ma and Anya behind. Not that he hadn't missed his father or brother. There had been those moments. Though Ma's kind, caring touch on everything she did and everyone she encountered had been sorely and notably absent.

And here he had returned to find Pa just as hard-headed as ever. The man's words had stabbed at Nick's heart. Deeply. How could he be so cruel?

That was not Nick's to take on. He knew he had to do what he was called to. And the Lord had certainly blessed his journey since moving on.

As Nick stood and stretched, he thought again about returning to Denver. His mission was complete, and he had embraced Ma and Anya. Would that be selfish of him? To run out on them after such a short reunion?

Again, Ma's deep brown eyes haunted him. And he knew. There was reason enough to linger. Perhaps he might manage a few more days.

Movement below the hay loft had Nick reaching for his revolver.

"Nick?" It was Anya's voice beseeching him.

"Up here." He resettled his gun belt and moved to the loft's ladder.

When he reached the edge of the raised ledge, he spotted his sister near the barn door.

She smiled up at him and gave a little wave. "How did you sleep?"

He climbed down the ladder as he responded. "Fair enough."

When he reached the ground and turned, he found her frowning, her eyebrows gathered.

"It's nothing to worry about. Who wouldn't prefer a bed to a gathered hay pile?"

He'd meant it as a jest, but the lines in her delicate features deepened. "I just wish you were more welcome."

Pulling her into a brief hug, he said, "Don't worry a bit about that. It's my doing."

As he released her, she stepped back and sniffled. Was she about to cry?

She managed on a shaky voice, "It's not you. It's Pa."

"I've been just as stubborn as he has." Nick said it to ease her guilt, but the truth behind the words rang loud for him.

Anya swiped at an eye as she looked to the side. An errant tear? That made his heart hurt.

"No, don't do that." Nick was quite certain he wouldn't be able to take that.

She sniffled again and faced him. "Ma wanted me to tell you that Pa left at sunrise."

Nick nodded. The man really did want to avoid him. Could he blame Pa though?

"She has breakfast ready for you."

He lowered his gaze. "I'm not sure I—"

"Don't you start that. I won't let you be pig-headed, too."

His regard shot to her face.

"That would break Ma's heart even more than this whole thing already has."

He nodded. Of course, she was right. This needed to be about Ma. Not him. Not his desire to sneak away again. He needed to stay. For Ma's tender heart.

"Glad we are agreed." She jerked her head in a nod and spun away then moved toward the door. A moment later, she looked back and pushed out exasperated words. "Are you coming or not?"

That drew a smile from him. "Right behind you."

They stepped outside and, soon enough, walked into the house. The aroma of Ma's flapjacks filled his senses. Those were his favorite. Always had been.

He gave Ma a quick squeeze before sitting at what had always been his seat at the table.

She set a plate before him that must have been stacked six high.

As he poured syrup on them, he chuckled. How odd. His father had made sure Nick knew he was not welcome, while his mother did everything she could to speak the opposite. Which would he allow to penetrate his heart? Now that was a question he hadn't a ready answer for. But as he put the first bite in his mouth, the sting of Pa's rejection melted just a little.

CHAPTER 10

Uncertain

Could anything be more humiliating? Betsy stayed close to her father as they stepped into the hotel. What exactly would he have her doing? Surely he wouldn't consign her to labor-intensive tasks...that would be too embarrassing.

"Very well now," Father said as they moved alongside the front desk where a dark-haired woman nodded at him before going about her business. "What shall we do today?"

Betsy eyed the woman. Her job didn't seem so difficult. Nothing that would get her hands dirty for certain. But would she want every person coming into the hotel to know she was an...employee?

A woman in a white apron walked through the lobby area, a duster in hand.

"I think I might enjoy greeting the guests and checking them in." Betsy's words rushed out before she considered them. Or how they would be received.

Father glanced at the dark-haired woman who had jerked her regard to Betsy. The woman's pinched mouth and furrowed brow betrayed a frustration.

"Nonsense," Father remarked, all but chuckling, "Dorothea has always done well. Besides," he said as he took Betsy's arm and steered her to the door leading to the back of house rooms and offices. "...you need to start at the bottom."

"At the...bottom?" Betsy swallowed, a bit fearful of what that might mean. They passed a broom and dustpan that must have been set to the side. Surely, he wouldn't ask that of her.

"Yes. Everyone does. And it'll be good to learn all the jobs at the hotel, don't you think?" He offered her a winning smile as he patted her arm.

She grimaced.

"Don't make that face, darling. It will be good for you."

That was her mother talking. How had she secured her hooks in Father? Betsy shrugged off Father's hand and looked down the hallway. Then it occurred to her. Even Mother said one would catch more flies with honey. When else would be best to utilize those better tactics?

She tipped her chin downward and peered up at her father through lashes. "I'm just worried that I will make a mess. I've never...cleaned anything." Then she batted her eyelashes and pushed her lower lip out. That always worked.

"Then it is high time you learned how." Father put a hand on her back and ushered her down the hallway until they reached a door at the far end.

The sound of sloshing water and the scent of soap gave Betsy pause. Was this the laundering room? He couldn't ask that of her...he wouldn't.

Father opened the door and revealed two women washing various linens in large vats of water.

"I thought I might find you here, Mrs. Thompson." He smiled at the elder of the pair.

She set aside her scrubbing and stepped around the large tub to approach Father and Betsy. "Do you need something, Mr. Callaway?"

"As a fact I do." He turned toward Betsy. "Mrs. Thompson, you know my daughter Betsy."

The woman nodded and smiled at Betsy. Though she had been taken aback by the events of the last several moments she could not find it in herself to respond in kind. So, she simply jerked her head down once, hoping that was enough to appease Mrs. Thompson and her father.

Father's eyebrows lowered, but they were quickly back in place as he continued the introduction. "Betsy dear, Mrs. Thompson heads the cleaning staff."

Betsy just stared. Surely, she still slept. This was nothing more than a bad dream...surely. She blinked a few times and pinched the inside of her good wrist. No such luck.

"It is good to meet you, Miss Callaway." The older woman ran her hands down the front of the damp and dirtied apron.

Would she extend a hand to Betsy? That would be unwelcome. No matter how she might attempt to dry them, they had been in the lye. It wouldn't do. But as Betsy watched, Mrs. Thompson simply shifted her focus to Father.

"I am glad to have been introduced to your daughter, sir," Mrs. Thompson said as she glanced back at the other woman tending the wash. "Though I do have much work to tend to, you see, one of my girls is down with a fever. That leaves extra work for the rest of us."

Father's eyes lit up. "How wonderful."

Mrs. Thompson's brow furrowed. "What, sir?"

"Oh...not that the girl is unwell, but it is good that Betsy is joining us today. There will be a place for her."

"What?" Betsy couldn't hold back the pained word.

Mrs. Thompson didn't appear to understand any more than Betsy did.

"Betsy wishes to learn and eventually take on a position here at the hotel."

"Oh." That was all Mrs. Thompson said as she passed a keen eye over Betsy.

For her part, Betsy shifted, twisting her fingers. What could she say? How might she retract her offer?

"So, wherever you can best utilize her, do so." Father appeared to be quite proud. Of her? Or of this plan? Perhaps both.

Betsy gritted her teeth as words to deny this situation ran through her head. Which ones to take hold of?

Father whirled back to Betsy. "Mrs. Thompson will find you an apron or something more suitable to wear." He glanced down at her dress. "No sense ruining that."

Mrs. Thompson nodded in her direction. But the woman seemed no more pleased than Betsy was at the prospect of them working together. Though was it truly together? No...the woman would be Betsy's overseer. She would tell Betsy what to do and how to do it.

This would not go well.

"I have much to tend to," Father said as he moved to the door. "I leave Betsy in your capable hands, Mrs. Thompson."

Betsy watched her father go, wanting to call out to him, to naysay this arrangement, or something, anything. But she clamped her lips shut. There was nothing to be said.

Her father turned a corner and disappeared.

Betsy swallowed and turned back to Mrs. Thompson, who reached behind the door and extracted a worn dress. It was brown and ugly.

"This might fit." Mrs. Thompson offered her a smile and held out the horrid dress. Not only was it the color of mud, but it was also stained. Though it did not seem possible one might differentiate such on that shade of dingy. Still, it had visible splotches in varying places.

Betsy held up a hand to ward off the passing of the garment. "I am well enough with what I'm wearing."

Mrs. Thompson looked her up and down. "You are certain? I'd hate for that fine dress to be spoiled."

Betsy chewed at her bottom lip as she peered down at what she had foolishly deemed appropriate for the work ahead of her. "I only need an apron."

"Suit yourself." Mrs. Thompson shrugged. And reached behind the door once more. The dress was gone then, but the woman pulled out an apron that must have at one time been white. It had become faded and worn until threadbare.

This grew worse by the minute.

"Let's start by helping Lydia with the wash."

"But my bandage..." Betsy held up her still wrapped hand.

Mrs. Thompson grimaced. "Very well. I have other things that need doing."

Betsy took the apron, but only stared at it.

"Pardon me, Miss Callaway. But I don't have all day. There are many things to get done and I have to make sure they do. Including what your father has asked regarding training you." Mrs. Thompson's look was not hard, but it was stern.

She wanted to ask the woman what she was thinking saying such a thing to *her*. Did she imagine that she had leeway to lord over Betsy. But as Betsy drew in a steadying breath, she saw the situation for what it was. There would be no escaping. Perhaps...if she made the best of it, Father would elevate her quickly. She could only hope.

Swallowing her revulsion at the thing Mrs. Thompson handed her, she slipped it over her head and tied it into place.

"My apologies." Though she offered those words to assuage any ire in the woman, Betsy's tone was grim.

Mrs. Thompson merely moved toward the washboard she had earlier vacated. "Now, then..."

Betsy listened as the woman told of the proper way to use a washboard. As if Betsy was a complete ninny. But all Betsy could think was how this would be a very long, very arduous day.

Nick walked down the main stretch in Cripple Creek. Strange how things had changed and yet had not. There, Mr. Yerby swept the walkway outside the General Store while all manner of miner and farmer strolled about the planked sidewalks. The dress shop was new, but the saloon had not changed. And there was the bank. He did not let his gaze linger there.

As Nick continued on his journey down the wide dirt packed road, Wyatt Sullivan waved with a smile from the clinic doorway before ushering an older man inside.

He waved back at Wyatt and moved on down the stretch. The boarding house lay just a few doors down from the clinic. A few more hat tilts to people in the area and he found himself at the establishment's front stoop. He looked at the well-worn stairs up to the porch and smiled. Yes, some things never did change.

Memories flooded into his mind...memories of him and Karl racing up and down those stairs, chasing each other with slingshots when they were supposed to be on an errand for Pa. The golden haze of looking back melted into a starker, darker realization of the rift between him and his brother. Nick could never be the son Pa wanted. But Karl was. That and more.

He sighed and pushed those thoughts to the side. This was no time to get sentimental. And though the stairs creaked with age, they held true as he ascended. Should he knock? An image of Mrs. Sager crossed his mind. She would come out to this very porch, broom in hand, and chase him and his brother away. There had always been a crinkle about her eyes even as she chided them for 'misbehaving.' They had known of her fondness for the town's children. Even if she hadn't any of her own.

Perhaps that was why. Too many times she had sneaked cookies into his and Karl's hands. Too many to count. That kindness was borne of something in her heart. Even if, he now realized, it was a place of broken dreams.

Would she answer the door? He paused at that thought. Would she indeed? Or would the years find the place abandoned or with another proprietor?

Only one way to find out.

He knocked and waited, glancing about himself. Though there were plenty of passersby, none seemed the least bit interested in what he was doing.

Redirecting his attention to the door, he wondered if he'd disturbed Mrs. Sager's cleaning. Maybe he should come back later. He turned and moved toward the steps. But the creaking of the front door told that it opened.

"Yes?" Came a voice that was much too young to have been Mrs. Sager.

Shifting his footing, he looked back toward the structure.

A middle-aged woman stood in the doorway, a question on her features.

"May I help you, sir?" she pressed out. Maybe he did disrupt her in the midst of her daily upkeep.

"Is Mrs. Sager still in charge of the boarding house?" What drew him to ask, he wasn't certain. But it was done. Now he waited for an answer.

The woman rubbed her hands in the cloth of her apron. "Mrs. Sager hasn't been in charge here for near five years or so."

He nodded then looked to the ground. "I hope she is in good health."

Brown wavy hair pulled up tightly shook as the woman spoke volumes with the movement of her head. "She passed a couple years ago, God rest her soul."

He glanced down the street. Yes, some things had changed. And not for the better.

"I don't mean to be unneighborly, but is there something I can help you with?"

That jerked him from his reverie. "Oh, yes. I need a place to stay for a couple of days."

"Oh." The woman's already lined face frowned. "I'm afraid we're full up."

"Oh?" It was his turn to frown. His gaze dropped to the porch boards. What was he to do now? He had told Ma and Anya he would stay for a few days, but this presented a very real problem.

"There's one other house that takes boarders—Mr. Snyder. But he sent a couple of people to me already as his house is full too."

Nick twisted his mouth as he considered what he might do. Even if his father was amenable to it, staying multiple nights in the barn did not appeal.

"There is always the hotel." Even she seemed apologetic.

Yes, it was an option. But how viable? It was quite a bit more expensive. Not that he didn't have the funds. However, there were plenty of other things he'd rather spend that money on.

Still, he nodded. "Thanks."

She settled on a small smile as she backed into the entryway of the house and closed the door.

He stepped back down the stairs. This would not do. But, he had given his mother and sister his word. And they were well worth the added expense.

That reasoning would have to suffice.

Looking up and down the street once more, he paused. Betsy Callaway's father owned the hotel. At least, as far as Nick could remember. And the awkward, uncomfortable encounter with the man the other night gave him reason to doubt a fair reception at the establishment.

Yet he was out of options. Unless he went to Wyatt and appealed to their somewhat friendship years ago in school. That wasn't going to happen. He would have no part of leaning on a former friend's generosity for his own purposes.

So, to the hotel it was.

And just in time. The sun hung overhead, bearing down on the whole of Cripple Creek, seeming to press onto his shoulders with a focused intensity. But that must only be his imagination.

Back down the main stretch, past the clinic, the General Store, the dress shop, and, yes, even the bank he went. It unnerved just the same to pass his father's place of business without giving in to the urge to glance within. Was Karl hard at work there? He hadn't laid eyes on his brother yesterday as he'd been banished to the barn before Karl returned home.

Would Karl be as firmly set against Nick as Pa had been? Or would the years have softened his heart? Either way, this was no time to feel that out.

After he crossed to the next street over, he spied the hotel that had likely been visible from much farther away. It was grand—a strong, well-kept white structure among the sea of browns, many in varying states of disrepair.

He took one moment more to press down his trepidation before pushing through the front door.

As he stepped within the fine building, he had the thought that he had likely never been inside. The painted walls and lush rugs covering the floors were quite fine. There was a sitting area to the left and beyond that a restaurant. A large, raised desk stood directly to his right. Could he even pretend he might belong here? It was as if he playacted.

"May I help you, sir?" A feminine voice off to the right called to him.

He turned to find a woman maybe a few years his senior coming around from behind the desk. Though he fully expected to be ejected from the building for his rough appearance, she smiled at him. He suddenly wished he had thought to check for any remnants of hay about his person.

Clearing his throat, he hoped his voice wouldn't fail him. "Yes. I need a room."

Moving behind the desk again, her voice lilted up as she said, "Yes, sir. Let me see what we have."

She flipped through a logbook of sorts and then beckoned him closer. "We have two rooms available. Would you prefer first floor or third?"

He wasn't certain what to think. What was he supposed to say? Was there something obvious he wasn't understanding about which room would be the better one? And while he hoped that his confusion looked like thoughtfulness, he would have to answer soon.

Giving her his best grin, he said, "No need to walk up extra stairs, right?"

She nodded. "That will be just fine, sir."

Had he guessed correctly? He couldn't discern from her rather pleasant affect.

She dabbed her pen in the nearby inkwell, then looked to him. "May I have your name?"

"Yes..." All of a sudden his mouth became dry. But he swallowed and tried again. It was just his name, after all. What was his problem? "Nick Hammond."

She wrote his name in the book with the loveliest script he'd ever seen. "Hammond. Any relation to our banker?"

How did he not think that this would come up? Cripple Creek wasn't that large, and his father was quite well known. Notorious even. "Yes," he said, ducking his head. "That's my father."

"How wonderful to host family of one of our most upstanding citizens." She offered another quick smile before turning to search out the room's key among those hanging behind the desk.

The door to her right moved and all but slammed open. Then a woman in a rather fine dress backed out, her arms barely encompassing a broom, dustpan, and a bottle of something. It appeared as if they would fall at any moment.

He rushed over, reaching for the broom. "Let me get that for you, miss."

"Oh…" the young woman said, her blonde curls fairly bouncing as she looked up. But any further words died on perfect pouting lips as her gaze collided with his.

"Betsy?" Could it really be her?

She pulled back, teetering precariously.

He grabbed for her arm, steadying her.

As he tugged her back to her feet and some semblance of balance, she jerked free.

What had happened with her father? Had he been cross with her? Had he decided to punish her? Because the Betsy Callaway Nick knew would never, ever be caught dead in an apron.

He narrowed his gaze. "What are you doing here?"

CHAPTER 11

Unexpected

Betsy decided that she must have done serious evil indeed to deserve this. Her jaw slackened as she stared at a perfectly composed Nick Hammond. And his hand was on her arm. Jerking free was her only option.

"What are you doing here?" He glanced about himself. As if he could escape from her predicament. He should.

What was *he* doing here? How could God be so cruel as to put her at the mercy of the man's judgment once more?

She coughed and took a step back, a rather difficult maneuver with all the things she held. And she tipped again.

Nick was quick to close the gap once more. But she tried to shake free though there was little doubt he kept her from falling yet again.

"I could ask you the same thing." She shot the words at him, hoping her tone may bid him give her more space. His hands were still on her arms.

His eyebrows rose. "Me?" He waved at the front desk. "I should think it was obvious. I'm trying to get accommodations for the evening."

That was strange. "You aren't staying with your parents?"

His features drooped and she became all too aware of the onlookers around them. Had she overstepped?

"Don't change the subject." He steered her in the direction of the corner.

Her back hit the wall and he stopped advancing, but now he loomed over her.

"Is this because of your father? Did he force you to work here?"

Her mouth opened and closed. Did she not have an answer? Or was it his closeness that sent her heart and mind skittering? Pressing her lips together, she swallowed past a dry mouth. "It's not like that." Why was her voice so timid?

His gaze scoured her features; his scrutiny was difficult to stand. It seemed as if he peered within her. How was that possible? And her body betrayed her, warming and tingling where his hands remained. As well, the heat radiating from him seemed to sear her through the front of her shirtwaist. Did he intend to protect her? From her father?

She caught on his gaze again. Now the blue pierced her soul. Her cheeks heated and she looked down at the small space between them.

"Then tell me how it is." His voice was breathy. It feathered across her cheek but bore no coolness.

Air. She needed air. But how? And where was her voice? As much as she wanted to push him away, she couldn't make herself do it. Had all her strength rushed out of her? Her knees became wobbly. Could she lean into him? Of course not! That would be unseemly.

Nick glanced over his shoulder at Dorothea then looked at the door Betsy had just exited. He wouldn't lead her back there, would he? She and Nick would be out of sight. It wouldn't be appropriate. But she doubted she would resist him. And that bothered her.

"Let's step outside."

She let out a breath. That would be best.

He reached for the space between them. What was he doing? But she couldn't move back any farther. Then he stilled. "I am just trying to help you with these things.

"Oh." She tilted her face up and watched as he lifted her burdens and set them to the side.

Then he took her arm with the gentlest touch and led her to the front door. He glanced at Dorothea and nodded. "We'll be back in a few minutes."

Dorothea looked between Betsy and Nick then dropped her regard to the books on the desk. What would the woman tell Pa? Would she go after him directly? That didn't give her and Nick very long.

Betsy let him lead her outside and to the side of the building just in the alley. Still visible to passersby, but less likely to be heard.

He dropped his hand and walked a couple of steps then back. So, pacing it was. What had him so wound up? When he had passed over the same piece of ground no less than five times, he paused and faced her.

"What happened after I left your folks' house?" His gaze was intense.

The fact that he seemed so concerned softened her brewing ire. Her tongue might ache to be snippy, but her heart wasn't in it.

"Nothing." She tore her gaze from his and peered opposite. The memory of the way she behaved toward her father brought heat back to her cheeks. Why? Why did Nick bring that out in her? She didn't like it.

He stepped closer. "Did he hurt you?" His voice wavered but the slightest bit.

She jerked her regard toward him. "No. Of course not." Why she was so defensive, she didn't know. She just...was.

He didn't flinch. "Then why are you doing maid service in his hotel?"

Did he think it was so beneath her? Why? But she knew...because she had always put on that such would be. In her way, she had always looked down on those who did such labor. Goodness. Now she was having to swallow that pride. And it hurt.

"I..." She dropped her focus to the dirt beneath them. "I have to make a place for myself somehow."

"Why?"

Did his questions have to be so pointed? Why must he remind her of how proud she had always been? But she didn't want to answer. Because she didn't want to admit it to him? Or to herself?

He let out a breath. Then put a finger under her chin and lifted her gaze to his. "Why, Betsy?"

"Because I can no longer remain an unmarried leech."

His eyebrows furrowed. "What? Did they say that to you?"

She wished he wasn't looking at her like that. It made all of this worse. And it knocked her off-guard. "No. Well...my mother would have if she had the nerve. But no. They want me to be able to make my own way in the world."

Was that enough or would she have to explain how she had tried to manipulate Father and it backfired?

His concern did not soften, but his words did. "I see."

Her eyes stung with unshed tears. What did he see? How humiliated she was? How pitiable she was? Or how much he wished to end any association with her? She could not bear to look at him anymore, but he held her chin in place. So, she closed her eyes.

She sensed him lean closer. What was he thinking? Would he try to kiss her? Holding her breath, she braced herself for the touch of his lips. That surprised. Did she want him to kiss her?

His breath was ragged as he exhaled.

And she parted her lips.

Nick could not lift his gaze from Betsy's mouth. He was drawn to her. Lifting his hand, he grazed fingertips over her cheek and jawline. That may already be more than he should have dared trespass.

The image of a flying insect going toward a lantern slipped into his mind. If he gave over to this attraction and kissed her, would he find himself lost to the fire that not only heated, but could burn?

Did he care beyond the touch of his lips to hers? Something made him want more. But he couldn't take the chance. Nor would he dishonor her by taking this moment to press in. This must stop. Now.

As he drew back, overwhelmed by the massive effort it took to do so, he let his hand drop. He sucked in a breath that he was only then aware he had been missing. His gaze fell on her features again, but he did not allow himself to close the space between them. It was too dangerous. It wouldn't be right.

"Betsy," he said, surprised at the thickness of his voice.

She opened her eyes. They glazed, filled with a sadness he had not expected. Was she distressed that he had not pushed on? She folded her arms in front of her, creating a more real barrier between them. He should be grateful for that.

As she looked to the ground, he caught a reddening about her cheeks. Had he embarrassed her? Because he had wanted to kiss her? Or because *she* had wanted it as well?

He shook his head. This was no time for that kind of thinking. "I'm sorry."

She shook her head and rubbed her arms though the day was quite warm. Was the shimmering in her eyes a welling of tears? He had not intended to hurt her. But he could not let himself console her. So, he stood and watched as she reined in her emotions. And he felt every bit the cad for it.

"Why...?" she said before sniffling then clearing her throat. "Why is it you aren't staying with your parents?"

When she met his gaze, there was none of the spiteful, demanding woman he had known her to be. There may just be more under the surface. More than he expected.

"Nick?" Her question broke into his thoughts, and he realized he had been staring.

Looking toward the street and those passing by, he tried to forget the sound of his name on her lips and how it warmed him. "It's not important."

Then she glared at him. "Was your family not pleased to see you?" There was something in her gaze that told him she suspected there might be more to the situation.

He set hands to his gun belt. "It's complicated."

"I see." She nodded.

The silence that followed became thick with unspoken words and whispers of the kiss they'd almost shared. Was that even possible? To regret something that should never have happened—and didn't?

"I'd best not keep you from your...work." He still couldn't fathom how it was that she had been made to work as a common employee at the hotel. What more was there to that story?

She glanced back to the front of the hotel. "Yeah."

"I'll walk you back." He stepped toward the boardwalk.

She held up a hand. "I thank you, but no." The sudden depth in her eyes gave him pause.

He nodded and remained as she spun and, with arms still firmly wrapped around her torso, walked back to the hotel and slipped inside.

Now that she was out of sight, he let himself fall against the wall. What was happening? What had become of their terse interactions? Would he trade this awkwardness for the spite she had sent his way before?

No, he wouldn't. For she was an enigma. And this softer side had become equally intriguing. He liked it. Very much.

But there was no place for him to entertain such thoughts. His dreams did not allow him to consider bringing along a woman for a few years yet. There was no place for a lady in his life. For a fine lady...probably never.

He straightened, shaking his legs to remove any last remnants of her presence. Despite what had occurred between them, he must go back into the hotel and settle his account. That did not seem possible at the moment.

It might be best if he took this opportunity to wire Sheriff Brandt about his plans to linger a few days. He prayed the man would be understanding. He would need the man's full recommendation to move things along on the road to becoming a US Marshal.

Even if a future with a woman like Betsy were possible, it was an unnecessary distraction right now. After all, he had a plan. And it didn't involve such attachments.

He pushed off the wall and stepped onto the dirt road. Finishing the needed tasks to secure his room would have to wait.

The walk to the telegraph office on the other side of Cripple Creek took mere minutes. As he neared, the door to the clinic opened.

Wyatt Sullivan nearly knocked him over as he rushed out. Then his eyes went wide. "My apologies, Nick. I didn't see you there."

"Not a problem." Nick wondered if perhaps he needed to pay better attention. For his thoughts kept flitting, unbidden, to blonde curls and a curt smile.

"I had hoped to run into you." Wyatt set his hat on his head.

"What?" Did the doctor really mean that?

"Oh..." Wyatt chuckled. "I mean, I hoped to catch you at some point and ask after your adventures."

Nick gave Wyatt a sideways look. Did the man tease?

"Last I heard from your mother, you took a deputy position in Denver. Gave up your ranch hand days." He smiled, a genuine grin.

Nick relaxed. "Yeah. At some point it became obvious that I wanted more than being a hired hand."

Wyatt nodded. "I can understand that." He turned back to the clinic and locked the door. "I'm headed to the café for some vittles. You hungry?"

Nick's stomach churned in response to the sound of food. "I suppose I am. I'd like that."

The two men moved off in the direction Nick had come from. Perhaps the wire to Denver could wait.

"How are you these days?" Nick didn't quite know how to ask about Betsy. Nor did he really want to hear about it, but something must have happened. For it had always seemed—in school at least—that she had her eyes set on Wyatt. Did something occur to change that?

"Good." Wyatt's voice indeed testified to that fact. There was no hesitation. "With a wonderful wife, active children, and a clinic that is too small for the town, I stay busy."

"Children?" Nick said, the word not feeling quite right on his tongue.

"Yes." Wyatt's tone warmed. "Katherine and I have three now."

"That's fantastic!" And Nick felt a tug of jealousy that he did not expect. His efforts were firmly trained on his goal. A wife and kids were not something he had factored in. A stray thought brought Betsy's face back into focus. Preposterous. Wait...had Wyatt just mentioned...? "Katherine? Katherine Matthews?"

"One and the same." Wyatt beamed.

Nick shook his head. "Last I heard, she had gone to San Francisco to continue her schooling."

"That is true. She came back. And we...well, it's a long story."

Nick resisted the urge to speak into the moment, giving Wyatt space to continue if he cared to.

But he didn't. And they soon stepped to the entrance to Mrs. Abby's eatery. Ushering Nick within, Wyatt gave Mrs. Abby a smile and a hello.

She looked at Nick curiously. Then her face lit up. "Is that little Nick Hammond?"

"I don't think he's all that little anymore." Wyatt clapped him on the back.

"That's for sure." Mrs. Abby all but purred. "It's good to have you back. Let me get you two seated." She led them to a table near one of the café's windows.

After they settled, Nick couldn't hold back the question burning in his gut. "I gotta tell you, I would have bet almost anything you and Betsy would have ended up hitched."

Wyatt frowned and peered out the window. The air around them became tense. "Good thing you're not a betting man."

Nick got the message. This was not a subject to dwell on. Had Betsy rebuffed Wyatt's attempts? It seemed that most of the interest had been on her part. Was she so fickle?

Wyatt adjusted his focus back to the table. "How long are you in town?"

"Only a few days." Nick fingered the napkin on the table. "I had a job to do and that's done. But I want to spend some time with my mother and sister."

Wyatt offered a half smile. "If you have the time, I bet Katie would like to see you."

"Sure." Nick wasn't at all certain, but it seemed like the thing to say. His gaze wandered out the window. "So much has changed." He mused.

"Sure has." Wyatt glanced about the eatery.

"But not everything."

"That's true."

"Say, whatever happened to Timothy?" They could always revisit school days and friends.

Wyatt was silent, almost pensive as he rearranged his fork and knife.

Again, Nick sensed he had mis-stepped. "I just—" A blur of movement out the window grabbed Nick's attention. When he turned in that direction, he saw that a few men had spilled out of the bar and were tussling in the road.

He stood abruptly. "That can't be good."

Wyatt was right behind him when Nick rushed out of the café.

CHAPTER 12

Clashing

Betsy flushed with heat as she thought again about Nick's closeness. She kept her head turned downward as she walked along the boarded planks that lined the street. Her father, beseeched by Mrs. Thompson, had given her leave after she stumbled one too many times in her chores. True, she was tired, but it was more than that.

She had been driven to distraction by Nick. And that had never happened to her before. Indeed, Betsy couldn't place where was her head was. She'd been both relieved and upset that he hadn't kissed her. And that didn't make any sense.

Brushing her lips with her fingertips, she remembered how his hand had grazed the side of her face, his mouth so close she could feel the whisper of his breath mingling with hers. Her insides stirred to swirling. She was out of control. That must not happen. She would not let a man drive her to such a place. This must stop.

She coughed. The dust that surrounded her thickened. What caused that? She looked up. Men rushed from the saloon and gathered in the road, fists flying.

Betsy shrieked and pressed against the outer wall of the building. What was happening? She struggled to make out anything with all the shouting and cracking as fists collided with flesh. It sickened her.

More, how could she slip by without drawing attention or getting caught up in the tussle? More men stumbled out of the vagrant establishment. She was not safe here.

Looking back toward the hotel, she considered running that way. But with several small fights breaking out between here and there, would that be wise?

The bank was closer, just down the alleyway to her right.

She'd best take that route while it was open to her.

Decided, she ducked into the slender space between the saloon and the barber shop and picked up her pace. If she never saw such a ruckus again, it would be too soon.

Her heart raced as she scurried along. She kept looking back, but no one followed her. Still, she would not stop. As she burst through the other side of the alley, she slipped quickly into the bank.

The pounding of her heart filled her senses. How long would it be before she could catch her breath?

"Miss? Are you well?" This from a masculine voice that sounded similar to, though not as deep as, Nick's pleasant baritone.

She jerked back from the extended hand as she shifted her regard in that direction.

A man in a fine suit stood before her. A man that oddly reminded her of Nick. Was she so delusional after their interaction that she would conjure up such an image on another person's affect?

"Betsy?" The man definitely seemed to know her.

She settled her gaze for a longer study of his features. And all she could discern were the angles that reminded her of Nick. Though, unlike Nick's scruffy jawline, this gentleman was clean shaven but for a well-kept mustache. There was something oddly familiar about him. Perhaps it was nothing more than the image of Nick she kept putting onto his features.

"Yes. Do I...do I know you?" She didn't have the wherewithal to realize how incredibly rude that sounded until the words were out. She straightened and ran a hand down her now-dirtied apron. "I apologize. I just...ran from a brawl in the street outside the saloon. I'm a bit out of sorts."

"Do not think anything of it."

She narrowed her eyes and tried to press Nick out of mind and conjure some memory of who this might be. "I am sorry, sir. I cannot place you."

"That's all right. You were a few years ahead of me in school. And I didn't have a mustache then." He waggled his perfectly placed eyebrows.

Her confusion only intensified. She had gone to school with this man? Again, she felt the heel. All of her attention during those years had been hooked firmly on Wyatt Sullivan. It was a miracle she finished her schooling at all. Especially as her mother's only emphasis was on finding a suitable husband.

She shook her head. "But you knew me?"

He tilted his head downward and peered at her with a wide smile that shone a couple of dimples in both cheeks. "Everyone did. Betsy Callaway has always been renowned as the loveliest girl in all of Cripple Creek."

Was it her imagination, or did the man's face redden?

"Oh. That is kind of you to say." Surely not everyone thought that. Wyatt hadn't. Nick hadn't. What was it with thinking about Nick yet again? Would he never leave her mind?

"I'm Karl. Karl Hammond. My dad owns the bank." He straightened his shoulders and tugged his jacket firmly as he said it. His declaration came with some measure of pride.

"How nice." Her heart stuttered, and she remembered where she had come from. She lifted a hand to tuck an errant curl behind her ear.

"Oh my!" His features clouded. "Are you injured?" He reached out the lightest touch to her bandaged arm.

"Oh, that?" She was touched by his concern. "It is an injury that is well healed."

His eyebrows gathered. "But you still need a bandage?"

She nodded. "A precaution at this point." She bit at her lip, wanting for a change of subject. "Might I...linger here for a bit? At least until the fighting is under control?"

"Of course." He grinned, showing perfect teeth. "Stay as long as you'd like. Hopefully Sheriff Jones won't have it under control too soon."

"What?" She furrowed her brow. Did he want the fighting to continue?

"That is…" He cleared his throat. "I wouldn't mind an excuse to spend more time with you." Then his smile fell and the red in his face deepened. "Forgive me, I am rather awe struck and far too forward."

"Not at all." She offered him one of her most charming smiles. Could this be Nick's younger brother? That small scrawny boy from their school days? Now he was a clean-cut man with the advantage of a rather wealthy family. Perhaps even due to inherit the bank. And he was fond of her. This was the makings of the best kind of…friendship.

"Please, come and sit." He waved her farther in. "You must be worn out from your close call."

"Thank you." She followed him to a bench at the far end of the room, suddenly fighting tears. She *had* had a close call. It had been horrid.

To her surprise, he sat beside her. Rather close. More so than he needed to. But she found it inviting, though it was a bit forward for him to assume she wished it.

"You still don't seem at ease. Shall I get you something? A glass of water perhaps?"

She waved him off. "Just sit with me for a few moments." Now who was being forward? She cringed at her words but hid it by looking away. Perhaps she only needed to appear interested and hope that genuine feelings would follow. Because her heart tugged at her, pulling her toward memories of Nick. And that was the last thing she wanted.

Shifting her focus back to Karl, she pressed on a sweet smile and attended his words with more eagerness than she felt.

Thwack!

Nick's head spun. Not only because of the rush of movement surrounding him, but also due to the well-placed punch by the man swaying to his right. Every time Nick separated two combatants, another pair became more aggressive.

His vision cleared and he glanced about for Wyatt. The doctor had no more luck than he.

A gunshot sounded and jerked most of the men from their angered stupor. It also snagged Nick's attention.

Looking in the direction the shot came from, he spotted Sheriff Jones. Even then, he dismounted from a patch-patterned horse as he lowered his revolver. "That's enough!"

Nick couldn't help but be relieved. The sheriff would sort this out.

Men came from around the sheriff and spread through the crowd. His deputies?

"Doc?" The sheriff's booming voice was closer now. "What are you doing here?"

A deputy pushed Nick. Without thinking, he spun toward the assault.

"Go on home." The cross man fairly spat the words at him. "That's not a suggestion."

"But I wasn't part of the—"

"I don't care." The man came closer until he was directly in Nick's face. As if that would do anything but rile him.

Nick scanned for Wyatt. They would surely trust the doctor's word. But Wyatt stood by the sheriff, chatting, with his back to Nick.

"Listen." Nick put his hands up in a motion of surrender. "I just wanted to help."

"You can 'help' by getting yourself out of my face. Before I lose my temper."

What was wrong with this deputy? Did he really expect such behavior would calm the situation? "I'm a—"

"I don't care if you're the king of England. Now, get!" He glared at Nick and made a shooing motion with his hands.

What were Nick's options at this point? As much as he wanted to give as good as he got, he would not do anything to make the situation worse. So, he nodded.

Then the deputy took a step back, folded his arms, and watched Nick.

"May I at least check on my friend?" Nick pointed at Wyatt.

A scowl covered the man's features as he shook his head. "Maybe I need to lock you up for a couple of nights. Would that straighten you out?"

Nick walked past him, bumping the deputy's shoulder as he did so. He didn't care if it wasn't his best move.

The deputy whirled around, grabbed Nick's arm, and threw a punch.

Nick ducked it easily. And, as he straightened, he shoved the man away.

The deputy had been thrown off balance by the force of his intended punch. And when Nick pushed him, he toppled.

There wasn't a sense of satisfaction filling Nick, but rather regret. That hadn't been necessary. What was his best course of action now? What would the Lord want him to do?

He pressed out a breath and closed his eyes, wishing away his tension and anger. Then he reached a hand toward the deputy. Would the man accept it? Allow Nick to get him to rights?

The deputy spat at Nick's proffered hand and the man's eyes narrowed. "You've done it now."

"Silas!" The booming voice of the sheriff called from Nick's right.

Nick spun in that direction.

A scrambling behind Nick begged him turn, but before he could, a large weight hit him from that direction, knocking him to the ground. As well, it pressed the air from his lungs.

Nick tried to remove the man's bulk from himself as he gasped for breath.

"That's only the start," the man called Silas sneered.

"Enough!" Sheriff Jones grabbed his deputy's shoulders. "Get up."

Silas paused but obeyed. But not before eyeing Nick one last time, a threat in his gaze.

Once the man was off, Nick sucked in air.

Wyatt held his hand out for Nick, who nodded and grabbed it.

Now on his feet, he scanned for Silas.

The sheriff was in the process of giving him a dress down to the left. All Nick could make out was the angry thrum of the sheriff as he poked a finger at Silas's chest.

And Nick almost felt bad for Silas... almost.

"You okay?" Wyatt leaned closer to look at the right side of Nick's face, probably red and swollen. It certainly smarted.

Nick nodded. "It's nothing. I've had worse."

Wyatt scanned the side of Nick's face. "Still, you might need something to help that heal faster."

Nick shook his head. "Don't worry about me. There are bound to be other injuries that need attention."

With an exasperated grunt, Wyatt moved onto those that remained about. He would have these men patched up and back in the saloon in no time. Not that their return to their rough life was Doc's fault. These men had their patterns. And they usually included warming a bar stool.

Nick ran his hands down his sleeves and shirt front, attempting to remove as much dirt as possible. He reached up to touch the side of his face and immediately jerked back. Throbbing heated pulsed strongly. Whomever had gotten that punch in had aimed well.

Settled that he wasn't more seriously injured, he scanned the area.

Men scattered, likely headed for their homes. Or the boarding house, Nick groused. He turned, hoping to seek out Sheriff Jones. But something caught his eye by the saloon.

He homed in on the couple walking by. The woman's blonde curls bounced, and the man set a hand to hers, which was wrapped around his forearm. Those curls belonged to none other than Betsy Callaway. What was she doing here? Wasn't she supposed to be at the hotel, far from this rowdy display?

Nick's glare drifted to the man. And an all too familiar face smiled at Betsy. Nick knew that look. And that face.

Regret sliced through him. Because Betsy walked with someone else? Or with *him*—the brother who had made it clear he never wished to see Nick again?

His heart squeezed and his whole chest tightened painfully. And he prayed that he misunderstood the adoring look Betsy tossed in Karl's direction.

Nick had to get out of the hotel...frequently. Avoiding Betsy while hoping to come across her had been an impossible goal. She was everywhere—in the scent of the flowers, the smoothness of the table surfaces, and the light coming in the window. So, he found himself seeking out his mother and Anya. Weren't they, after all, why he had delayed returning to Denver?

Even now he turned his head to the side as his mother reached for his bruised cheek. "It's nothing, Ma. Honest."

"Don't tell me that. I have eyes, don't I?" Gingerly, she fingered the swollen area. "Did you see Dr. Sullivan about this?"

"He was there when it happened...as I mentioned before." Nick pulled back from her touch yet again. "He didn't seem concerned, so I did nothing further." Glancing at Anya, he prayed she could see his plea for assistance.

Anya nodded. "Ma, we don't have much time to spend with Nick. Let's not waste it arguing."

Ma looked at Anya, then back at Nick, and set her hands in her lap. "If you are certain."

Nick laid a hand over Ma's. "I assure you. I am fine." Then he offered Anya a smile.

In the next moment, Ma stood. "I have to get something started for supper."

"Ma, you can't be serious. We just finished lunch." Nick tipped his head at their plates, still sitting on the table.

Ma and Anya exchanged a look.

Then Ma sputtered, "There is just a bit that I need to do."

Nick's eyebrows lifted as he peered at Anya. "Something special happening tonight?"

Ma stilled, then shifted her shoulders and continued into the kitchen. Obviously, she wasn't going to tell him. There were other ways to find out. He was a trained deputy after all...how hard could it be to get information from his sister? She had never been good at keeping secrets anyway.

He rose and reached for his hat. "I think I'll go check on the wagon. See what I can do about that wheel you complained about."

Ma looked in his direction. "That would be nice." She seemed a little at a loss. "Unless you need to get back to town."

He shook his head and peered at Anya. "No. No need to get back right away. Besides, I'll have to head back to Denver day after tomorrow. This might be my only chance."

Ma froze and found his gaze. A frown created deeper lines in her face. "Nikolai...are you sure you have to leave so soon?"

As he stepped toward Ma, he offered a smile he didn't feel. "You know I do. Sheriff Brandt grows antsy. He needs all his deputies to manage such a large city." He embraced her and spoke into her shoulder. "But I'll be back before you know it."

She sniffled and leaned away. "You promise?"

It wasn't fully up to him if or when he came back. But he couldn't avoid her question.

"As soon as I can."

Ma patted his arms. "That's the best I can hope for, I suppose."

He smiled. "Perhaps next time you see me, I'll be a U.S. Marshal."

Her smile fell. That did not surprise. She wanted her baby chicks, now all grown, to stay close and safe. But that wasn't him, hence the need to strike out on his own.

Planting a soft kiss on her cheek, he muttered, "It will be fine. I promise." Then he shifted his regard from his mother's eyes, already welling with moisture, to his sister. "You care to help me?"

Anya gave him a curious look, her eyebrows furrowed and mouth tight. "I—"

"Thanks. I appreciate your assistance."

"But I—"

He waved a hand. "I won't ask you to do much. Maybe you can just keep me company."

She glanced at Ma. Something passed between them. But by the time he peered at Ma, she had turned toward the oven.

If Ma thought she could keep Anya quiet about whatever had them so stirred up, she was sorely mistaken. Which, in all honesty, she probably knew.

Nick stepped to the front door and held a hand out for his sister.

She hesitated a moment, then, fisting her hands in her skirt, she all but stomped in that direction.

It wasn't long before they were strolling to the barn. In silence.

That wouldn't do.

"How is Ma, really?"

Anya set a hand on his arm. "She is...well enough. She just wishes you were closer to home. You know how she is."

Nick nodded. They slowed as they approached the barn where the wagon sat. It leaned hard to one corner. So, that's where he started.

A cursory glance told nothing other than it bore more weight than it should. Something with the axle perhaps? He crouched to get a better look.

"What about Karl? How is he?"

Anya was quiet.

Nick stretched to look over the wagon at her.

She bit at her lip.

"Come on, one of us had to bring him up at some point." He shrugged and dropped back down to examine the axle. "So...how is he?"

Anya cleared her throat.

Nick imagined she was measuring her words carefully.

"He is well."

Nick popped back up to shoot a hard look at her. "That's good. But you and I both know you are dodging something."

Anya let out a long breath. "He is working at the bank with Pa. Every day he goes and every evening he comes back."

"Come on, Anya, I could have guessed all of that." He ducked to feel along the axle. "If he won't see me, I just want to know how he is faring. He's my brother too, and I care about him."

The post of the axle, where it connected to the wheel, was bent. But not enough so as to have caused such a drastic shift.

"He really is well." Anya's words were gentle and soft. So much so that the lightest breeze would have swallowed them up. "Pa is very proud of him and how he is handling everything."

Her words brought a sharp pang in his chest.

Proud. Pa was proud of Karl. The man who used to be proud of Nick. Before.

He pushed those thoughts to the side and dipped lower to reach farther under the wagon. Grunting, he said, "I'm glad."

"Are you?" Anya's bold question was his due.

He looked down as his fingers searched for any abnormalities. Was he indeed? Just because he couldn't have Pa's favor didn't mean he begrudged Karl's having it. Did it?

Even so, that wouldn't help matters. If he ever hoped to reconcile with his brother—or his father—he would have to die to what he wanted, to the hurt that their good relationship brought him.

"Honest. I am happy for Karl. He's found his place in life."

And in this family, Nick mused.

Anya leaned against a nearby post. "Will you miss Betsy?"

"What?" he sputtered as he coughed.

"Betsy Callaway." Anya leveled her gaze on him. "Come now, you followed her to Cripple Creek...the viper."

"Excuse me?" Now he stood upright, eyes seeking her face. "That was nothing more than an offer to see her home safely. Nothing more. Besides, it brought me home."

Her features scrunched as if she disapproved. "She's nothing but trouble."

His brow furrowed. "I think she is misunderstood." Then he turned back toward the wagon.

"Truly?" Anya's voice held the scowl he couldn't see. "You didn't have to watch the way she threw herself at Doctor Sullivan. It was absurd. And him married to Katherine. Such vile, sinful, manipulative..."

Nick glanced her way again. "Did you ever consider that she is just trying to protect herself?"

"Did you ever consider that she is just an evil woman? Taking advantage of men when and where she can?"

He shook his head and dropped beside the wagon, resuming his search. "We maybe should treat her with the same kindness Christ showed. Even if we don't agree with her...behavior."

Anya pushed out a breath but said nothing further.

His reach neared the point where the axle, inside the skein, ran to the center of the underside. Something didn't seem right—with the axle or with whatever his sister held close.

A sharp pinch caused him to jerk his hand back. He lost his balance, precarious as it was to begin with. Pitching forward, he knocked his head on the wheel, then fell back and onto his rear.

Anya was by his side in a moment. "Nick! Are you all right?"

"I'm fine," he said with a grunt. He used an elbow to ease her back a bit. Then he got to his feet.

"You're bleeding." Anya stepped closer.

He used his uninjured arm to hold her at bay. It had been a long time since he'd let anyone baby him like this. "It's fine."

"No, you're not," she fumed. "Let me take a look at that."

Between her insistence and the white-hot pain, he gave in and held his hand out.

She seethed. To be fair, it was a lot of blood.

Turning, she grabbed for a blanket that had to be covered in horsehair and dirt. Regardless, it was something.

So, he let her press the corner of the blanket to his cut. How deep was it? Would he need stitches?

"Keep this on it. I'll go get Ma." She spun in the direction of the barn door.

He grabbed for her arm. "No, you don't."

She whirled back toward him, a question in her eyes.

"Before we get Ma all stirred up, let's see how bad it is." Even as he spoke, he grimaced.

She nodded with some reluctance.

He leaned against the wagon, holding the cloth in place. "Looks like we have some time to kill. Why don't you just tell me what you and Ma are hiding? You know you want to."

Wide brown eyes stared up at him. She *did* want to tell him.

"Your head," she said on a gasp while reaching fingertips toward his forehead. "You're going to have quite the—"

"Anya," he said a bit more harshly than intended as he leaned away from her. "Just tell me."

She finally looked at him in the eyes. "I—"

The rumble of horse hooves on the packed dirt road reached them and grew louder.

Anya jerked her regard that way.

As did Nick.

A surrey approached, led by a chestnut mare with darker, nearly black hair—Karl's horse.

Nick narrowed his gaze to get a better look. Was it Pa and Karl? Home early perhaps? But one of the figures wore a dress.

Did Karl have a sweetheart? Then it occurred to him—what he had seen after the saloon brawl. Was that...Betsy?

He tore his gaze from the fast-approaching couple and to his sister. "I have to go."

"Nick, don't be so rash. You need tending." She gripped his forearm.

He didn't want to shake her off, but he couldn't stay and see Karl with Betsy on his arm. And just why not? The thought was a wonder. Something for him to consider later. Not now.

He glanced at his sister's pained expression. What did she know? Did she suspect he had a care for Betsy? And more...did he?

Betsy let Karl help her down from the seat of the fine buggy. She offered him a smile that was surely about to crack her cheeks. It didn't, but it made the muscles of her face ache just a bit.

He, in turn, grinned as he assisted her.

"Thank you," she said, fluttering her eyelashes. Was it so wrong to take the feelings she had and push them to their limit? It wasn't lying... exactly.

Voices in the direction of the barn drew her attention that way.

Nick stood just within, arguing with a young woman who held his hand between hers. What was that about? And why should it bother her so?

She shook free of that thought and looked at Karl. That's where her focus needed to be. But his gaze seemed to have followed hers. And he frowned as he now glared at Nick.

Setting her mind to be pleasant and nonchalant, she sighed. "What is Nick doing here?"

He jerked his regard to her. "How do you know Nick?"

His grip on her hand tightened.

Betsy winced. Her hand no longer required bandaging but was not so healed that this did not hurt. She needed to remedy this...fast. It would not do to push Karl away. Or give him the impression there was anything beyond curiosity in her question. Was there?

Giving his arm a gentle squeeze with her other hand as she stepped closer, she forced a smile onto her face. "I was in school with him."

Karl's features relaxed, as did his hold on her. "Oh...that's right."

She slid her previously injured hand out from his grip and looped it through the crook of his arm. If she didn't fess up to more, Karl would find out and wonder why she omitted the whole of it. In fact, she wondered why she had the urge to hold things back from him. Was there more to her consideration of Nick? Such nonsense! It was not worth the risk. Not now, when she had finally found a prospect that was well established and had money—just the kind of man her mother would approve of.

"He also escorted me home from Denver after that terrible stagecoach holdup." She pushed out her bottom lip in a perfect pout. "You remember, those horrible bandits that wounded me."

He set his other hand on hers, giving them a gentle pat. "That's right."

For some reason, she was drawn to look in Nick's direction again.

He and the rather lovely young woman had stopped arguing and stared in her and Karl's direction.

A pulse flowed through her, the thrum of something not altogether unpleasant.

Though Nick's narrowed eyes and furrowed brow told much.

Betsy cleared her throat and forced her regard back to Karl. "Isn't Nick your brother?"

"Not anymore." Karl's voice was steady and steely.

She wanted to ask him to tell her more but thought better of it. "Shall we get out of this heat? Go into the house? I am so very eager to meet your mother." With gentle movement, she tugged him toward the steps.

He resisted at first but obliged soon after.

Though she should not, she peered in the direction of the barn again.

Nick and the woman were gone. It gave her a bit of a start. Where had they gone? What was between them? What had happened while she had been focused on Karl?

As quickly as the questions came, she dismissed them and let Karl assist her up the porch stairs and to the door.

Betsy grinned at him and slipped a hand free to straighten her blouse and touch her curls, ensuring each hair was pinned in place. Meeting Karl's mother meant a great deal to him. She would not diminish the importance nor let herself be distracted by Nick and whomever he conversed with.

Karl shifted toward her. "Are you ready?"

Pushing the portion of her hair that remained down over her shoulders, she nodded. "Of course."

"Don't be worried. She will love you...almost as much as I do."

Betsy paused. He had not said that before. Did he love her? How could that be? They had only been courting for nearly a week. Was he so taken with her?

Something in her struggled with that prospect. Was it truly right for her to lead him on? Perhaps, if she didn't intend to marry him…but that wasn't the case. She was committed to seeing this through.

After all, he was perfect. Right? Everything her parents wanted. Wasn't he?

Then why did her heart ache?

There was little time to think on it. For Karl swung the door open.

A warmth that went beyond the heat of the fireplace greeted her. Along with the aroma of stewing beef.

Karl closed the door behind himself, cutting off her last escape.

She eased in a few steps and offered him another smile. Was she supposed to wait for an introduction before proceeding farther? But as she scanned the area, she couldn't find anyone in the immediate rooms.

"Mother?" Karl called as he moved into the kitchen, looking both ways. "Anya?"

Who was Anya? Oh, yes, their sister! Was that who had been speaking with Nick?

"I wonder where she could be." Karl's face scrunched. He wasn't pleased. But he had never been more than a little upset when he'd come upon such situations before. There was no doubt his composure would return soon enough.

"Wait here. I'll see if she's in the back." He strolled toward the back hallway, calling for his mother. His voice echoed off the walls as it diminished.

Betsy ran a hand down her skirt for lack of anything better to do.

Footsteps on the stairs to the left of the kitchen caused her to look up. Long legs became a figure that was more familiar than she'd have cared.

"Nick?" The word escaped before she could stop it. How had he made it into the house and up the stairs so quickly? Was there a back door she didn't know about?

He stalled just moments from the bottom step. His features slackened. Did he know why she was here? "Betsy."

Why did he have to say her name like that? Like there had been an entirely too intimate moment just a couple weeks ago? Like he was more familiar than he should be?

She looked away, unable to take in the blue of his eyes any longer. "Karl is looking for your mother."

"Oh." Nick glanced back up the stairs to the second level. Only then did she notice that he held one of his hands and that it was bandaged. What had happened?

She shook her head. It wasn't her place to care. And she didn't.

He stepped down the remaining stairs and moved toward the door. "I'd best get out of your way."

As he passed, she reached out before she could register her movement.

He paused and caught her gaze with his. There was more there than she wanted to see—hurt, confusion, and disappointment.

Why should she care? But she did. "Are you all right?"

She had meant the bandaged hand, but as she spoke, she realized how it sounded. Though she couldn't correct herself. Her heart beat harder at his nearness.

"I'm fine." His words were soft.

"I can't seem to figure out where my mother..." Karl came back into the main room. And then his footfalls stopped.

A thick silence fell over the space as Betsy turned her head in his direction.

"What are you doing?" Karl's words were thick and edged with sharpness.

"I..." Betsy started but couldn't seem to conjure anything else.

"Answer me." Heat suffused his words.

Nick pulled out of Betsy's grasp. "I was just leaving."

Karl closed the distance between himself and Betsy in a few strides, inserting himself between her and Nick.

Nick backed up. "Really, Karl, I was about to—"

"Don't." The single word Karl emitted was harsh. "You think you're entitled to everything that is mine."

Nick glanced from Karl to Betsy and back again. "That's not true. I have never wanted what you had. Never."

The tension only thickened. Betsy was caught between wanting to soothe Karl's ire and her heart which hurt for Nick's obvious pain.

Karl's eyes narrowed. "That's what *you* say."

More thumping on the stairs belied that others came.

Betsy looked in that direction to see the young lady from the barn and an older woman who froze, her eyes widening.

Karl didn't seem to notice that they'd been interrupted, but Nick shifted his focus.

"I just want to leave." Nick once again moved toward the door.

Karl flew across the space and a cracking sound told that his fist collided with Nick.

"Nikolai!" the older woman screamed.

The young woman rushed to the base of the stairs.

Betsy's feet placed her in the thick of it without giving her a chance to think. She reached for Karl's arm, trying to pull him back.

Nick slumped against the door, a hand pressed to his face.

"You aren't going to fight back?" Karl yelled.

Nick's clear blue eyes flashed in Karl's direction. "Not with you."

Betsy continued to tug at a resistant Karl.

The other young woman moved in their direction. But before she could assist, Karl rocked back and loosened from Betsy's grasp. Not in time for Betsy to catch her balance.

Her body slammed into the floor, her wrist on fire upon impact.

"Betsy!" Nick called out.

Karl spun as she looked up. He moved in her direction.

Nick grabbed Karl's shoulder. "If you *ever* lay a hand on her..." He held back the rest of the sentence.

Karl turned on him. "You'll what?"

Nick's eyes became as fire. "Just don't."

Karl fumed. "You can't tell me what to do."

Nick stepped closer to his brother.

"For the love of all that's holy!" The older woman—perhaps their mother—stepped forward, but their sister barred her from coming closer.

Nick glanced over Karl's shoulder toward the women and his face eased. Then he moved to the door, cast one last look at Betsy. Anya leaned over her, supporting her and helping her to her feet.

"Don't come back," Karl seethed.

Nick paused.

Betsy feared the exchange would continue.

But Nick went out the door, shutting it soundly behind himself.

CHAPTER 14

Disoriented

Nick stirred and came slowly to consciousness. But he didn't want to. The stupor of sleep was much preferable to his thoughts. The memories of the previous day's encounter with Karl and Betsy gave way to an aching heart.

He sat up on the edge of the bed. Everything was still dark. Typically, he preferred the dark greet him in the morning. Perhaps it lingered from his ranch hand days, but there was something fulfilling about waking before dawn and getting things done.

But this day he sat and stared at the dimness beyond the window. Though he hadn't requested any particular view, his room had a winning view of a shrub. Not even that thought could turn his mind from the difficult moments this trip had brought.

He shouldn't have come. His father didn't care about him and would not forgive Nick's impulsive youth. And his brother...well, Karl hated him. Plain and simple. One of those, he merited. The other, he wasn't certain was his due.

Something rose within him. But it wasn't the urge to get out of bed. More like the desire to return to the safety of the covers, to trade the darkness of the room for the darkness of unconsciousness. He grimaced.

And a sharp pain filled his features. He tenderly touched the eye that had been hit while breaking up the bar fight. Then, remembering his brother's fist late yesterday, he felt along his jaw. It smarted even more.

What was he to do? Sit here and lick his wounds? Pretend that those on his body were the only ones?

Denver.

That was all that was left to him. And while he certainly did not want to leave Anya or Ma without a proper farewell, he couldn't make himself return to that house. He wasn't wanted there.

Lord, what are You doing to me? I thought I followed Your path. And now everything is chaotic and...just too hard.

His prayer was heartfelt, but simple. There was nothing more he could think to say. It didn't matter...his foundation in the Lord was firm enough that a dispute with Him about how things progressed would not make Nick the wayward prodigal that his father and brother had decided him to be.

With all the strength he could pull from within, he stood. Forcing a stretch he didn't seek, he was pleased when blood rushed through his limbs and refreshed his muscles. He stepped closer to the window. For what, he wasn't sure. To see the leaves of the bush better?

Even as he bit back a snarky comment for no one, he peered at the sky. The lightest hint of morning peeked through the clouds. The window faced westward, so though he may wish for the light rays to portend a colorful sunrise, it would not come. Streaks of yellows, purples, and pinks would be on display for the world on the other side of the building. But not for him. Seemed fitting.

Though in his mind, the streaks of yellows curled and became flaxen. In the next moment, gold flecked green eyes flickered and an image of Betsy formed. He allowed himself a few moments of indulgence. Her features were soft, well-shaped, and...perfect.

She was beautiful. That had always been her failing. Too attractive for her own good. And she relied on it, utilized it as a weapon. Yet there was more beyond that...and he knew it. He had glimpsed it many times in these last weeks.

Why wouldn't she let that out? Why did she shut down those more vulnerable places? As if they were a weakness. Indeed, that was not how he saw them.

He sighed. Once again, it didn't matter. She had chosen which path she would take. Karl was everything she wanted...or at least thought she did. Due to inherit the bank, he would be able to care for her in the way she had been accustomed. The way she deserved.

Unlike Nick.

His sights were on a job that would lend itself even less to stability than being a deputy. His hope to join the U.S. Marshals and bring justice to territories sorely in need of it was counterintuitive to a wife. But it was there he could be of the most service and make the most difference.

Not here. Not now.

So, while he may find Betsy an intriguing puzzle, he could not begrudge her a better life...with Karl.

Dressing quickly, he then went through the motions of gathering his things. How would he pass the hours before the stage would leave Cripple Creek? It wouldn't be until much later this afternoon. Might he dare trespass on his father's house again? That, again, was not likely.

Should he seek out the church? Spend some time praying? Yes, that would be best.

But first, he needed to secure his passage to Denver.

He splashed water on his face and ran a hand over the stubble along his jawline. Should he shave? It wasn't truly necessary before traveling. And God didn't care about his outward appearance...just his heart. His wounded, bruised heart. Though he had brought that to God many years ago, he felt a deep ache that penetrated what he had believed to have been made whole.

Finally finished with his ablutions, he slipped out of the room. He prayed with every step he took that he would not come across Betsy in the lobby or entryway. But when he made it outside of the hotel without spotting her, he couldn't deny his disappointment. Shoving that out of mind, he strolled in the direction of the stage office.

Wagon wheels crunching on the dirt of the road drew his attention. Wyatt Sullivan directed his horse down the main stretch. This time, Katherine, holding a young child, sat beside him.

Without thinking, Nick waved. Then jerked his hand down, regretting his action. He didn't want to linger in conversation with his former schoolmates.

Wyatt halted the wagon by the livery and dropped down before helping Katherine.

Though as Wyatt took care of the horse and cart, Katherine waved at Nick and rushed over. "Nick? Nick Hammond?"

He smiled. And was surprised that it was more genuine than he'd expected. "Katherine Matthews...that is, I mean...Sullivan."

She waved a hand as if to bat his mistake to the side. "You call me whichever." Her breaths came rapidly from her quick pace.

The child in her arms reached up to touch Katherine's braid.

A smile engulfed Katherine's face as she tugged her hair free of the little girl's hand and tossed it over her shoulder. "Wyatt said you were in town. I'm glad I got to see you."

He let the warmth of her words curl his lips. "So am I. And who is this?"

Katherine made a motion to turn the child to face him but met with too much resistance as the chubby hands gripped onto the front of her dress. "This is Miss Ellie Mae."

That tugged at Nick's heart anew—to remember the tragedy that befell Ellie Mae. It reminded him why he had formed such a bad opinion of Betsy in the first place. She had been largely at fault for the incident with the way she taunted and teased Katherine, goading her into a dare that never should have been posed.

"That's..." He cleared his throat. "That's perfect."

Katherine hugged the girl closer and offered a smile that brightened her eyes. It, too, warmed his heart. He had never thought Katherine would get past the death of her friend.

"I'd love to have you to the house for dinner. How much longer are you in town?"

He looked at the ground. "I'm actually returning to Denver today. Sheriff Brandt gave me leave to visit, but I need to get back and resume my duties." Why he felt the need to omit the part about escorting Betsy, he wasn't sure. But he did.

Katherine's smile fell. "I'm sorry to hear that. Do you have plans to come home for the holidays?"

How was it possible for her to hit all the sore spots?

He shook his head slowly. "I do not."

"Surely your mother and father..." She paused.

What did she know? What did all the townsfolk know of his departure a few years ago?

"I'm sorry." Her features tightened.

"It's all right." He looked toward the livery, wishing for Wyatt to come help him in some way. But the doctor was caught up in his own conversation with the livery owner. So much for that.

"Did you see your mother? And Anya?"

He nodded. "Our time was brief, but good." He folded his arms.

"Do you have anything planned between now and the stage?"

He shook his head. "Nothing I can think of."

She looked back and, getting Wyatt's attention, waved him over before returning her attention to Nick. "Then I think we owe you breakfast...or at least a cup of coffee."

He wanted to refuse, but he craved this connection with his past. Even if it wouldn't last longer than a trip to the café. He needed it. "I think I can manage that."

Wyatt joined them shortly thereafter.

Katherine nodded at Nick but spoke to Wyatt. "We are taking Nick to breakfast."

Wyatt looked from his wife to Nick. "Well, what are we waiting on? I'm starved!"

Nick chuckled as his own stomach grumbled. Maybe his final hours in Cripple Creek wouldn't be half bad.

Today held every promise. Betsy admired herself in the mirror. She had pinched some color into her cheeks, and the rosiness of her appearance had no equal. Her long blonde curls had been swept up and the brilliant green dress she wore highlighted the brightness of her hair.

Her mind flitted to the exchange yesterday between Nick and Karl. What disturbed her the most was how her heart went out to Nick, not Karl. Nick had been visibly pained by his brother's words. So had their mother. Though, after Nick left, the tension had melted. Still, Karl had continued to bristle. It made her formal introduction to his mother and sister—and later his father—a bit strained.

It was no matter...parents always loved her. She was beautiful and capable as a homemaker. No other young woman in Cripple Creek could cook, mend, or tend house better than her. What else could a man want in a wife?

Karl certainly seemed interested in making their courtship more permanent. Why else would he bring her home to meet his parents? As he had said goodnight that evening, he'd asked once more about meeting her parents.

She had kept a smile on her features and didn't show how inwardly she had balked at the suggestion. And always did when he asked. But why? If she wanted them to be affianced, she would need to bring him home to officially be introduced as her beau.

What held her back? Again, her mind wandered to Nick's clear blue eyes. Not altogether unlike his brother's deeper shade of blue. But when she allowed her thoughts to wander, they would find their way to Nick —to his kindness, to the way he had wanted to rescue her and help her learn to defend herself. As if he thought she was able to be more independent.

Was that what she wanted?

No. She shook her head. A secure marriage was what she needed. Karl could provide that. He would provide that.

Not only had Nick never expressed a desire for a commitment, he hadn't even seemed to like her. Well, except for that almost kiss that still made her pulse race when she recalled it.

"Betsy?" Mother called to her from the lower level. "Are you ready yet?"

"Yes, Mother," she yelled back. Rising from her vanity, she smoothed a hand down her vibrant emerald skirt.

It may be a little much for going to town to see to a few things with Mother, but she intended to also make a stop at the bank and see Karl. She had to reassure him that she cared only for him. And not for how her traitorous heart pulled at her. Her will was stronger. Besides that, she fully knew what was best for her future.

Spinning, she checked that the lace collar at the back of her dress lay just right. Everything was in place.

Then she walked out of the room and down the stairs.

"Gracious, girl," Mother said as Betsy appeared in the great room. "You do doddle so."

Betsy smiled. "I wanted to be my best when I see Karl today."

Her mother stepped closer and set a hand to her cheek. "I am so blessed. My daughter has found a fine suitor. Probably the most sought after marriageable man in the town."

Betsy tightened her smile so it would stay in place.

Her mother's treatment had changed quite drastically when she'd informed Mother that she entertained Karl's suit. Was that how her mother saw her? Valuable for the match she could make?

She shook her head. That was nonsense. Her mother loved her.

"When will you bring your young man home for a family dinner? I have an inkling he might propose shortly thereafter."

Betsy had to turn away from her mother. Her stomach churned at the thought.

That was the same as butterflies, right? Just because her stomach became fluttery around Nick didn't mean anything. Karl's affection definitely brought out some movement in her stomach—though maybe not as pleasant. But it was there.

She made a show of arranging the pillows on the settee. Could she look at her mother while the anchor in her gut grew heavier? There was little chance she could maintain a genuine smile.

"Well, I for one, am glad your father released you from that job at the hotel. You will soon have a wedding to plan."

Again, her stomach lurched. Still, she forced a reply. "All in good time."

"If you are ready, let's get going. No time to let the young man's attention wane."

What did that mean? She turned to her mother and was thankful that the woman had moved toward the door and didn't see the grimace Betsy certainly wore.

At length, Betsy stood straighter and held her head up as she made her way to the front door as well.

Soon enough, they were off in their fine surrey.

Conversation as they traveled to the heart of town was mostly on her mother's part. She doted on how amazing a catch Karl was.

Betsy nodded along but could hardly think of anything but Nick's gaze when he'd watched Karl take her hand.

But it didn't mean anything, she was sure of it.

They dropped the horse and cart at the livery and strolled to the General Store.

Mother spotted one of her friends and rushed to her. They took up easy discourse while Betsy waited, her own thoughts and questions assaulting her.

She had to see Karl. Now.

Waiting for a break in the conversation, Betsy excused herself and, smiling, said, "I think I will take my leave to check on my account at the bank."

Mother's smile stretched as she turned to her friend once more. "She's not going to check her account. It is something else entirely that takes her to the bank. Or some*one* else."

Mother's friend grinned as well. "I have heard. What a wonderful match they will make."

Betsy's face heated. As much because of the stirring in her middle as her embarrassment.

"Go on, dear," Mother said, waving a hand in the direction of the bank.

Betsy gave a jerk of a nod and moved off. Though as long as she was in earshot, her mother continued to fairly swoon over the situation.

As Betsy greeted the few people she passed on her way to the bank, she considered their responses. The townsfolk in general seemed to have moved on from her overzealous pursuit of Wyatt years back. And she could now breathe easier among them.

Or could she? Every step that brought her closer to the bank made her chest tighten.

Stop this! She admonished herself. There was nothing for it.

Nick had never been an option. These thoughts of him were just nerves. Karl was her future and that was that.

In a few moments, she stepped through the front door of the bank. A quick scan had her waving back at Mr. Hammond, who spoke with a customer. But Karl was nowhere to be found.

She sighed and the pent up air left her rather relieved. Perhaps she should wait for her beau. Despite her anxiousness, that was why she came. And why she would stay.

Settling in a chair, she watched the back office door. It wasn't but a minute or two before Karl came from the hallway behind the counter, buttoning his jacket. He looked a little on edge himself.

Was that still about Nick? If so, it was her job to reassure him.

Standing, she made sure her movements toward him were a glide. Yes, she must exude grace and beauty.

When Karl caught sight of her, his eyes widened, and his features shown a moment of surprise before an uneasy smile settled on his face. "Darling!"

Why did it sound more a question than an exclamation?

He closed the distance remaining between them. Placing hands on her arms, he leaned in to press a kiss to the side of her face. "What are you doing here?"

Even as he said it, his gaze wandered to the area behind her. Should she have come during a break in his day? He seemed distracted by potential customers. And who wouldn't be? He had a job to do.

"I only wanted to see you. Is there anything wrong with that?" She put on her most becoming smile.

"Of course not." His gaze caught hers again. "I am glad to see you."

He seemed a bit dismissive. Was he so upset about Nick? There was one way she could think of to move past that.

"I won't stay long, but I wondered if you would like to have dinner with my family. Perhaps tomorrow?"

He still seemed distracted, but those words caught his attention. Looking at her again, a real smile filled his face. "That would be lovely." Then he set her hand to the crook of his elbow. "And I have been ever so eager to do so." He stepped toward the front door but paused to let the customer that had conversed with Mr. Hammond pass.

"Excellent." She hoped she sounded pleased. "I will make something extra special for you." Then she gave him a charming smile, one she knew was apt to have men drooling.

He stopped and leaned closer. "I am looking forward to it even more then." His voice sounded deeper and more husky than it ever had. A tingling spread from her core. This was what she wanted to feel, right?

Karl resumed their movements toward the door. "I don't wish to take up any more of your time."

That was odd. Did he think more of this interaction? Did he sense she but appeased him?

Then it struck her—he had declared his love for her yesterday. And she hadn't responded in kind.

"Karl," she said, setting her other hand on his arm and halting him. "I do care for you. Very much." She lowered her gaze and made a pouting face. "And I have many hopes for more dinners with you."

He looked down at her and smiled. A quick glance around and she noted that no one else watched. Gazing into her eyes, he said, "There is nothing I'd like more." Then he moved his face toward hers. Would he kiss her? Right here?

Much to her surprise, he did brush his lips against hers. It was light and it was but a moment.

Though she couldn't deny she was glad when he pulled back. That must be her sense of propriety.

He grinned again and tapped her on the end of the nose. "Have a wonderful day, dearest. I know mine is much brighter because of your visit."

Why was it so difficult for her to force her lips to curl up into a smile? Still, she nodded and let him direct her to the door.

But the door flung open before they could reach it.

A man in the midst of pulling a bandana over his face pushed within.

Her heart thudded. What was going on here?

The man raised a gun, holding it in her face. But he looked to Karl. "Bring me someone who can open the vault. Or my trigger finger might slip."

All the blood drained from Betsy's face, her knees became like jelly, and the world swirled. Was she going to faint?

She forced her head to steady. Karl was here. He would surely save her.

Then why didn't she believe that?

CHAPTER 15

Danger

Nick shoved the last bit of his bacon into his mouth. Mrs. Abby's café never failed to satisfy. Never. He hadn't had flapjacks this good since...since his mother last made them. And suddenly, his heart dropped.

Would he ever see Ma and Anya again? Dare he chance a trip to the homestead to say good-bye? Didn't they deserve as much?

But it was too hard. Much too hard.

Nick tried to follow the conversation between Katherine and Wyatt, but he struggled. It didn't help that they passed knowing looks along the way. Would he ever have someone to share such secret glances with?

Shaking his shoulders, he attempted to free himself of that thought. Though as he shifted his gaze back to his dining companions, he noted that Katherine watched him. But it wasn't Katherine's features. It became Betsy's.

Blast it all! This would not do. He refused to be caught up in this fatal attraction to a rather flaky woman. For certain, his heart couldn't stand it. And wouldn't.

"Nick? Are you all right?"

Betsy's features disappeared in a moment and Katherine's concerned gaze bore into him.

He reached for his coffee cup. "I'm fine. Just...distracted."

Katherine sent another meaningful look at Wyatt.

The doctor cleared his throat. "Are you sure you need to leave today?"

Nick made every effort to extend his sip of the dark brew. Only when he couldn't hold his breath any longer did he put the mug down. "I'm certain I am quite well. And whether I want to or not isn't the issue. The sheriff needs me back. As he clearly expressed in his last message, he's been working with one less deputy for long enough."

Wyatt nodded as he reached a hand out to his daughter.

The child cooed and set her gaze on her father—an adoring, happy gaze. It tugged Nick's thoughts dangerously close to Betsy and what possible future could be there.

Refusing to lose his mind in such wanderings, Nick set his cup down and looked out the window near their table.

People passed by, more in a hurry than usual. And something about their reactions gave him pause.

He leaned to look beyond the window and scanned what he could from his vantage point.

Indeed, the townspeople moved in a wave in the direction of the southern part of town. Had something gone awry?

He narrowed his gaze and studied the odd happenings more closely. Yes, everyone fairly scurried. Women held their young children close to their skirts and men wrapped arms around their wives as they pressed on.

"What's the matter?" This was from Wyatt. Wooden chair legs scraped the floor. Did he push his seat back?

"I don't know…" Nick managed that much as he rose, pushing his own chair back.

Then his gaze homed in on the source of the crowd's attention—the bank. That had to be the apex of all the rush. Was something going on at the bank? Something about the situation made him uneasy. But he couldn't see anything more from his position.

Wyatt came closer to where Nick stood by the window. "What do you think it is?"

The stirring in his stomach became heavier. Something wasn't right.

Very few things would cause such a reaction. One of them being an attempted bank robbery.

Could it be? Fear seized him. His father was in that bank. And his brother. He couldn't let anything happen to them.

Without another word, he weaved through the café, checking to make sure his weapons were secure and available. Soon enough he was out in the street, fighting the crowd. He heard Katherine and Wyatt call after him, then Katherine beseeching Wyatt to stop.

Though nothing would halt Nick. Not only did he have a sworn duty as a lawman, but he also couldn't let anything happen to Pa or Karl. He just couldn't.

Now rushing through the street, he maneuvered around the fleeing people. Few people would move headlong into danger, but a trained deputy was one of them.

It took longer than he could stand to thread his way to the bank.

The window's shades had been drawn. His heart pounded as his body prepared for whatever he might face. He couldn't just burst into the bank, weapons blazing. That would get someone killed. What was left?

Then he remembered a small side window high on the wall facing the alley. Perhaps the would-be robbers wouldn't have noticed—or cared—to bother with it. Moving into the narrow passage, he grabbed a couple of crates, stacked them, and jumped on top.

More figures filled the bank lobby than he'd have thought. A man whose features were obscured by a cloth stood in the middle of the large area with a gun raised and pointed at Karl and...*no!* It couldn't be.

Nick blinked.

It was... Betsy stood on the other end of the revolver, white as a sheet and trembling. Nick wanted to curse, but that would not help anything.

As he watched, thinking through his options, he spotted movement at the back behind the teller counter.

Another man with a bandana over the lower half of his face pushed Pa out of the back offices. What had Pa given them? What would he? And would they simply leave without harming anyone if they got what they came for?

Nick couldn't take that chance.

Once more, his gaze settled on Betsy. She reached for Karl, but he, too, was frozen in fear. In fact, he side-stepped to put Betsy between himself and the gun.

Nick's heart thumped hard. But he couldn't truly fault his brother. Karl was thrown off balance to say the least.

Either way, Nick had to get in. *Now.*

"What do you see?" came a harsh whisper from the right.

Nick jerked in that direction, nearly losing his footing.

Sheriff Jones stood below, a determined look about his features.

Nick's pulse settled a little at the realization. Still, how had he let someone sneak up on him like that?

Hopping down, he wanted to quietly tell Sheriff Jones what he'd seen. He landed on the ground and, in a low voice, said, "There are at least two bandits inside. They are armed. And they have Karl, my father, and..."

Why did his heart have a sickening thud at the thought of Betsy at risk?

"And what?" Sheriff Jones's words were curt. He was not prepared to be patient.

"They have Karl, my father, and Betsy Callaway."

The sheriff's gaze altered in an odd way as Nick said her name. But there was no time to think on it. Now was the time for a plan. For action.

"You know the bank better than any of my men. I need your help on how to best proceed." Sheriff Jones studied Nick's expression.

Nick nodded, grateful he would be working with the law on this one.

The sheriff had every right to insist he step down. And Nick had every right to ignore him.

"Where are your deputies?" Nick wanted to know the whole of the situation.

Sheriff Jones waved at a couple of men crouched at the corner of the building.

What could they do to overcome these bandits? How would they get in? That wouldn't be the toughest thing they faced.

Nick knew about a dozen ways to get in. But what to do once they were in? How to capture the men without putting Pa, Karl, and Betsy in even more danger?

There was not time to dwell on his loved ones and their possible fates. If he and Sheriff Jones were to be successful, he had to keep his head straight and think.

"I have an idea..." Nick looked at each of the deputies and then the sheriff. "But it won't be easy."

Even as he started sharing his plan, he was unable to shove Betsy's panicked face out of mind.

I'm coming. No matter what it takes.

Betsy's legs went from porridge to solid blocks of ice. She couldn't make them move. How was this happening to her? Again? Two robberies so close together...it didn't seem right. Why would God do this to her?

Karl laid a hand on her shoulder. But she didn't feel any strength or comfort from his fingers clamping on her. And had he moved behind her? That was odd.

Maybe he planned something. Though that thought did not give her any confidence. In her mind, she saw Nick riding to her aid atop his horse as he had those weeks ago...and chasing away the bandits that had robbed the stagecoach. If only he could be here now. Surely, he would know what to do.

Unless Karl had a plan, it would be up to her. Or should she let these men take what they wanted if it meant she and Karl would be left alone?

Something riled within her. There was no way she could stand by while these men took the townsfolk's money. She wouldn't.

Squaring her shoulders, she glared at the man holding the gun in her face. "Excuse me..."

A rustle of movement drew her—and the bandit's—attention toward the offices in the rear of the bank.

Mr. Hammond was shuffled out from the back and pushed into the lobby.

"Tell me where it is," the bandit shoving him demanded.

"Where is what? I've let you into the vault...what more could you want?" Mr. Hammond's gaze caught hers. They were wide and glassed over. His features deepened almost in a regretful way when his gaze met hers.

The bandit jerked Mr. Hammond as he rammed the revolver into the banker's back. "You know what I'm talking about. The jewels!"

Mr. Hammond frowned.

The man holding the gun on her grabbed her arm and jerked her to himself. "Tell us or the lady will get a mouthful of lead."

Mr. Hammond's features slackened. He seemed defeated.

Betsy pushed against the dirtied clothing on the chest of the bandit caging her with his arm. "Just a minute now—"

A shot rang out from beyond the front door.

She jerked her regard to the window that had been covered by a shade. Grinding her teeth, she wished for an edge about herself that would intimidate these men.

The man dragged her to the window, keeping his gun on her. "Pull the shade." He indicated she should tug it from the window slightly so he could see out.

She ground her teeth. "No."

"What?" The man pulled her more firmly against his filthy chest. Had he ever bathed? "What is the matter with you?" He pressed the gun into her side.

It hurt. And she wanted to cry out but wouldn't dare give him the satisfaction. Clenching her teeth even harder, she shot out, "I said no."

She tried to turn so as to see the man better. But he whipped her like a rag doll before jerking her to himself once more. "You'd better try that again. If you want to come out of this with no additional holes in your body."

No one would use her as a hostage. She remembered the things Nick had shared. What was it? Closing her eyes, she kicked backward, the heel of her boot connecting with the man's shin.

He hollered and gripped her all the more tightly as a slew of curses flew from his mouth.

She pulled back, preparing to spit in his direction. Something had taken hold of her. And she would not back down.

The man seethed and raised his gun.

Karl stepped forward, hands in front of himself. "Don't harm her. I'll help you."

The bandit looked at Karl. Goodness, the thief smelled awful too. But would he give up his revenge on her for now and listen to whatever help Karl offered?

Roughened hands flung Betsy to the floor forcefully.

She landed hard on her hip; a cry escaped her lips before she could bite it back.

Karl gently tugged at the shade as the bandit looked out.

The man's gruff voice was exasperated. "It's the sheriff! How did he get here so fast?"

Betsy thought that was perhaps the dumbest question ever. Men approaching the bank with bandanas over their lower features...how could it remain a secret? Her snarky thoughts fought to be released as verbal ammunition.

The bandit looked back at his fellow criminal and then at Karl.

Then Sheriff Jones called out, "You are surrounded. For your sakes, come out with your hands up."

"How many are out there?" The bandit holding Mr. Hammond asked gruffly.

"At least three." The first bandit groused.

"I ain't leaving without those gems."

Again, Mr. Hammond's features scrunched. What was that about?

The bandit with Mr. Hammond shoved his gun into the banker's face and cocked the hammer. "Enough of this. Tell me now. Where are the jewels?"

Karl raised his hands. "Don't hurt them. I will show you."

For whatever reason, that seemed more cowardly. Though Betsy should find it brave that he would do what he could to keep her from harm.

The bandits watched Karl move toward the back office, arms still raised. "Please...let me just...show you."

Mr. Hammond pulled away from the revolver.

For a moment, the bandit looked angry enough to let a bullet fly.

But Karl rushed forward. "I will show you…if you'll not harm them."

The bandits exchanged a look.

"Go with him," the one nearest Mr. Hammond said. Something was oddly familiar about his voice. "I'll keep an eye on these two." He smirked at Betsy before waving his gun at the banker, urging him to move to where she now lay on the floor.

Mr. Hammond did so. And, as he drew near, he reached for her. "Are you all right?"

With his efforts to support and lift her, Betsy was soon on her feet. And aching. However, she didn't think that information would help anyone. "Yes."

Karl and the other bandit, with a discernable limp, disappeared into the back rooms.

Another shot rang out. "We're coming in."

The remaining bandit grabbed Betsy. "No they won't." He looked between Betsy and Mr. Hammond. Then shoved her into a seat and said, "Tie her to the chair."

"With what?" Mr. Hammond objected.

Betsy noticed that the bandit had started to perspire.

"Your belt should do fine," the man groused before swinging the gun in her direction.

Mr. Hammond took off the belt and moved to Betsy.

"Tie her hands behind her back and through the back slats."

Mr. Hammond, hands shaking, did as instructed.

The pull of the leather on her flesh would certainly leave marks.

She wanted for something to say, some way to challenge the man. But she came up short. The pain searing from her side and hip were horrid. And now her shoulders ached as well from being pulled.

The bandit came around and checked that Mr. Hammond had tied the belt securely.

A banging on the front door drew the bandit's attention.

"Hurry up," he called toward the back rooms. Then he turned to Mr. Hammond, raising his gun again. "Tell the sheriff to back off."

Mr. Hammond's wariness and fear were evident in his eyes.

"Don't do it," Betsy pressed out, glaring at the bandit.

The filthy thief was at her side in a moment, grabbing a fistful of her hair and jerking her head back. "You must have a death wish."

Betsy spit in the man's face.

He drew his gun hand back, fire flashing in his eyes. Would he bring that down on her head? Did she care?

Instead of the gun, he swiped the back of his hand against her face.

The world spun, and she struggled to find her bearings.

Mr. Hammond raised his hands. "Please, don't. I'll say whatever you want."

The bandit calmed a bit and gestured at the front of the bank.

Mr. Hammond stepped to the door. "Sheriff Jones, don't come closer. These men have my son and Betsy Callaway in here."

Quiet followed.

"Give it up," Sheriff Jones called out. "There's no escape."

The one bandit shoved a chair against the latch, securing it from the inside, and then he paced to the other side of the teller counter where he yelled, "I'm gonna need you to pick up the pace."

Nothing.

"You hear me?" the bandit called again.

Still nothing.

Had Karl taken out the bandit? Why did that seem so unlikely?

The bandit grabbed Mr. Hammond by the arm and pulled him toward the back.

Even though she was woozy, Betsy tugged at her bindings. She couldn't just sit here...helpless. There had to be something she could do. But the more she pulled, the more her flesh burned.

She hung her head, overcome and disoriented. And defeated.

Footfalls whispered against the floor.

When she looked up, Nick stood over her with the oddest look in his eyes. Was she dreaming this?

He leaned toward her, and his strong hands worked at her bindings. "Are you okay?"

She shook her head. "I wish you were really here."

He released her wrists.

Still she sat.

He cupped the side of her face, his lips so near. "I am here. And I need you to move."

She raised her arms despite the pain that bit at her from her shoulders. Resting her hands on his chest, she set her forehead to his.

His breath was warm and his hands so comforting. Could she stay here forever? But she realized...she couldn't. Not even if he were real.

He lifted her to her feet.

She cried out as he put pressure on her injured side.

His eyes darkened with concern. "Can you walk?"

Testing her balance, she nodded. He eased her toward the front door.

"Going somewhere?" A gun cocked from across the way.

Betsy peered over Nick's shoulder.

The dirty bandit had returned and now leveled his gun on her would-be rescuer.

She moved toward the robber, but Nick slid in front of her, blocking her with his body.

Nick raised his hands. "I don't want more trouble. Just let the hostages go and you can take anything you want."

The man's eyes narrowed. "You might talk a nice game, but I'm wise to you. How did you get in?"

Nick remained silent.

Something slammed into the front door, causing wood splinters to shower the area.

Nick grabbed Betsy and, pulling her to the wall, crouched over her and shielded her again.

Gunshots fired off from both sides.

In her frustration, Betsy wanted to scream. But nothing would come. She clung to Nick and pressed into him.

And just as suddenly as it had started, the shooting stopped.

She tried to peer around Nick, but he wouldn't let her, holding onto her tightly. At length, he stood and drew Betsy to her feet.

The bandit that had assaulted her was laid out on the floor, bleeding. But the sheriff and deputies seemed unharmed.

"What about my father and Karl?" Nick called out.

Sheriff Jones nodded and directed his deputies to join him as he moved into the back rooms.

Betsy moaned. Her legs wobbled.

Nick's arms came around her, pressing her to his chest. And his warm breath was in her ear. "You're safe now."

Tears filled her eyes. Wasn't she stronger than this?

"It's okay," he mumbled. "I've got you."

She leaned into him, trying to ignore how the heat of him soaked into her body, wrapping her in a warm cocoon of sweetness. How could this strained ordeal give way to such a moment? It didn't make sense.

He pulled back slightly and looked into her eyes.

It was as if he could see to the core of her. Could he?

His gaze flicked to her lips for just a second, then back to her eyes. "You are one brave lady."

The words seemed joking by his tone, but there was a fierceness in the blue looking down at her.

She sniffled. "I knew you'd come."

A throat clearing to the right stilled her heart. She turned in that direction to confirm what her heart suspected.

There stood Karl, eyes flashing and frown chiseled into his face. When had he stepped out of the back? Regardless, he was most assuredly not happy.

CHAPTER 16

Fallout

Nick froze at Karl's harsh remark. It was more than that...it was somewhat of a snarl. And though he knew his brother and Betsy were officially courting, he could not let her go. Something in him wanted to keep her from his brother. And he still wasn't sure why that was.

Karl's glare leveled on the places where Nick's body was perhaps closer to Betsy's than necessary.

Betsy removed her hands from Nick's shoulders and backed up a step. She looked down as her face colored. Was she embarrassed? And if so, was it because they had been caught or because she was in Nick's embrace to begin with?

He did not have time to entertain either thought. Not after what had just happened here. Between them. Not to mention, the fact that a robbery may have just taken place. Did the bandits get anything?

Nick swallowed, then found compassion for his brother's plight. He stepped toward Karl. "Are you all—"

Karl held up a hand. "Don't."

Nick stopped his forward motion. Then watched as Karl's hard gaze landed on Betsy.

"I thought we had an understanding."

Betsy stepped to Karl. "I believe we do. That was only an expression of gratitude for saving me from the horrid man."

She either gave good lip service to Karl. Or play-acted well to Nick, who, for his part, wasn't any more certain than Karl. As much as he wanted to turn and try to determine the veracity of her words, he dared not.

"Karl?" Betsy's voice had a pout to it. The kind that men always fell for. Perhaps she *had* only pretended to be caught up in the moment.

"Get out of my sight," Karl said through clenched teeth.

"You can't mean that." Betsy's voice wavered.

"Not you." Karl's tone remained spiteful. "My broth—" Karl paused. Then drew in a breath. "This interloper."

Interloper, was he? Karl couldn't seriously think that. Nick had just helped stop a bank robber that very well could have caused the deaths of Betsy, Karl, and Pa. As much as he wanted to challenge Karl's words, something held him at bay.

Karl took a step and grabbed Betsy's forearm, tugging her to himself.

Betsy let out a sharp cry then silenced. Had Karl hurt her?

Nick closed the distance. "You're hurting her."

Karl glanced between Betsy and Nick, his glare settling on his brother. "That's none of your concern."

Nick seethed, focusing on breathing in and out.

Betsy had pulled her lower lip between her teeth as if she tried to stop from emitting another sound. But even Nick could see that Karl's fingers dug into her flesh.

Nick leveled his gaze on Karl again. "Do not make me do something I will regret."

Karl stared at him. Then, after a moment, laughed—a long, rather dismissive sound. "Something you will regret? That's rich. You mean you intend to add to the mountain of regrets you have built for yourself?"

Nick had never wanted to strike anyone more than he did in that moment. His hands curled into fists in preparation, but he held back. This wasn't about him. It was about Betsy.

"I am fine," she said, her words sounded forced.

"Are you certain?" He wanted to argue, to make Karl release her. But it wasn't his choice. If she would take this kind of treatment, who was he to step in?

She nodded, but he noticed that she pressed a small smile onto her features.

He shrugged, then set the hardest glare he could muster on his brother. "Don't hurt her again." Then he walked in the direction of the back offices.

But he questioned every step he took that brought him farther away from Betsy and Karl. His heart tore at him. But Karl was right, it wasn't Nick's concern.

Then why did he feel responsible? Why did his heart sink until a crater opened in his chest?

As he neared the back office, he heard Pa speaking.

Nick listened for a moment.

His father seemed to be detailing to someone what had happened.

Pushing through the doorway, Nick exchanged a look with his father and with Sheriff Jones.

Then the lawman waved him over.

"What are you doing here?" His father's eyes narrowed.

Nick startled at his tone, but said, "Someone had to do something."

Pa's eyebrows knitted together. "What?"

Sheriff Jones looked at Pa. "It was Nick's plan that quite possibly saw your lives saved.

Pa's eyes widened. "You...?"

Nick wanted to take hold of the gentler word and soak it up. But he held back and nodded.

Pa looked at Sheriff Jones, who nodded. "I...don't know what to say."

"It was my duty as a deputy to prevent a crime I could stop." Nick's response was simple and, he hoped, devoid of emotion.

Pa looked to the ground. Did he want Nick to express more? Or did those words alone make him uneasy?

Nick set a hand on his revolver. But something seemed off. "Where is the other bandit?"

Sheriff Jones answered, "It seems he got the slip on your brother."

Nick blinked. "He would have had to go quickly. Did your men try to track him?"

Sheriff Jones nodded. "We think he got out the back door. From the prints in the back alley, we assume another member of the gang waited nearby back there with the horses. We lost them."

Nick had not seen anyone suspicious, but that didn't mean anything. These types of men lingered in the shadows. And, in all honesty, he had been focused on stopping those within the bank before anyone was hurt.

That brought Betsy to mind. Would Karl treat her harshly? Or would he give way to her charm?

Why did that make Nick so nauseated?

"I need to get a statement from Karl." Sheriff Jones looked from Pa to Nick and back. "If you'll excuse me."

Then the sheriff strode out of the office, leaving the two Hammond men alone.

Nick shuffled his feet and looked to the ground. With the weight in his stomach, could he even risk conversing with his father?

"I...suppose I owe you my gratitude." Pa's words surprised Nick.

He looked up and found his father's gaze everywhere but on him. "Of course."

Pa fidgeted for a moment.

Nick decided that a talk about the crime might ease things between them. "Were they after whatever monies you had in the safe?"

Pa nodded. "And Mrs. Iverson's jewelry." He looked at the empty office safe and then seamed his lips. Had he let that detail slip? Was it a secret then?

"Jewelry?"

Pa sighed. "Yes, Mrs. Virginia Iverson is passing through Cripple Creek. And left her jewels in our possession while she lingered for a few days."

As reluctant as Pa was to speak of it, he latched onto this detail. "Who knew about the jewels?" A new, sick feeling filled his gut.

Pa shook his head. "I'm not sure. I didn't think anyone did. She and I spoke privately." There was a slight wavering in his voice. Was he nervous about Nick's questions? Was that because he had a guilty conscience? For the risk to his reputation that the robbery might be? Or something else?

Nick's thoughts whirled. And, with them, his stomach. He didn't want to tread in the places his mind was taking him. But could he not?

Betsy stared after Nick. What would happen with him? But the force of Karl's grip on her arm turned her attention back to him. The press of his fingers dug into her flesh, and she tried to tug free.

His grip held.

"You're hurting me," she managed.

"And you aren't doing the same to me?" Karl's eyes were darker than usual. What would it take to make him forgive the moment he walked in on?

Did she want him to?

Yes.

As much as Nick moved something in her, there was no future there. Karl was her best hope. Maybe her only hope.

She stilled. "I am truly sorry for that." Pouring all the sincerity she could into her expression, she prayed he would relent.

Indeed as she gazed at him, his grip eased and she was able to pull her arm back.

He shook his head as if to clear something from it. Then his gaze was on her again, his eyes more of a bright blue.

"I apologize. I just..." With slow movements, he set hands on her shoulders. "I just care about you so much." He set a hand to his chest. "It...drove me crazy to see you in my brother's arms."

She set gentle fingers on his chest, her movements tentative and unsure. But she forced herself to put thoughts of his harsh hold to the side. "I know." Reaching up, she stroked hair back from his forehead. "It was an unimaginable situation. I was just so scared."

He rubbed his hands up and down her arms.

She tried not to wince when he touched the place where he had no doubt bruised her.

Leaning forward, he set his forehead on hers. "I don't want to be a jealous fool."

Her hand slid down to his cheek. "I don't want to give you any reason to be one either."

"But you have to understand..." His hold tightened.

She grimaced but eased her features quickly.

"When you told him that...that you knew *he* would come and save you...it did something to me."

She nodded, only a slight movement. "I do understand. I was so overcome..." She wanted to push out words that assured him she thought only of him. But something restrained her from speaking that lie.

Karl sighed and settled into their embrace. "I can see that." He pulled back and cupped her face. "I was so worried. If anything had happened to you, I..." He cleared his throat. "I don't know what I would do."

She let her lips curve, but her heart wasn't in it. What did that matter? "I know."

Movement from the back gave her cause to draw away from their more intimate interchange.

Karl did not release her as easily. But, after some moments, he did.

Sheriff Jones stood in the doorway to the back office.

Betsy set her hands in front of her. The man would certainly want to speak with them. Was she ready for that? She was numbed within by the swirling emotions of the last several minutes, and her head ached from the bandit's rough handling.

She was thankful that Karl kept a hand on her arm. This time, it anchored her.

"I hope I'm not interrupting anything." The sheriff's gaze passed over them. Did he judge their closeness? Or was he simply wary from the robbery?

Karl shook his head. "Of course not. I was only...tending to Miss Callaway."

She nodded, hoping that would reassure the lawman.

Sheriff Jones moved toward them but paused by the bandit's body.

Betsy's hand flew to her mouth. She had completely forgotten that a man lay so close, bloody and dead.

Karl turned concerned eyes on her. "Do you need to sit?"

She waved him off. "I'll be fine." As she spoke, she prayed that her visage matched her words and not the pounding anxiety filling her.

The sheriff bent to one knee, his body fairly creaking as he did so. He wasn't as young as he used to be. Sheriff Jones afforded her a glance. "Are you certain you won't let Mr. Hammond here escort you outside?"

She gave it some thought in the following seconds, but something rose within her. She wanted to see the face of the man who had tried to kill her. So she offered the sheriff a calm voice when she said, "I want to stay."

Sheriff Jones shrugged and tossed a look at Karl.

He shrugged as if he were less sure of her ability to withstand what would follow. Did he know her at all?

Fighting the urge to give the sheriff a tongue-lashing, she squeezed Karl's hand. "I'll be all right."

Sheriff Jones settled his focus on the bandit. He turned the body over.

Betsy's stomach roiled. Maybe she should step outside.

But as she opened her mouth to speak, she noticed that the bandit's mask was partially pulled down. An eerie feeling washed over her, and she could do nothing more than stare as the sheriff tugged it the rest of the way off.

Betsy's vision blurred. How was this possible?

She closed the distance between herself and Karl, gripping onto him.

He wrapped an arm around her and watched as she pressed her hand against her lips and jerked forward, bending at her waist. "Betsy!"

Her stomach held as he directed her to a nearby chair. She barely registered that it was the same one she had been bound to.

"Are you all right?" Karl knelt in front of her. "Let me call for Dr. Sullivan."

She shook her head. Her breaths came rapidly. She fought to steady them lest she faint. "You...you don't understand."

Sheriff Jones's gaze fell on her again. Did he discern there was more to her words?

She settled her full attention on Karl. And, even gasping, pressed out, "That...is...one of the men...that robbed the stage."

CHAPTER 17

Trouble

etsy held back a shriek. How was this possible? Did the vile men follow her to Cripple Creek? Had they attacked the bank because of her?

Karl stroked her arm. "You don't look well."

She pressed a hand to his shoulder and focused on his features, which had carved deeper crevices in his face. He was truly concerned for her.

"I'm fine, I assure you. Just...a little shocked is all."

If only that was all.

Sheriff Jones stood with some difficulty. "Miss Callaway, am I to understand that you know this man?"

She turned toward the sheriff. "Yes...I mean, no...I mean..." Closing her eyes, she took in a deep breath and let it out. Then she rose.

Karl remained at her side. Perhaps closer than he needed to be, but she must allow for that. He was worried. Understandably so. Certainly, her behavior must seem strange. He kept a hand on her arm and his other claimed her opposite hand.

Only then did she realize how much she trembled.

"Miss Callaway?" Sheriff Jones did not appear as prepared as Karl to give her leeway. "What do you mean to say?"

She cleared her throat and tried to step forward, but Karl's limbs entangled with hers, preventing easy movement. "On the way to Denver some weeks ago, the stagecoach I traveled in was held up by this man and two others."

The sheriff's eyes lit up. Why?

Then it occurred to her...he knew about the others. Before she could stop herself, she sputtered, "There were three involved in this, weren't there?"

Sheriff Jones remained silent, pensive almost, but by the way his eyes cut to the back of the bank, she knew she was right.

"The man that took Karl to the back...is he...?" For whatever reason, she couldn't finish that sentence. It wasn't that she minded the idea of the miscreants being killed, was it? She glanced at the man on the floor. No. It shouldn't be like this. Didn't people deserve a chance to make things right?

Didn't she?

She shook as emotions coursed through her.

Karl gathered her in his arms and turned her away from the body. "Don't look, darling. It's too ghastly."

Still, she wanted to know about the second bandit. And where had the third man been? "But—"

"You don't have to be so brave," Karl said, pulling back to look at her. He touched her cheek. "Let me take care of you."

The desire to know what had truly happened here waned. She couldn't let that get in the way of her primary goal—securing Karl's affection and devotion. That was the only way to make any sort of future for herself. Settling her attention on him, she softened her hold and leaned into him.

She nodded. "Please, take me away from here."

Karl pressed her head to his shoulder with a hand. "Of course, darling. Anything for you."

Sheriff Jones spoke up as they moved toward the door, "You can't leave just yet, I haven't finished—"

Karl paused and looked at Sheriff Jones. "Miss Callaway is in no condition to answer your questions. I am taking her to be seen by Dr. Sullivan."

That was the last person Betsy wanted to see, but she dared not protest.

Sheriff Jones shook his head. "I can't let you leave, Mr. Hammond. I need your statement while it's fresh in your mind."

Karl's body tensed. Was he so protective? "I intend to see to Miss Callaway's well-being first."

Betsy watched Sheriff Jones's face over Karl's shoulder.

The older man frowned. "Is there some reason you won't talk with me, son? Something you're hiding?"

Karl's breaths came heavily. "I do not care for your insinuation, Sheriff. I am a law-abiding citizen. My family's bank has been trespassed upon and plundered, I was nearly killed, and the woman I love was accosted. If you can't see fit to let me ensure she is properly cared for then I'll—"

"I can see her to the clinic." Another voice, strong and sure, came from behind them.

Betsy didn't need to turn to know it was Nick. The stiffening of Karl's entire form would have alluded to that fact even if she hadn't been able to make out the deeper sound of Nick's baritone.

Karl's breaths punctuated as he turned and said, "Not an option. The sheriff will need your statement just as much as mine."

"Already got it." Sheriff Jones watched Karl with wary eyes.

What was happening here? Betsy kept her gaze on Karl. She couldn't risk looking at Nick. She was afraid of what Karl might see.

She shook her head. It wasn't as if she couldn't control herself. Turning, she glared at Nick, trying to keep all semblance of frustration for Karl in the forefront of her mind. But as their gazes met, her knees weakened.

His eyes were intense, and full of compassion and...something else. Did he care for her more deeply than he'd let on? Did that change how she regarded him?

Karl's arms wrapped more tightly around her. "Sheriff, every minute we linger, Miss Callaway becomes less able to hold her own. I promise, I won't be long." He stepped toward the front door.

Footfalls stomping on the wooden floors warned that Nick neared.

But suddenly, his hand took her elbow opposite Karl. "I assure you, I will see to her care."

Karl stalled.

Only then did Betsy realize that a deputy had stepped in front of Karl's path.

Tightening his grip on Betsy once more, he looked between the deputy, her, and Nick. He shifted to face her and cupped the side of her face. "Will you be all right if..." He glared at his brother for a long moment. "...if Deputy Hammond takes you the clinic?"

She thought for a few seconds. Why did the thought of being in Nick's care warm her and set her at ease more so than Karl's dutiful oversight? Though the memory of the attack on the stage now pricked at the edges of her mind, she met Karl's gaze. She pressed a kiss to his hand briefly and nodded. "I will. But only because you asked me to."

A small smile teased at the corners of his mouth. He leaned forward and set a kiss to her forehead. "That's my girl."

He released her, but not before his eyes darkened as they met Nick's. "Be careful with her," Karl said in a warning tone.

Two heartbeats' length pause seemed to stretch as the brothers eyed one another.

Nick took her arm, his hold more gentle and secure at the same time. How was that possible? And as Nick tore his gaze away from Karl, Betsy allowed him to lead her out the front door.

But she couldn't look at Nick. Every thought was on the forthcoming encounter with Wyatt. No matter how much time had passed, each interaction with him was awkward and strained. It had every right to be. After all, she had tried—more than once—to separate him from his wife. Even after they spoke vows. Not Betsy's finest moment...or moments.

That would forever haunt her, bearing shame down upon her shoulders. And her heart.

Nick held his arm stiffly as he escorted Betsy.

She'd seemed rather reluctant to go with him. Was it because she left

Karl behind? Did she not want to be with Nick for the duration of the time it took to walk to the clinic?

That did not warm his heart. Still, it tugged at him. Why? Because he wanted something more? What that might be, he didn't know. Maybe that wasn't the case. This *was* only physical attraction after all. She certainly was beautiful and had a comely figure.

He shook his head. There was no benefit to that line of thinking. It was best he push all of his thoughts to the side. So, that left him and Betsy with nothing to say on their walk. And nothing between them but tension.

She slowed markedly. It was noticeable in the way she pulled at his arm. And how she lingered.

He thought to ask her but didn't want to tempt himself by looking at her.

Then she stopped altogether.

What could he do but inquire after her interrupted pace? Though as he glanced over his shoulder, he found that her breathing had become rather shallow.

He furrowed his brow and puzzled on what manipulation this might be. But his heart pulled at him. *The traitor.*

Her breaths came in gasps. And...was she crying?

He turned more fully to face her. Indeed, her eyes pooled with moisture.

Blast! He would hate himself for this later, but he couldn't ignore her. Not anymore.

"What's wrong?" He gentled his hold and stepped closer. Why the latter was important, he wasn't sure. But it had been.

She sniffled and turned away. As if she didn't want him to see her tears. Was that a sign she didn't put on some act to sway him? Or was this, too, part of the manipulation?

He couldn't bear to watch her spill her emotions, so he looked to the ground. But something bade him raise his gaze to her once more.

"Tell me." His words were soft, almost reluctant.

She sputtered a laugh and faced him. "You wouldn't understand."

He took her hand and tugged her farther out of the sightline of passersby. She didn't need their stares. Or their questioning glances.

She looked around as he did so. Then she set her gaze once more on the ground.

He touched her cheek; it seemed the most natural thing. "How can I possibly understand if you won't tell me?"

She shook her head. "Maybe I don't deserve any such kindness."

"Why wouldn't you?" He watched as her shoulders slumped and affect fell. It made him ache.

She continued to tremble.

He tipped her chin so she had to look at him. "Why wouldn't you? You are one of God's creations. He has a purpose for you, the same as everyone else."

Her mouth turned downward, her lower lip pushing out in a pout. It made him want to lean in and rub a thumb over her lips...and then touch them with his own.

"I don't know that I can believe you." Her words were serious and low. And her eyes reflected that as well.

He'd rarely seen her so sedate. Usually she was spouting with snark and condescension. Not now.

But her tone concerned him...and confused him. Did she think so little of herself? That surprised. "Of course, you—"

"Just stop." Though she snipped a bit, nothing more than resigned sadness filled her voice. "You don't know all I've done. The things that make me unfit for anyone. Even God."

"That can't be true." His heart went out to her. She was in such obvious pain. It didn't seem right.

"You don't know," she repeated, her words soft and numbed.

Perhaps this was a bad idea. Still, words came that betrayed his softening heart. "You're in pain from being mistreated. You've just been through a horrid experience...and you're not thinking clearly. Let me get you to Doc."

He reached for her arm, but she jerked it away.

"I...I can't."

He tired of this. Yet he couldn't force her onward. It wasn't in him.

Rain drizzled from the sky. Still, she didn't move.

He tried again to urge her forward. "Let's go to the clinic before the rain worsens."

She wouldn't budge but looked up at a sky spewing droplets on them. She closed her eyes and let the drips of water trickle down her face. Were some of those trails made by her tears? There was no way to determine what was what.

The rain intensified. Not that she noticed.

Forget the clinic, then. They needed better shelter.

He glanced about and spotted the café. Perhaps they might wait out the deluge there.

Moving in that direction, he wrapped an arm around her shoulders. "Here."

Her shirtwaist was already damp where he touched her.

"Let's get you inside."

She resisted until he angled in the direction of the café entrance. Only then did she allow him to lead her to the drier interior.

He nodded at Mrs. Abby. "We just need a couple cups of coffee."

Her eyes widened. "I heard about what happened at the bank. Are you—?"

"Please, Mrs. Abby," he said, keeping his voice firm. But he didn't demand...yet. "The coffees."

She shut her mouth and nodded, still her features belied that she wasn't happy about it.

Regardless, all of Nick's being focused on Betsy. He steered her to the closest table and shrugged out of his wet jacket. His shirt hadn't become too drenched under his jacket, but Betsy's dress had been without protection. Her hair, which had already started falling from the pinned-up style she'd worked that morning, now had pieces dangling about her face, sticking to her cheeks and forehead.

Though she was a mess, he couldn't deny how much more attractive she was to him. How much more vulnerable a picture she made. It caused something to rise in him he wasn't sure he wanted to embrace.

Shaking out his jacket to eliminate the worst of the moisture, he eased Betsy into a chair and set his outer covering over her shoulders.

She gripped the lapels of the jacket and tugged it closed over her chest.

Nick glanced about. Where was that coffee?

Betsy shivered. From the chill of the rain? Or from her earlier mood?

He grabbed the other chair at the table and dragged it closer to her. Then he turned her chair so that she faced him. As he sat, he gathered her cold hands in his and rubbed warmth back into them.

Her gaze fell to their hands. Did she wonder at his actions? Or marvel at the growing current between them, pulling him to want to gather her in his arms?

"I...don't want to..." The slight chatter to her teeth made speaking more difficult.

"Shhh." He lifted a hand and pushed some of the hair off her face. "You don't owe me an explanation."

"But...I do." Her voice wavered.

He tucked the jacket more tightly around her.

She reached out and gripped his wrist. "You need to know."

Why would she say that? Did she really think that? Why? Was she as drawn to him as he was to her? Either way, he couldn't deny her.

"Very well." His tone softened. "I'm listening." He set his gaze on hers. Something strong moved in the space between them. Would he be able to pull away unscathed...even if he wanted to?

She drew in a shaky breath.

It took great effort on his part to keep still. His hands, as much as his heart, wanted to soothe her.

A rustling of skirts alerted him that Mrs. Abby drew near.

He turned and spotted her crossing the dining room with a tray.

She set two steaming mugs in front of them. And, without so much as a glance in their direction, spun and moved back to the kitchen.

Then they were alone. And as much as he wished to grab the hot mug and let the warmth of the coffee fill him, he didn't. His full attention was on Betsy.

CHAPTER 18

Truth

Betsy watched Nick. How could she do this? Yet how could she not? Dare she bare herself? To him of all people? Would it be any worse than holding it in?

She studied him. His blue eyes were filled with concern. And something else. Could it be that he cared for her? How was that possible? After what they had been through and how she had tried to distance herself from him with venom. Yet he still sat with her, warming her hands, and asking her to lay her burdens on his shoulders.

Incredible.

She licked her lips.

His gaze dropped for a moment. And when his eyes found hers again, the intensity became too much.

Glancing down at their hands, she considered her options. But the truth burned within, needing to break free. She couldn't cage it any longer, seal it in as if it never happened.

"I...have sinned against God and against Wyatt and Katherine."

His eyebrows arched. "What do you mean...sinned?"

She chewed at the inside of her cheek, wishing she might take the words back. But she had cracked the door to her muddled past and there was no closing it. Hurt seeped from her heart. Would he see it?

He withdrew his hands. Did he already regret his feelings? Perhaps even resent her? Soon after, however, calloused fingers touched her chin and drew her face upward.

"Tell me." His words were so gentle it stoked an ache in her chest.

It grew until it became a cavern, an emptiness. But hadn't it always been there? She couldn't remember the last time she had been seen...and loved.

She cleared her throat and looked over his shoulder.

His thumb directed her gaze back to his. "Look at me and tell me."

That was too much. Surely, she wouldn't be able to do that. But she would try...for him.

"I did what I could...all that I could to come between them."

He didn't move, didn't jerk back or withdraw as he clearly should. What was this? It wasn't possible that he could want to hear more.

She let out a sigh.

"How so?" His question was spoken with a firm quietness. And she couldn't escape it. Perhaps it was time to let it all out.

"I...attempted to make Katherine look incapable. I..." She eyed Nick. "...flirted with Wyatt, contriving a situation that would see us alone. And I...kissed him."

Nick's features altered in a way she couldn't discern. His brows were heavier as the lines about his mouth deepened.

He disapproved. And why shouldn't he? Her actions were unforgivable. "That doesn't seem like—"

"Doesn't it?" The rise in her own volume surprised her. "I knew he was married. *Knew* it was wrong, but I made up excuses...excuses that permitted me to act the harlot." She slapped a hand over her mouth.

There. She'd said it. And she couldn't take it back. There was the awful truth of what she had become, and what she remained—forever stained by her conniving.

Nick drew in a long breath and eased it out as he set his hands on his knees and leaned back. His judgment would soon follow.

And he would be right in it. No explanation would make what she had done understandable. What did she expect?

Leaning forward, Nick set his elbows on his knees. "That is quite the confession."

Her hand dropped from her mouth. Being open and raw before him was more than she could bear. But this was her penance, and she must accept it. "I wouldn't blame you if you want to leave now."

His eyebrows lowered, furrowing over his perfect eyes. "Leave?"

She sniffled. When had she started crying? "I can't expect an upstanding man like you—a righteous man of faith—to tolerate my behavior."

He looked at the floor then back up with nearly clear eyes. "You know, Jesus said 'let he who is without sin cast the first stone.'"

She shifted. The lack of condemnation made her more uneasy than her confession. "Well, yes. But I can't ask you to keep company with me. It may...tarnish your good name."

He moved his hands to clasp hers. "But I'm not going anywhere."

It was her turn to be taken aback. He couldn't mean that. Still, his eyes spoke to the veracity of his words.

Only then did she realize how close their faces were. He'd scooted forward and she had shuffled until she now sat on the edge of her seat.

She looked at their hands to find their fingers had interlaced almost as if of their own accord. Was he to blame? Or was she?

When she set her gaze on him again, there was that pull. "Please don't sacrifice yourself for me."

He closed a fair portion of the distance between them. "There is no sense in it, but I..."

For the first time she could remember, he seemed to lose his words.

Her lips curved only slightly before she schooled them not to. This was no time for levity.

When she looked at him again, his gaze had become intense.

The air between them was thick.

"Nikolai, I..."

Relishing the sound of his full Christian name on her lips, he leaned closer as if a moth to a lantern.

She loosened a hand from his and set it to his chest, creating a much-needed barrier. "Don't do something you will regret."

His now freed hand cupped the side of her face. And he wiped at her tears with a thumb. "I won't."

With that promise upon his lips, he claimed hers.

Nick pressed into her. And, as she leaned into him, he lost any remaining resolve. Wrapping his arms around her, he pulled her against himself.

Something screamed from the recesses of his mind. But he ignored it while every part of him clung to this moment, a moment of bliss...a moment of abandon. No one else mattered. Nothing could tear him from it.

She wrapped one arm around his shoulders, and one tentatively examined the scruff of his face.

He allowed the sweetness of the moment to envelope him. And he gave himself to the sweetness of her. She tasted of honeysuckle and smelled of lilac. How could a man want more? Yet he did...

Suddenly, reality crashed in on him. This was wrong.

She courted his brother. And here Nick was forcing himself on her.

Although, in that moment, it didn't feel that way.

Overcome, he used every ounce of strength within himself to pull back.

She whimpered as he did so.

Then her large green eyes were on his. Though there was no question in them, only understanding.

"I...I shouldn't have done that." His words came between gasps for air. How long had they remained locked in that embrace?

"I know." Her head dropped.

He tilted her chin up. "It's not what you think."

Her mouth twisted. "It's not?" It was obvious she didn't believe him.

"No," he said, allowing his hand to linger on her jaw. "I don't want to take advantage."

Her eyebrows pinched. "Advantage?"

"You are in a vulnerable situation. As your friend..." He coughed. "I should be helping you see yourself in light of God's grace."

"Oh." The glow in her eyes dimmed. Did she still think herself so unworthy of God's love?

They needed to talk about something else...anything else. "Have you...spoken to Wyatt or Katherine since then?"

Betsy looked down and shook her head.

It ripped at his heart to see her so dejected. He leaned forward but was mindful to keep some space between them. Mostly, he didn't trust himself. "That may be where we need to start."

"We?" There was a spark in her eyes.

It pained him that he couldn't let it be what she'd assumed. "I meant...you."

A frown weighed on her lips.

"Don't you see? You have the chance to make this right."

Her features fell. "Make this right?"

"Go to Katherine and Wyatt. Tell them what's in your heart. How sorry you are. They will listen. And—I truly believe—they will forgive you."

She shook her head, a look of dread filling her eyes. "I...I can't."

He took her hands again. "You *can*. You are the strongest woman I've ever known."

She gnawed at her lower lip. Because of his confession? Or because of her doubt?

Finally, she spoke. "But what if they hate me?"

"You know that's not like either of them."

Her eyes were as those of a deer caught by a hunter.

"But what if they don't hate you?"

That didn't seem to bring her any measure of peace. Either way. She still had every appearance of being lost...and alone.

The urge to pull her to himself again almost overwhelmed his good sense. That wasn't what she needed.

Reaching up, he tucked a strand of hair that had started to curl on her cheek behind her ear. "I believe in you. There is more in you than you care to see."

Her gaze caught his. And there was that heat. How did it not sear him completely through?

But there was also confusion in her eyes. "I think you're in denial."

I think I'm falling in love. The silent admission startled him. That couldn't be. Or could it? Despite his best efforts to steer clear, he did feel for her. Deeply. So, he only cleared his throat.

She watched his movements. What went through *her* mind? When she spoke at last, her voice was hard. "I have only scratched the surface on my sins."

He swallowed, rapidly becoming overwhelmed with emotion. Leaning forward with elbows on his knees, he forced himself to look at her. Dare he speak of what was in his heart? "Betsy, I..."

He paused. This was ill advised.

Her eyes widened. The trails left by tears shimmered in the emerging sunlight.

"Betsy, the thing is...what I wanted to say was that I think—"

Laughter from behind cut him off.

Betsy's gaze jerked in that direction, and her mouth gaped open.

He turned, afraid he knew what he would find. Sure enough, there stood Katherine and Wyatt, smiling and chattering at the entrance to the café.

They looked about the room, catching sight of Nick and Betsy.

Wyatt nodded and Katherine waved.

But Nick worried more about Betsy's reaction. He spun back toward her.

She had dropped her head and her hands squeezed together more tightly.

Again, he wanted to take her clenched fingers in his, but that would not be invited.

Footfalls moved toward them.

"Are you two all right?" This was from Wyatt.

"We heard about the bank robbery. For some reason, Sheriff Jones thought you'd be at the clinic," Katherine added. "Is everything okay?" Her gaze, filled with sympathy, moved between the two.

Betsy's hands became white, and she tilted her head so that the back was all that remained visible to Katherine and Wyatt.

Katherine settled a hand on Nick's shoulder.

He needed to speak. To tell them...tell Wyatt that Betsy should be examined. But his tongue stuck to the roof of his mouth.

Wyatt came over and stood with his wife.

With the Sullivans standing behind Nick, it must make Betsy feel small, perhaps even confronted.

"Betsy," Nick started as he reached for her. But as soon as his fingers made contact, she jerked away, standing as she did so. Her chair clattered to the floor.

"No." Her trembling hands clasped again. "I..." She looked at Katherine and Wyatt briefly before turning her focus to the floor. "I'm sorry. I just...I can't do this." She rushed across the dining room and out the door.

Nick rose, but Wyatt clamped a hand on his shoulder and pressed him back down. "Don't."

"But she—"

"Just let her go." Katherine's voice was quiet, but firm. "She has to find her own way."

Nick leaned down, pulling away from Wyatt. And prayed.

Sunlight streamed through her small bedroom window, assaulting Betsy's senses. Who had drawn her curtains to the side, allowing the blasted light to intrude on her solitude?

She looked in that direction briefly before allowing her head to fall back onto her pillow. Setting a hand to her forehead, she groaned. Perhaps...maybe...no, likely...it was rather that she had not pulled them closed last night.

Betsy rolled over. What had the previous day wrought? Oh yes, the bank robbery. Even then, she could see Karl's anger and frustration in her mind. Had he been angry with her? Or with Nick? Did she care?

And the kiss. With Nick. Nikolai, as she had called him. A brief taste of wonderful.

Then she'd fled. Ran away from Katherine and Wyatt. From the right thing. From Nick and the feelings he stirred in her.

She pulled the pillow over her face. How could she possibly brave the day...after her cowardice and confession to Nick? It wasn't possible.

A solid knock landed on the door.

Oh dear...

That would be Mother or Maria. Father never disturbed her privacy...never seemed to be so bothered by her doing or not doing whatever he needed her to. Indeed, he lacked the consideration to care. There was little need to dwell there, though.

"Yes, Mother?" She guessed.

The door creaked open, and her mother stepped inside. "Do you plan to sleep all day?"

Dragging herself upright, she dropped her feet over the side of the bed. "No, ma'am. I just..." Her head pounded unforgivingly. She pressed the heel of her hand to her forehead.

"What is it?" Mother's tone was demanding.

"Just a bit of a headache." Betsy blinked and tried to clear her vision.

"What is with you, girl?"

"I...had a bit of a trying day."

Mother moved to the window, settling as much as she ever did. Her straight, perfect posture gave the impression that she didn't quite know how to relax. Such it was with her uptight ways. "Mr. Hammond has been waiting to speak to you for nearly an hour."

Betsy jerked herself into a similarly stiff posture. "Nick?"

Her mother turned and set narrowed eyes on her. "No. Mr. *Karl* Hammond."

Betsy dropped her regard to the floor. Her face heated. What had she revealed in that moment?

Mother took measured steps in her direction. "Whyever would *Nick* Hammond be calling?"

Betsy shrugged, not trusting her voice.

The points of Mother's boots came into view. Then a long finger on Betsy's chin forced her face up.

"Are you not courting Mr. *Karl* Hammond?"

Betsy cobbled together what nerve she could. "I am."

"Then I fail to see what concern you could have for his wayward brother."

Betsy swallowed and nodded. There was little benefit to fighting with Mother. As Betsy well knew, it would go nowhere. "Please tell Mr. Hammond that I will be out in twenty minutes."

One of Mother's brows arched. "You will be out in ten."

"But I..." Betsy scanned the room, searching for a dress that might suit.

"Very well...you may have fifteen. But make them worth Mr. Hammond's while." That was the final word on the matter.

Betsy stood and shuffled to her armoire. "Can you send Maria in?"

Mother halted in her progress to the door, a hand on the latch. "Maria is busy elsewhere. I would advise you to make the most of the time I've given you without assistance."

"Yes, Mother." Though Betsy was tempted to sulk, it would not add to her time nor improve her mother's mood. So, she pulled a dress from its hanger and set it on the bed.

The door clicked shut and Betsy let out a long breath. This was impossible.

But she dared not waste another second moping. Karl waited. As did Mother...somewhat impatiently, as it would be.

Rushing through her ablutions, she then glanced at her reflection. Her hair could use more pins and the fabric of her dress could stand some ironing. But there was no time. The question remained—was she decent enough?

There was no time to consider it.

Mother's boots clipped on the hallway boards.

Betsy rushed to the door as she smoothed a hand down her shirt-waist. Likely to no avail.

She strode from her room and past Mother in the hall as if the woman wasn't clicking her tongue. That would cost her later, but she had a job to do—relieve any worries Karl might have about what befell her yesterday.

After stepping into the parlor, she paused as Karl stood.

He was well polished with a slight bruise on his forehead and his bowler hat in hand.

She had no need to guess where he had gotten that shiner. But beyond that, he appeared none the worse considering what they had experienced.

"Betsy," he said as he stepped toward her. He stopped an arm's length away and gave her a once over. "Still disheveled from the robbery, I see."

Mother sighed loudly behind her, then moved forward. "Yes, Mr. Hammond, she is still recovering from such a fright."

So, Mother had known about the robbery...and had not bothered to ask Betsy how she fared this morning. But that was typical.

"I am certain," Karl said, letting his gaze wander to Mother for a moment. Then he put out a hand. "Let me get you off your feet."

Betsy nodded and set her fingers to his palm.

He closed his hand over hers and tugged her to the settee. Though he did not take the chair to the side as he ought, but sat close beside her, still holding her hand captive.

She opened her mouth to protest, but Mother cut her off. "I will see that the tea is coming along."

With that, the older woman moved on, leaving her and Karl unchaperoned.

That pinched at Betsy, despite the fact that she had been in company with Nick without benefit of oversight. Somehow, that did not bother as this did.

On that note, she had been alone with Wyatt as well in the clinic years before. But that was before...

Before what? Before she cared? Before her heart had softened? What was happening here?

"What did Dr. Sullivan say about your injuries?" Karl's gaze was intense. But in a way that made her shudder.

"He...didn't say much. There were others with injuries more dire than mine." The simple untruth scraped against her conscience. That was new.

"I shall have a talk with him. Your wellbeing is of utmost impor-tance." Karl's eyes darkened.

"No." She set a hand to his arm. "That's not necessary."

His eyes widened.

"That is, I wanted him to move on to the others who needed his attention."

Karl shook his head. "You are truly too good."

A wave of regret washed over her. She was nothing of the sort. What did Nick think of her after she had run off? What greeted his heart this morning?

Shaking her thoughts free of him, she focused on Karl.

He had let his regard drift downward. Then he took her hand once more, and, licking his lips as his gaze caught hers, said, "I am so very sorry I wasn't able to protect you."

"What could you have done?" She caught the sound of her words as they escaped. "That is, you did everything you could. Everything anyone could."

He nodded. "If only you knew how much you mean to me..."

The thick stream of guilt pounded into her heart. How could she do this?

A loud thump reverberated as the parlor door flung open. Mother led Maria in with a tea service.

"You two are bound to need refreshment. My apologies for the delay."

"Nonsense," Karl said, letting his lips curl slightly. "It is appreciated."

Betsy watched him. Did he mean anything he said? Or was he simply a nice façade for the lies he told?

A pang shot through her. What of her own behavior? Did she make an equally fancy façade for her sin? For her dishonesty? Perhaps she deserved no better after all. What did she know of love? Of truth?

This was the world she belonged in. Might she as well play the part?

Nick walked down the dirt packed road through Cripple Creek. Years of horses and carts pounding down the widened path had made it what it was. But as straight as this road ran, his heart traveled a winding path with an obscured destination. Yet onward he went. To his own detriment.

He had extended his stay at the hotel. As much as he wasn't certain about running into Betsy there, he had no other options for boarding right now. And he couldn't, in good conscience, leave Cripple Creek without resolving this issue of the bank robbery.

Besides, it was connected to the Denver search for the stagecoach bandits. How did they end up here? Had they followed him? Or Betsy? That seemed unlikely, but how else could he explain the coincidence?

Either way, the telegram had been sent to Sheriff Brandt...words he couldn't take back. Nor did he wish to.

However, if he were to be honest with himself, would he find that he stayed for Betsy as much as he did for the investigation? What was this pull he felt toward her? This growing tenderness in his heart?

She was the last person he would have expected to develop any such feelings for. Yet, here he was, wanting to deny what was quite obvious.

"Deputy Hammond, I didn't expect to see you today."

Nick didn't have to look to guess who had spotted him. But he did.

Sheriff Jones stood in the doorway to the jailhouse, confusion marking his features. "I figured you'd have caught the first stage to Denver."

Nick smirked. "I wouldn't leave without helping wrap up this mess."

"I'm glad for it." Sheriff Jones glanced over his shoulder. "I was just about to go out to the Callaway place and talk with Miss Callaway. Her witness statement was not fully taken yesterday." Then the sheriff eyed Nick curiously.

Nick only nodded.

"In fact, I never heard talk of what happened after you took her to see Dr. Sullivan."

Now that was a story. But aloud, Nick said, "She didn't want to be seen."

Sheriff Jones put a hand to his chin. "That don't seem right. Wish she'd have come back and given her statement then."

"She was...ah...rather emotional after everything." Nick didn't want to lie, but how much was he ready to reveal to the older man?

The sheriff continued to watch Nick. And Nick felt every bit of it. Not only in his body, but in his conscience, which pricked with the half truths.

"Care to join me?" The sheriff indicated the direction that would lead to the Callaway home. It wasn't really a question.

What did the older lawman suspect? Did he know what went between Nick and Betsy? Did he wonder if Nick held out on him from a misplaced effort to protect Betsy? More, Nick wondered himself if he did.

Truthfully, he would rather not go. He had a very real desire to see Betsy, but he also wanted to avoid her. Which would win out in the end?

Either way, he needed to accompany the sheriff—if for nothing else than to ease his suspicions.

"Did you hear me?" Sheriff Jones's voice took on a gruff edge.

"Yes, sir, I did." Nick turned his attention back to the sheriff. "I was just...thinking."

"Oh? About what?" The man's gaze narrowed. Would the investigator in him keep him questioning Nick's loyalties? He probably should.

"Same as you, I suppose...wondering how it's all connected." Nick prayed that his eyes testified to the truth of his statement. Or at least what he believed to be true.

Sheriff Jones nodded and waved him over. "Grab one of my deputy's horses. We'd best get on our way."

Nick nodded and followed as directed, selecting a painted mare from those tied to the jailhouse post.

Sheriff Jones mounted his tan steed with some effort and, with a nod, moved out.

Nick's heart raced. And he wondered himself if it was because of what lay ahead...or who.

CHAPTER 20

Discovery

Betsy set her teacup down. Was anything more nonsensical than the conversation around the tea service? It was on the surface... and it was dull. Most of the talking was done by Mother and Karl. Betsy smiled here and there to emphasize a point one or the other made. Or to comment to ensure they thought she followed along. At least more than she actually did. For her thoughts were rampant.

But there was a large part of her that wanted to escape...to somewhere else, to somewhere of consequence. Was there a place where this shadow of propriety evaporated?

That place turned out to be her memory of Nick's kiss. It had enraptured and moved her more than she would have expected. She had been fully wrapped in the moment, in the feel of him holding her close, in the touch of his lips on hers...taking and giving, with a tenderness in his hands on her. As if he feared she would break.

Did he truly cherish her so?

Then her heart dropped. It didn't matter what had happened. She'd turned her back on him, on whatever it was he stirred in her...and ran away. How could he still care for her after that...and after knowing, in part at least, her sin?

"Betsy, darling." Mother's sharp voice cut through her wonderings. "Is something the matter?"

Betsy's gaze flew between Mother's hard stare and Karl's confused expression. Had she missed a question aimed at her?

"I'm...sorry. I was distracted."

Mother pinched her lips and took a sip of tea.

Karl reached for Betsy's hand. "Of course, you were. I am asking too much of you in your current state. Perhaps you should rest."

Betsy nodded slowly as she set the teacup and saucer on the side table. "I think you are right. I do have a bit of a headache."

"I would expect no less. Certainly, after what you've been through. Forgive me for being an oaf and suggesting you entertain me." Karl's words were kind, but his features told another story. The lines about his eyes and mouth were strained.

Betsy dipped her head. "I thank you for understanding." She dared not look in Mother's direction again. Judgment oozed from the woman's pores. Palpable even from this distance.

Karl stood and tugged gently on Betsy's hand, prompting her to rise as well. "I shall—"

Maria rushed into the parlor without warning. How had they not heard her coming down the hall?

The servant dipped in a slight curtsy. "Forgive my intrusion. But two men are here to speak with Miss Callaway."

Karl narrowed his gaze as Mother got to her feet. "Miss Callaway is in no condition to be seen."

"Begging your pardon, ma'am, it is the sheriff. And he said he won't be dissuaded."

"Well, I *never*..." Mother set a hand to her chest. The movement seemed as if she were shocked at such treatment. But Betsy knew it was for show. Just as *she* had known Sheriff Jones would come this day, Mother had to suspect the same.

Karl said, clenching his teeth, "I insist they come another time."

Betsy set her other hand to his forearm. "Do not trouble yourself so. I can speak with him." Then she turned to Maria. "Please, show them in."

Mother huffed.

Betsy had committed an offense in bypassing her mother's permission, but it had to be done.

Maria nodded and moved off down the hall without closing the parlor door.

Mother bristled but plastered on a smile for Karl's benefit. "My sincere apologies for the intrusion."

Karl waved his free hand. "Do not worry yourself. If Miss Callaway is at liberty to speak with the sheriff, I will not stop her." His voice was tight, and his grip now clamped on her no longer bandaged hand.

She knew better than to even attempt to wiggle free. But she turned back to him. "He may need to speak with me privately."

Karl shook his head. "I will not allow it. You will have my full support. I will not be removed from your side."

She wanted to sigh. This had gone beyond ridiculous. Still, she kept her breathing even and offered a small smile.

"And I intend to stay as well." Mother's clipped words did not invite debate.

Several sets of footfalls in the hall warned of Maria's return with the sheriff and, likely, one of his deputies. Betsy steeled herself for their appearance. What would they ask of her? Could she hold firmly to herself as she relived the events? Even the interaction with Nick?

Sheriff Jones appeared in the doorway slightly ahead of Maria. Still, the woman did her pathetic excuse for a curtsy and announced, "Sheriff Jones and Mr. Hammond, er, Deputy Hammond."

Then the broad-shouldered Nick came into the room.

Betsy slowly sat more upright, at alert, as she watched him. Though he seemed to avoid her eyes. Why was he here? Her face flushed, but she hoped no one noticed. How could she face him? Now? Why had she permitted this?

Maria grabbed the set aside teacups and slipped from the room.

If possible, Karl's grip tightened even more. Would he bruise her again? How was he so ruffled by his brother?

Mother glided toward the men. "Sheriff Jones, Deputy Hammond, how might we assist you?"

"Thank you, Mrs. Callaway. I apologize for the unannounced visit, but we need to speak with your daughter."

Mother sighed then. "I apologize, Sheriff, but she is none too well today." She waved a hand in Betsy's direction.

Dare she contradict Mother? Then she felt Nick's gaze on her. She looked at him and saw the naked concern there. He did care. And he wasn't even trying to disguise it. The real question was—did *she* care?

Karl's thumb rubbed across the back of her hand. Firmly. So much she flinched.

Nick's brows lifted and he glanced in the direction of her and Karl's joined hands.

"I am sorry, Miss Callaway, but the sooner we can get your recounting of the events, the better. Memories tend to fade."

Betsy nodded as she set her gaze on the sheriff. Could she avoid Nick in such close quarters? Maybe not, but she didn't have to look at him.

Mother shot Betsy a disapproving glare. That wasn't new.

Betsy wasn't certain she wanted to put the sheriff off again. He seemed rather determined. It may be best for her to just cooperate. "Very well, Sheriff. I will answer your questions."

Sheriff Jones moved to the seat beside Betsy's position on the settee —the chair that Karl should have occupied.

All of a sudden, she was embarrassed at Karl's closeness. It spoke of an understanding she wasn't sure they had...yet.

"First, I'd like you to just tell me, if you will, what you saw and heard yesterday. Starting from your arrival at the bank. And why you were there." The older man's eyes were kind, fatherly almost.

Betsy knew better. This was a means to an end for him. Did everyone just want from her?

Not everyone. Thus far, Nick only gave.

That thought stung her heart. And, though she refused to look in his direction again, she sensed his movements as he walked to the window. So, he intended to merely listen.

She shook off her trepidation at his presence.

Though she doubted Karl did. He scooted closer and set an arm around her. "I'm right here if you need me." He squeezed her hand and then loosened his grip. *Thank goodness!*

His gesture was a kindness, to be sure. But was it genuine? Or more for show?

Betsy nodded at him before she faced the sheriff and sucked in a deep breath. Then she began.

Sheriff Jones was largely quiet for the duration as she shared what she remembered.

She resisted the urge to glance at Nick when she mentioned how he had rescued her. Though Karl's arm about her shoulders tensed.

Once she finished, she pulled in a cleansing breath and prayed this would be over soon.

Sheriff Jones leaned forward, setting his hands on his knees. "Where again was Karl when Nick came in?"

"He was in the back office. With the bandit."

Karl's hand clamped down on her shoulder.

"He was sacrificing all for my sake...to keep the bandit from hurting me." Did she actually believe that? Or had he done it to save his own skin? She wouldn't dwell on that. It could serve no purpose.

Karl's fingers relaxed.

"And...Mr. Hammond? Where was he?"

"In the bank lobby with me. He was forced to bind my hands with his belt."

"Ah, I see." The wheels turning in his head were quite nearly visible. "And...what did you say you went to the bank for?"

"To see Karl." She looked to him.

The furrow in Karl's brow eased.

"Any particular reason you needed to see him that day?" The sheriff just would not relent.

Betsy shifted under his scrutiny. Indeed, she sensed Nick's gaze as well. "I...can't quite remember. I just...needed to ask him something." She kept her attention on her lap. Could the sheriff sense that she withheld information? Did Karl?

"There you have it, Sheriff," Karl spoke up. "You've had your accounting done and your questions answered. I must insist that Miss Callaway be given leave to rest."

Sheriff Jones's glare fell on Karl. "I am not finished."

"I must also insist," her mother said as she stepped forward. "What more do you want?"

The sheriff's gaze went from Karl, to Betsy, to Mother, then to Nick. Unbidden, Betsy's regard followed the sheriff's and caught on Nick, who studied her. Was he disappointed? Concerned? Or prepared to dismiss her and any tender feelings or thoughts he may have had?

"Sheriff Jones, I think we may have all we need...for now." Nick stepped to the older man.

The sheriff jerked around to face Nick. Some unspoken message seemed to pass between them. What was it?

Sheriff Jones shrugged and shifted his focus back to Betsy. "My apologies, Miss Callaway. It is not my intention to disrupt your recovery." He stood. "But I may have further questions."

Before her mother or Karl could respond, she nodded and rose. "I thank you. And I will, of course, be available."

Karl also got to his feet, keeping his hand on her back.

The sheriff and Nick moved toward the door.

Without warning, Sheriff Jones halted and turned. "One last thing, Miss Callaway..."

Betsy nodded and set her gaze on the sheriff.

Nick stood beside him, but she couldn't risk glancing his way.

"You mentioned that you recognized the one bandit from the stagecoach robbery. Did you recognize either of the other two?"

Betsy startled.

Nick's intense gaze was on her again.

Sheriff Jones cleared his throat. "Miss Callaway?"

"Sorry," she said as she drew in a breath and let it out, calming herself as much as possible. "I only saw one other. But the other man I saw kept his bandana over his face. Besides, I didn't get as good a look at him during the stage robbery either."

"Any reason you could identify the one bandit but not the other?"

"Other than the bandana over his face?"

"Yes." The sheriff seemed to be short on patience.

She held up her hand. "That was the vile man who stomped on my wrist."

Karl's muscles tightened again; his stance stiffened beside her. Was he upset by what had happened to her? Perhaps he did truly care.

The sheriff's eyes softened and his features relaxed. "I understand. Again, I apologize for disturbing you."

She nodded. "I wish you well with the investigation."

Mother sniffed loudly and shot her a warning look. If she wanted to steer clear of Mother's ire, she would stop talking.

"I will see you out, Sheriff." Mother stepped into the hall, brushing past Nick, but not acknowledging him.

Betsy looked to the floor again but felt every bit of Nick's stare.

Then he was gone. And she all but collapsed onto the settee.

Nick kept his regard trained on the meadow before him. The greenery reminded him of Betsy's eyes. The way they spoke of life and rebirth. He prayed that she would find that in God. But being with her, seeing her with Karl, it had been difficult to say the least. Especially after the kiss they had shared. An anchor weighed in Nick's gut. Was he nothing more than something for her to toy with?

"I don't like it," Sheriff Jones's gruff voice shot out.

"What?" Nick looked in the man's direction, but he didn't need to. It was rather plain what bothered the lawman.

Sheriff Jones's gaze hardened on Nick. "You know she's not telling the truth."

"Perhaps." Nick shifted his focus back to the area ahead of the animal.

"You disagree?" Sheriff Jones's voice was incredulous and held an edge.

Nick thought for a moment. After all, he had done too much acting on impulse. That's how he worked his way into this mess of things—sweet on a girl that fancied his brother.

The sheriff *harrumphed* and pulled at the reins, turning his horse right.

Where were they headed? Nick had assumed they would return to the jail. But this was the wrong direction. Regardless, he tugged at his horse's reins and followed. It was little work to catch up to the sheriff again. Then he set eyes on the man. "I *don't* disagree."

A quirked eyebrow met his gaze. Did Sheriff Jones find something odd about his response?

"I just...I'm not sure *what* she is being less than truthful about."

The sheriff bobbed his head and frowned as if considering Nick's words. "You make a good point."

Nick urged his horse to pick up its step. "I mean, could she be lying about the details of the robbery? Yes. But it's also possible she isn't being honest about her reason for being there."

Sheriff Jones nodded once more. "Yeah." His voice dropped. "I wonder that, too."

Nick shrugged. How was he to delve deeper into Betsy's alleged deception without giving away more of his interactions with her than he'd like?

Nothing readily came to mind. Perhaps changing the subject would work.

"Where are we going?" Nick watched the scenery change. It wasn't as if he didn't know this path, but where exactly were they headed?

"I have a few questions for the Iverson woman," the sheriff quipped briefly.

That made sense. With her being the one with the most to lose in the robbery, that would be a logical next step. Who was she? And what brought those jewels to Cripple Creek? It didn't fit together easily.

Even if her property was a primary target of the bandits, what did that have to do with the stagecoach hold up that Betsy had seen these same men at? Were the two connected? How likely was such a coincidence if they weren't? That seemed less likely.

"Who is Mrs. Iverson anyway?" Nick thought it best to gather such information before getting to wherever she was. Was she in the outskirts of Cripple Creek? Or would they go as far as Victor?

"She is Mrs. Abby's sister." The sheriff didn't bother pausing or even looking in Nick's direction. Word was that at one time Sheriff Jones fancied Mrs. Abby. Might have even been sweethearts at one point. But something created a rift. There was much speculation about the pair now that the sheriff was recently a widower.

"Oh?" Nick tried to keep his tone even but heard a slight lilt on the end of the word. For a man that purported of late not to care about anyone beyond his civic duty, Sheriff Jones seemed to know a bit about Mrs. Abby's comings and goings.

The sheriff grunted and looked away.

"She in town for a visit? Wonder why she would bring such expensive jewels with her."

"That's what I intend to find out," Sheriff Jones's gruff response gave no room for further conversation.

Just as well, Nick figured. He wasn't in the mood to talk himself and hadn't the slightest desire to hound the man.

They continued in silence until Mrs. Abby's cabin appeared on the horizon. They called her Mrs. Abby as she had been married to Old Fred Campbell, though it had been short-lived. The frail man just hadn't the constitution for much. Certainly not to live through the hard winter that visited Cripple Creek back when Nick was a boy.

So Mrs. Abby had lived in the Campbell home for the many years after...alone. Perhaps her love of cooking wasn't the only thing that had driven her to take charge of the town's most prominent eatery.

The men dismounted and walked their horses to the waiting posts.

Pausing, Sheriff Jones turned to Nick. "Now, this is a friendly call."

He nodded. "Of course."

"And as you can guess, I doubt Mrs. Abby will be home."

Was that a twinge of disappointment in his voice? Again, Nick nodded, but this time, said nothing.

Sheriff Jones stepped onto the small porch and knocked.

"Coming," a distinctly feminine voice called.

Nick swatted at a fly that buzzed by. Probably looking for a morsel.

It wasn't but a few seconds before the door opened.

Nick couldn't hide his surprise that it was Mrs. Abby standing on the other side.

Her face flushed just a bit. "Bernard?"

Bernard? Nick bit at the inside of his lip to keep from smiling.

She stepped out a bit, her gaze settled on the sheriff. "What brings you—?"

Her regard then fell on Nick. As quickly as possible, she smoothed her hands down her apron. "That is...how might I help you, Sheriff?"

"We need to speak with Mrs. Iverson." The sheriff held his own, Nick would have to give him that. He didn't sound or look the least bit hindered by her appearance at the door.

Mrs. Abby, on the other hand, frowned.

"It's about the robbery," Sheriff Jones added quickly.

And just like that, Nick fought another smile. Why did the man feel the need to qualify his interest in her sister if not to appease her curiosity?

"Virginia," Mrs. Abby called into the house. "Sheriff's here to see ya!" Then she turned an icy glare on the sheriff. "Won't you come in?"

Nick bit into the side of his mouth to keep from smirking as the woman moved and let the sheriff, then him, pass.

This was going to be one interesting chat.

CHAPTER 21

Digging Deeper

Nick looked around the small cabin that, to his recollection, he had never been in.

Sheriff Jones, or *Bernard*, on the other hand, moved as if he had. Curious.

A woman a few years older than Mrs. Abby with brown streaking her graying hair stepped into the great room that seemed to take up all the space in the house. Were there bedrooms in the back? Or perhaps there was only one back there.

"Oh, Sheriff Jones, how good of you to come!" The lady Nick assumed was Mrs. Iverson rushed toward the lawman, holding a hand to her heart. "Have you heard anything about my jewels? I just knew you would find them."

Nick could not miss the stony look Mrs. Abby shot her sister. What was that? She wasn't...jealous, was she? Again, he had to fight a smile. This time, by holding his breath and counting in his head.

"Actually, Mrs. Iverson..." Sheriff Jones took off his hat after a glance at Mrs. Abby.

It was nearly too much for Nick to swallow.

The sheriff focused once more on Mrs. Iverson and finished his thought. "I came to ask you some questions."

"Questions? Why ever would you have a need for that?" Her brow furrowed.

Sheriff Jones waved a hand. "It's fairly typical. I need all the information I can get in order to better trace what's happened to your jewelry."

"Abby dear, will you get some coffee for these fine gentlemen?" Mrs. Iverson motioned in the direction of the kitchen.

And though Mrs. Abby seemed anything but prepared to obey, she stomped off toward the stove.

Mrs. Iverson commanded the room, that was for certain. She came from money to be sure. As if the pricey jewelry in question had not been enough to support that inference.

She maneuvered to a well-worn settee and sat on one side.

Would she invite the sheriff to sit with her in front of her sister? Perhaps she had no knowledge of their past entanglement. Or maybe... she did.

But when she set a hand to the space beside her, it was Nick who caught her gaze. "Deputy, please do have a seat."

He gulped and shot a look at Sheriff Jones.

It was the older man's turn to stifle a smile. Not that he did it very well.

"Come, come, Deputy. I don't bite." She lifted an eyebrow and offered him a sugary smile.

He had the sudden urge to tug at his collar. My, the summer sun made the indoors warm. "Actually, Mrs. Iverson, we've been...um, riding for quite some time. I prefer to stand."

Nick felt Sheriff Jones's gaze on him, but he refused to give in to the temptation to glare back.

"Suit yourself, handsome." She winked at him. Actually winked.

He shuffled his feet, trying to find a better placement for his limbs... to no avail.

"Now, Sheriff, how might I help your investigation?" Mrs. Iverson glanced at the man.

Sheriff Jones sat in one of the armchairs. The one that was less weathered. Perhaps it had belonged to the ill-fated old man Fred.

"We just wanted to ask a few questions about your visit and your jewelry."

"Ask away." Mrs. Iverson looked across the room as Mrs. Abby brought two cups of coffee—one for Mrs. Iverson and one she passed off to Sheriff Jones without looking at him directly.

This was getting them nowhere. Nick cleared his throat and pushed out what he believed to be a fine question. "What brings you to Cripple Creek?"

"Isn't it obvious, sugar? I'm here to see my sister." She grinned widely before sipping from the cup.

Then she spit the dark brew back. "For heaven's sakes, Abby. What did you do to this?"

Mrs. Abby called from the kitchen. "Is something wrong?"

"It tastes like...like...salt."

"Oh my, did I mix up the sugar and the salt again? My apologies." Although the woman didn't sound the least bit sorry.

The sheriff was mid-sip when she spoke. He pulled the mug back and looked at the steaming coffee.

"Hand that back," Mrs. Iverson commanded as she rose, reaching for the cup. "I'll get it fixed."

"Mine tastes fine." He looked over the rim of the mug as he took another swig.

"You must take yours without sugar." Then Mrs. Iverson caught herself. "Did Abby ask you how you take your coffee?" Her gaze narrowed.

Abby returned to the great room in a flash, another cup in hand. "I, uh, have waited on the good sheriff many times...at the café."

"Yes, of course." Sheriff Jones smiled a little too broadly.

Mrs. Iverson's gaze moved between the two for a moment.

Mrs. Abby stepped to Nick. "This is for you."

He smiled and accepted the cup. He did take sugar in his coffee but was rather leery about the portion he'd been given.

"Back to my question..." Nick interrupted the glares being thrown about. "If you are here for a visit, why did you bring your jewels?"

Mrs. Iverson waved a hand. "I am visiting as I pass through."

"I see." Nick wasn't sure he had all the pieces yet.

"And where might you be headed next?" Sheriff Jones took up the mantle.

"My Henry, God rest his soul, passed near three months ago. I am moving to join my daughter and her husband in Denver."

Denver? That was an odd coincidence.

"And so, you placed your jewels in the bank for safekeeping in the meantime?" Nick said slowly.

The look she cut him was nothing short of patronizing. "They sure don't grow 'em as smart as they used to. You are quite fine to look at though."

His face heated. "What I mean, Mrs. Iverson, is to verify why you placed them in the bank and for what reason. Did you take them out at any point during your stay?"

She looked toward the ceiling and shook her head. "Not at all."

Mrs. Abby piped up then. "Didn't you take them out a couple of weeks ago? To prepare for your trip?"

"Oh, yes, you're right." Mrs. Iverson shifted her focus to Nick. "I had intended to leave for Denver a couple weeks back. But I came down with some sort of fever. And I had taken them out in order to put them in the lock box on the stage."

"Two weeks ago, you say?" Nick's breathing quickened as the pieces slid into place.

"Yes..." She still spoke as though he couldn't understand plain English.

But Nick didn't care. He exchanged a look with Sheriff Jones. "And you would have been on the stagecoach to Denver that next day."

"Yes. That *is* what I said." Mrs. Iverson frowned and shifted, seemingly agitated.

Sheriff Jones jumped in. "Who knew you had taken them out of the bank?"

"No one." Mrs. Iverson's gaze bounced between the two men. "Oh, except for Mr. Hammond, of course."

Sheriff Jones's mouth became a thin line, his features grim.

Nick's pulse raced as another part of the puzzle fell into place. But he wasn't sure he liked what they had discovered here.

Betsy strolled down the boardwalk. As much as she found Karl's attentiveness kind and as much as she had always wanted her mother's approval for her choices—which, now thanks to Karl, she clearly had— still, the whole morning had left her feeling rather suffocated. By Karl's constant touch and her mother's watchful eye.

She had begged off any further insistence for rest by her mother in declaring she had to get to the hotel and check on Father. And that she was supposed to be working...though she hadn't been back to work in the last several days.

Karl had looked at her rather curiously—perhaps the same look he would give a child who couldn't possibly understand him. And her mother had all but rolled her eyes.

Betsy could still hear Karl's words. "You won't need to do that much longer, darling."

He had planted a kiss to the side of her head before releasing her and taking his own leave of the Callaway home.

Mother had risen and left the parlor, clapping for Maria as she did so.

It was no use. Was her mother only pleased with the match she might make? Would Betsy never find approval for just who she was? Maybe she wasn't enough after all.

Not for Mother. Not for Father. Not for anyone.

Her thoughts drifted to Nick. Would he be at the hotel? Or still out galivanting around with the sheriff, doing important work? *He* was valuable. He was needed.

Would there ever be a time when he saw anything of the kind in her?

She jerked her head. That was nonsense. Mother and Father would never consent to her involvement with a deputy. No matter how much she...

That thought needed to just fall into the void. No use in following it. Not only was it doubtful such would come to fruition, it would only torture her to admit to herself that there was anything...*anything*... between them.

Nick was honorable, righteous, good, and...so much more than she deserved.

She slowed as she approached the front door of the hotel. Drawing in a deep breath, she steeled herself for the chance she might encounter Nick. As she exhaled, she stuck out a hand and pushed the door.

The air inside the hotel was lighter and a tad cooler than the scorching of the day on the street. She straightened her shirtwaist and moved toward the side door, to where she would find the back offices.

"Excuse me, Miss Callaway." The receptionist stepped in front of her. "Is there something I can help you with?"

"No, thank you. I just wanted to find my uniform and get to work. I've been...otherwise engaged these last several days."

The woman gave her a pitiful smile. "Yes. Well, it seems Mr. Callaway found a young lady to take your place."

"What?" Betsy stepped back. Had her father only been appeasing her? Playing some game with her? "But I...I am willing to help and I—"

"Oh, my dear." The woman settled an arm around Betsy's shoulders and steered her away from the portal to the offices. "I think your father accomplished his goals in the time you were with us."

"What does that mean?" Betsy furrowed her brow.

"You didn't realize?" The woman's gaze scanned the lobby before settling on Betsy again. "Mr. Callaway had told us to be understanding. Even when you made messes here and there. We were instructed to give you leeway and clean up after you." After smoothing over her dress, the woman offered Betsy a half smile.

Betsy had nowhere she could look but the floor. "I see. Well, I...am so sorry."

"No harm done, dear." The woman straightened her posture and looked at the front desk as if desperate to return to her post and wash her hands of Betsy. "It's all behind us now. Water under the bridge and all that."

Nodding numbly, Betsy shuffled toward the front door.

"Have a grand day, Miss Callaway. We hope to see you again soon."

Betsy wanted to scoff. The woman couldn't even afford her an original farewell? Just the rote words she uttered to every guest and visitor that passed through this lobby?

Blindly, Betsy walked out the door, her vision blurring. Where she was headed, she didn't know. Perhaps she should just return home and resign herself to her fate—a life with Karl that would put her in a tidy place and in a role with clear boundaries...and limitations.

Not yet.

She couldn't make herself go home. So, she turned opposite and moved off. The clomp of her shoes on the boards of the bridge told that she crossed over the stream that ran along the outskirts of town. How long she had walked to get there, she wasn't certain. Yet even then she didn't stop.

Not until the intensity of the sun bearing down on her gave her reason to seek shade...only then did she pause. By that time, however, she was quite a bit beyond the center of town. Glancing about, she wondered about her location, but wasn't certain. Perhaps it would be best if she returned the way she came.

As she looked in that direction, she became less sure about that however.

Then she remembered the stream. She had crossed a simple bridge over it.

Closing her eyes, she held her breath. Might she hear the tripping of water over stones? If she could find the stream, she could follow it back to town.

The faintest tickle of splashes was audible. There was little chance she could discern what direction that came from.

Was she completely useless?

Though her legs ached, she pushed herself to go back in the direction she could best figure she came.

The narrow path around the trees opened into a field dotted with purples and yellows, wildflowers that stood guard over the grasses that bent to the gentle force of the wind. It was lovely. Had she been here?

Looking to the horizon, she spotted the brown, wooden church steeple. It beckoned her as she had never known. She breathed easier. She had found her way.

Stepping in that direction, something caught her arm and caused her to stumble.

Hands, rough and firm, grabbed for her, keeping her on her feet.

But her heart raced all the same as she fought to turn. Who had trespassed?

Jerking her head around, she flung her wayward hair to the side. And found blue eyes on hers.

CHAPTER 22

Breaking Down

Nick watched Betsy's eyes shift to recognition. He hadn't intended to startle her, but she had completely taken him. Standing in the field between him and the place he sought—the church—her light waves breaking free from their pins and flowing around her in the wind. It had rendered him speechless. All he could manage was to reach for her and confirm if his vision was real. Indeed, it was.

And now he had alarmed her.

"Nikolai?" His name on her lips nearly undid him. The word was soft and filled with emotion. Was it possible there was more to her consideration of him than a simple care? Dare he hope?

"Betsy, I…" He swallowed. What could he say? Best to start with the truth. "I didn't mean to sneak up on you like that."

She glanced downward. "It's all right. I…had just been wandering about and found myself in this place." She waved a hand at the flower-dotted open space.

The sky was blue and filled with puffy clouds. Picturesque. But he had to admit that he was most drawn to her beauty. And that was dangerous.

She looked up and licked her lips. Why did she have to do that? The kisses they had shared haunted his dreams. And now they were all he could think about.

Her gaze landed on his hand, still wrapped around her arm.

"My apologies," he said, willing himself to let go.

But as his hand dropped, she grabbed for it. Lifting it between them, she ran fingers over the callouses. Almost as if in awe, or that she revered the marks of hard work.

The light brush of her fingertips captivated him. His breath caught. "Betsy..."

Her name emitted more as a groan than anything. Did she know what she did to him?

She met his gaze, the green of her eyes darkened, stirring something to life in him. Something he didn't fully trust.

He stepped closer. Then his other hand, as if moving of its own accord, traced the side of her face.

Her eyes slid closed, and her breath stuttered.

How could any man resist? With a grunt, he pulled her against his chest.

Eyes that had been sealed, opened. And delved into his. As if she asked for more. As if she wanted more from him.

He tilted his head and leaned in; his mouth so close to her lips. Would he take them?

Suddenly, she lifted slightly and claimed his mouth.

Her searching was tentative and gentle. As if her experience was not what everyone imagined. Was it not?

But blood pumped through his veins with a force that belied his body's ability to sustain it. A swirl of pleasure enveloped his chest, warming him and urging him to seek more.

Wrapping his arms around her, he pressed into her with his own search. The kiss was more forceful than he'd intended, but he had restrained his longing for too long, and now it overpowered him.

She moaned, and every part of him vibrated with need.

His hands were in her hair, digging into the silken gold. Indeed, she was far more precious than any gold in these hills.

As the desire for more filled him, he pulled back. He lay his forehead on hers and took several deep breaths.

Her fingers sought the stubble of his jaw.

No. He couldn't. No more. He stepped back and held her at arm's length, fighting to maintain that distance.

She laid her hands on his forearms and pushed against them.

He quite nearly relented. But, shaking his head, he held fast. "Betsy, we can't. It's too much."

"It doesn't have to be." Her voice was barely audible above the thundering of his pulse in his ears.

"I...can't." He dropped his hands from her shoulders and turned away.

"Can't?" Her words were shaky. Did she feel this thing coursing through her body too?

But he refused to turn, kept his focus on the far side of the field... where the church steeple stood. "I can't...and I won't."

She gasped. "What?"

"You don't know, do you?" He angled his head in her direction.

Her wide-eyed gaze communicated enough.

"I tried, Betsy. I honestly did." He ran a hand down his face. This wouldn't do.

"I won't trouble you any longer." She turned, but the faint sniffling sound was not disguised.

"Trouble me?" He spun.

She had increased the distance between them. Even as she walked away, he spotted that she held a hand to her face, and one to her midsection. What game was this? Or...was it not a game? Had he injured her pride...or her heart?

"Wait!" Against his better judgment, he rushed after her. As he turned her once more, her pain was laid bare before him in red-rimmed eyes that already swelled from emotion.

"You don't care for me. And you don't have to pretend you do." She looked to the side, swiping a tear from the side of her face.

"Care for you?" He could hear the exasperation in his own voice. Looking to the ground between them, he took some breaths, trying to level his head. Then he met her gaze again. "I...I tried. Lord knows, I tried to walk away. To not feel anything. To not give in. But I failed."

She rubbed her nose and hiccupped. "What?"

He wanted so desperately to wipe away her tears. Instead, he gentled his hold and let one hand graze her hair. "Betsy, I love you."

Her eyes widened, and she sucked in a breath. "Don't say things you don't mean." Was that...hope...in her gaze?

"You fill my dreams and haunt my waking moments. And as much as I told myself you could never feel the same for me, it doesn't matter...I can't change what is in my heart." He cupped the side of her face.

She laid a hand over his and held his gaze. "But I do care. So very much. Nikolai, I do."

He leaned forward and claimed her lips, careful to keep some distance between their bodies. And this time, the kiss was gentle, loving, affirming. And achingly sweet.

When he pulled back once again, there were more tears in her eyes. He ran a hand down the curve of her face. "What is it?"

"I've never been so...wanted. So loved. It's so...perfect." She gripped his wrist near her chin and tugged to bring him closer.

But he resisted. "I...can't. I'm only so strong, sweetheart." He let the corners of his mouth lift as he tucked some of her errant strands in place.

A small smile captured her as she let out a breath. Then her face fell. "But...I'm...courting your brother. I...have led him to believe there is a future."

Nick's hand dropped. "Is there?"

She pulled her arms to her chest, folding them in front of her. "I..."

Fear seized him. Could he bear it if she rejected him after his admission? "Betsy?" He wished his voice wasn't so pleading.

She gripped the lapels of his shirt. "I don't love him."

He relaxed...a little. "And the other? The fact that you are courting Karl?"

She glanced across the field. Her gaze drew his attention to where she looked—at the church.

What was he doing? This couldn't be right. But then why did his heart feel as if it were?

"I can't do this. I...I'm sorry, Nick. I have to go..."

And when she pulled away and ran off toward town, he didn't stop her. But he watched her as she went, fading into the distance.

His heart lay in pieces. Shattered. How could he have been so blind? She needed the security of marrying his brother more than she wanted Nick's love. That was painful. His gaze caught on the steeple once more, and his initial intent resurfaced.

He needed guidance about the investigation, about his father, and, more now than before, about his heart bending toward Betsy. Stretching out legs that felt sluggish from the recent encounter, he trudged toward the church. And to the only hope he had left.

Betsy's vision blurred as she rushed to Cripple Creek's center. Nothing mattered. Nothing.

Why had she just walked away from Nikolai? Everything in her heart cried out for her to turn back and go to him. Not only was she destroying her happiness, but his as well. And that hurt more than anything.

But was she good for him? That was certainly a no.

It would be best if she did not infect his life. She could never forgive herself if she prevented him from finding true happiness with a woman that was better than she. More upstanding. More kind. More...just more.

For she was a broken-down shell of a woman. Empty. Lost.

That was no match for a man such as Nikolai. That brought to her mind that perhaps she didn't deserve Karl's attention either. But something about that situation didn't feel the same. She didn't love him, that was for certain. Yet, why did she feel that she wouldn't be stealing his future happiness?

Pushing on, uncaring of what others thought of her raw emotional display, she didn't bother to swipe at her tears. She had but a short walk remaining to get to the safety of her father's hotel just on the other side of town. Then she could escape altogether to her bedroom.

Nothing could harm her there...well, not physically. But would she be free of the hardships that plagued her heart?

"Betsy Callaway," a voice called from behind and to the right. "I'd like a word with you."

Despite her desire to ignore the entreaty and continue on, Betsy drew in a breath and turned.

Nick and Karl's sister Anya stood, watching Betsy.

Striving to gather her emotions, Betsy wiped at tear-stained cheeks.

Then Anya strode to her, closing the distance with determination clouding any of the usual pleasantness about her features.

"Anya, how good of you to—"

A slap was the young woman's greeting.

Betsy held a hand to the stinging side of her face as a couple of the townsfolk around them gasped and whispered.

"Why did you do that?" Betsy's confusion surely echoed in the space between her and Anya. It wasn't exactly as if Betsy didn't deserve to be publicly humiliated. But she had not anticipated it to come from Anya.

The girl's features darkened. "How dare you play with my brother's heart!"

"Play?" The shock in her own voice sounded more intense than she felt. Again, it wasn't as if she hadn't earned redressing in this town.

Anya stood with fists clasped at the end of arms straightened at her sides. Would she strike again?

"I am sorry for any misunderstanding, but Karl and I are courting and I—"

"Not that brother." Anya's eyes narrowed.

Betsy dropped her regard to the boards beneath her feet, uncaring about the clusters of women and men watching.

"How could you?" Anya's voice wavered, betraying the more tender emotions beneath her ire.

"I..." How could Anya know what went between Betsy and Nick? Had she seen them just now? That wasn't possible.

"I knew your reputation. I knew you were no good." The verbal barbs struck their target. "Everyone does."

Shame overwhelmed Betsy. Yes, this was her due. "I...didn't intend to hurt anyone. Certainly not—"

"Come now," Anya said, eyes flashing. "You mean to tell me that you didn't try to come between Katherine and Wyatt? Didn't want to break a marriage forged in sacred vows to God?"

Betsy swallowed. Was there any recourse? Anything she might say to defend herself against such accusations? Especially as they were true.

"Don't have anything to say to me?" Anya fairly seethed.

"I...don't want to hurt Nick."

Anya threw her head back and pushed out a burst of air before leveling her gaze on Betsy once again. "Pardon me if I don't believe that. Not for one second. How could I?"

Betsy drew her arms about her torso. As if that would hide her from the many stares and whispers.

Anya pressed out further words. "Nick is decent and good. And has a tender, caring heart just ripe for the likes of you to take advantage of."

Betsy let out a shaky breath. There was no way to answer. She'd best just take this berating. Again, she had earned every bit of it. For Katherine and Wyatt. And for Nick. Perhaps even for Karl's sake. Yes, she was no good for anyone.

Anya took a step closer, steel in her eyes.

Betsy backed up before realizing she did so.

Anya's narrowed gaze held Betsy as guilt pierced her heart, tearing a path through her.

The younger woman pushed through clenched teeth, "Stay away from my brother."

Betsy released the last of her tension and hung her head and nodded.

Long moments passed between them. Anya's harsh breaths and the low voices of those gathered were the only sounds...except the pounding of Betsy's heart. Would it ever recover? She most certainly would not walk away unscathed.

She quite nearly opened her mouth. To say what, she wasn't sure.

But the whirl and whish of Anya's skirt seared the air about Betsy.

As the seconds ticked by, Betsy felt the distance grow between her and Anya. And sensed that others moved on as well.

Dare she fall apart? Sink to the ground in tears as she so wanted to? Would that make her appear the victim?

She wasn't. She was anything but the victim.

And she would pay for her sins. For the rest of her life.

CHAPTER 23

Hardships

Nick's time at the church had been refreshing, but it hadn't taken away the sting from his encounter with Betsy. The kisses they shared had been full of hope, of promise...all to amount to nothing. She didn't love him. And, while she may not love Karl either, he was the more appealing offer.

Did it matter, though? Nick intended to be a U.S. Marshal one day. Hadn't he already decided that a family and the trappings of settling down didn't fit well with that life? Perhaps her rejection was a blessing.

He maneuvered around townsfolk moving down the main stretch of Cripple Creek. The Callaway family's hotel was in the distance. He tried not to stare. For it only reminded him of Betsy. But he'd have to continue his stay there. At least for as long as this investigation went on.

The jail was a few paces away, but Nick's destination was the bank. That's where the mystery was. That's where they needed to find answers.

Deputy Gyles stepped out of the jail and directly into Nick's path. The man jerked away from Nick as if he feared injury would befall him from a surprise attack.

"Sorry, Deputy," Nick tugged at the brim of his hat.

"My apologies," Deputy Gyles sputtered. "I didn't see you there."

205

"That was obvious." Nick grinned despite the heaviness overshadowing him. "Is Sheriff Jones in?" He motioned at the small building.

Deputy Gyles shook his head. "He went to the bank. Had some questions for Mr. Hammond."

Nick glanced down the road in that direction. "That so?"

Gyles's attention shifted to the right.

Nick glanced that way as well.

A commotion of some sorts occurred just beyond the General Store. Clusters of people had gathered, blocking his view of whatever exchange occurred.

"Should we see what that's all about?" Nick tried to catch Gyles's eye.

"Don't worry yourself. I'll investigate. You go join the sheriff." The man stretched out long legs and moved off.

"If you need assistance, come get someone. Don't be a hero."

Deputy Gyles waved him off. There was little cause for concern. The man was reliable and smart about how much he could reasonably take on himself.

Nick didn't worry with it one second more. He resumed his walk toward the bank.

There was little of interest to pull his thoughts from Betsy and less reason to push such thoughts away. Except to pray.

And so, he lifted yet another request for God to soothe his heart and bind its broken places. Soon enough, he halted his steps. The bank loomed before him.

He pushed in and was greeted by a calm conversation. The voices, though, filtered across the space—Sheriff Jones and Karl.

His brother was not unexpected but was still the last person he wished to speak with right now. After...

Nick shook his head. It did less to remove Betsy's image and taste from his mind than he'd hoped.

The voices silenced.

Nick looked in their direction to find their gazes on him.

"Care to join us?" This from Sheriff Jones.

Karl's glare tore through Nick. Did Karl know what had delayed him? That he and Betsy had shared such intimacies? It wasn't possible.

Besides, Karl always looked at him that way. Nothing different about it.

Nick nodded and stepped to where they stood, near the teller's desk.

"You were saying..." Sheriff Jones turned back to Karl and urged him on.

The intensity of Karl's gaze on Nick did not diminish for several moments. Then he shifted his focus back to the sheriff. "Yes, well...I'm afraid I don't have anything else I can say that would help."

"And there was nothing taken other than what was in the vault and the office safe?"

"As far as we can tell." Karl truly appeared bored with the whole thing. "Look, Sheriff, I don't mean to put you off, but we are trying as best we can to put our bank back together.

"My sincere apologies for any disruption we have caused, but—"

"Who knew the jewels were in the smaller safe?" Nick pressed in.

Karl met his gaze, iron and fire in his eyes. "You are not ignorant to the workings of the bank. Father knew. I don't know how anyone else would have found out. He put them in, as usual, and he secured the safe. I'm not sure how anyone would even know about it, tucked away in my father's office as it was."

That was not reassuring. Nick swallowed but kept his features stoic. This was not the time to face off with his brother. Was that what Nick sought here?

Sheriff Jones looked him over as if attempting to quiet him.

Nick ignored the man. Something crept over him—fear, discomfort, uncertainty. Or perhaps the inability to believe his father capable of bringing something like this upon the town. And putting Betsy at risk.

There she was again. Could he not escape her?

Karl cleared his throat and turned his attention back to Sheriff Jones. "If there is nothing further—"

"Who led the bandit to the vault?" Nick shot out, refusing to be dismissed.

Karl's jaw muscles twitched. He held Nick's gaze and then released a long breath. "My father."

Sheriff Jones glanced toward Nick, an apology in his eyes.

"And I know what you're thinking, but—"

The door to the back office opened and Pa stepped out. He scanned the room, some strain about the area around his eyes. "Sheriff, Deputy, how might we help you?"

Nick shuffled his feet, praying the sheriff would not be too quick in acting on his suspicion.

"Mr. Hammond," Sheriff Jones said, stepping closer. "I have to put you under arrest."

"What?" Pa's wide-eyed stare fell on Nick. "I..."

"That's preposterous," Karl called out. "What sense does that make?"

But Sheriff Jones ignored them both and reached for Pa's arm. "Do not make this harder than it needs to be."

Pa tore his gaze from Nick and to the sheriff. "Do me this favor," he said calmly, "Do not drag me to the jail like some common criminal. I will go with you willingly."

Sheriff Jones nodded and released Pa's arm. "Deputy Hammond, if you will lead the way..."

Nick nodded slowly. He didn't have to look in Karl's direction to feel the heat of his glare. Neither could he look at his father, the disappointment in his eyes would crush any remaining piece of Nick's strength. Though he had just spent time in prayer, his heart felt heavier than ever.

What of his mother? His sister? His father's livelihood and reputation in this town?

For certain, this would only make things worse. Much worse.

Betsy allowed the ricketing of the surrey to bounce her about, vibrating her very bones. Mother was in some sort of all-fire hurry. She'd heard about Anya's display. Not from Betsy's lips, though she wondered why Betsy hadn't told her. Thank goodness, there was less reliable information about the nature of Anya's verbal attack.

Mother insisted they go straight to Karl and tell him before he found out elsewhere.

Betsy was embarrassed by the exchange and even more so that

Mother would force an interaction with Karl about it. And if that wasn't enough, the bank had been closed, oddly in the middle of the day. So, now their buggy carried them to the Hammond homestead.

The chance of coming across Anya at the Hammonds' home was great. And Betsy's stomach roiled at that thought. That was truly the last thing she wanted. Would Anya be furious? Would she lash out again? This time laying bare for Mother and Karl her suspicions about Betsy and Nick? That would be awkward to say the least. The only hope, only prayer that Betsy had, was that Anya might not have returned home.

Yet the day had moved onward into afternoon. It was rather unlikely she wouldn't have returned home to tend to her mother and the house's needs.

"There." Mother's terse voice shot toward Betsy, who had been hugging the side of the surrey. "Seems Karl's carriage is here. I wonder what caused him to close the bank early."

Betsy shrugged and tried to swallow against the tightness in her throat. Just as Mother had said, Karl's buggy and chestnut mare stood outside the house.

"No matter. We'll have this thing straightened out. If you intend to be his wife, you'll have to insist his sister respect you."

"Mother..." The word came out weak. Betsy's heart wasn't in this. None of it. More and more, she felt done. Defeated. Numb.

But she couldn't stop this. Couldn't run from it. Best put on a brave face. Straightening from her hunched position, she looked forward. And tried to not get sick as her heart sank deeper.

Mother slowed the horse and came to a stop. And waited.

Betsy moved to step down and Mother's hand shot out and grabbed her arm, her fingers digging in.

Mother wouldn't look at her though.

"Why aren't we—?"

"We wait to be assisted." Mother's voice was harsh.

Betsy blew out a breath. "What if they don't know we are here?"

"They know." Mother sat ramrod straight, watching the front door. Several long moments passed.

"This is unnecessary," Betsy said low. Dare she defy her mother?

Still, they sat.

The horse shifted. Perhaps even she was restless.

"I'm going in." Betsy slid closer to the side.

The front door slammed open, the door clattering as it was thrown with such force.

Karl emerged, followed by Mrs. Hammond.

The older woman pled with Karl, "Slow down. You need to see this from your—"

Then her eyes snagged on her guests. "Karl..."

He spun, his face reddened and fists clenched. Would he attack his mother?

Mrs. Hammond's gaze, however, stayed on Betsy and Mother. She even offered a slight smile.

Karl turned in their direction, then back to Mrs. Hammond. "This is not over." He then tugged on his jacket as if ensuring it was in place. Running a hand over his hair, he stepped to the surrey. "Betsy, darling, I did not expect to see you."

Betsy glanced between Karl and Mrs. Hammond, confusion and concern vying for dominance.

Karl took her hand, his hold tighter than she'd expected. "As much as I appreciate the call, it may be best if you came another time."

Betsy gritted her teeth, fighting the urge to pull free.

Mrs. Hammond remained on the top step, the picture of contriteness—hands clasped at her waist and face turned toward the ground.

"We have come from the comfort of our home to speak with you." Mother's grating words pressed out.

Karl looked at her. "I understand that, but we...that is, my family... has a bit of a challenge on our hands."

Mother's hawk-like gaze took in the scene. "Still, I insist we speak with you. It is a matter of great import."

The lines about Karl's mouth became strained. From the effort of holding back his desired response? She couldn't be sure.

Movement from just within the house, boots landing on the floorboards, preceded a voice, "Karl, I can't let this lie—"

Nick emerged and, as his brother and mother had, laid eyes on Betsy and her mother.

Mother bristled as he appeared.

Karl did as well, jerking his regard to Nick. "I will *not*..." He took a breath. "I do not wish to discuss this further."

"Will someone please tell us what is going on?" Mother demanded. "And for heaven's sake, help us alight from the buggy."

The Hammond brothers exchanged accusing glances.

"Please," Mrs. Hammond stressed the word. "We have guests. Have you two taken complete leave of your manners?"

Silence strained the air.

"Of course." Nick stepped forward. But even as he moved toward the surrey, he would not look at Betsy.

That made her ache all the more.

Karl jerked around, reaching for Betsy with the hand that wasn't clamped on her already. "My dearest," he said, tugging at her hand, "May I?"

She forced herself to stay focused on him, to not glance at Nick. Karl may see too much in her eyes. For certain, more than she wanted him to.

Nodding, she angled herself toward him and let him assist her down. But his hands on her were rough and possessive. Did he know? Was there truly anything to know?

She swallowed, then eased her breathing.

But once her feet hit the ground, Karl did not release her. He shifted and led her to the porch.

She sensed his eyes on her the entire time. It was unnerving.

The surrey creaked slightly. Perhaps from Nick helping Mother down. But Betsy would not look back. Not for anything.

"Please, do come in." Mrs. Hammond's lips lifted at the corners, but the muscles remained tight. Was her smile so forced? What had gone on between the family members? Mrs. Hammond led the way, calling ahead of her, "Anya, put on water for tea!"

Betsy stumbled.

Karl wrapped an arm around her, grabbing for the curve of her waist. "Are you all right?"

She offered him what she hoped was an apologetic look. "I think my foot caught a rock."

Karl glanced about the ground. "Oh?"

Tugging him forward, she said, "It's nothing. I must pay better heed with my steps. But I thank you for catching me." She forced her own smile then.

As they neared the front door, the swish of Mrs. Hammond's, and probably Anya's, skirts filled the quiet that strained.

Could she face Anya? She needed to gather herself. But how would that be possible?

She leaned into Karl, "Mr. Hammond..."

His face drew near hers as he laid his other hand on her captured arm. "For the last time, call me Karl."

She put on a small smile. "Karl..."

He grinned but lifted his eyebrows.

"I...don't know how to say this. But I need a moment."

His brows gathered. "A moment?"

"To visit the privy."

"Oh!" He looked away. "Then I'll walk you around to it."

"No!" The word came out sharper than she'd intended.

He stared at her, eyebrows raised once more.

"That is..." she said as she tucked an errant strand of hair behind her ear. "I don't wish to keep you from your respite."

The muscles in his jaw worked.

She pressed against his side, trailing a finger from her free hand along his that still held her too tightly. "Please, do go on in and secure my seat with you. I'll only be a minute."

The dark that shadowed his features lifted. "Very well. Don't be long." He tugged her closer and pressed a kiss to her forehead.

She couldn't help but steal a hopefully unwatched glance at Nick.

The man focused on assisting her mother up the stairs, not on Betsy.

Just as well.

Betsy squeezed Karl's arm and bit back a gasp of relief when he let go of her. Gripping her skirt to keep it out of the worst of the dirt, she moved to the side of the house.

The privy was just to the side of the house, off angle from the barn.

She wanted to rush but also resisted hurrying this errand. She'd have to face Anya soon enough.

Moments later, she closed herself within the small structure. This was the oddest place to catch her breath, but as she leaned her back against the door, that is exactly what she did.

Counting several breaths, more than she should remain here for, dread climbed in her chest.

There was no escaping what lay ahead. She ran hands down her waist where the seam of her skirt met her blouse. Sucking in a breath that neither refreshed nor soothed, she turned and cracked the door. Would Karl have come outside? Or, worse, Anya?

No one waited outside for her.

Closing her eyes, she thanked God—should He actually care—for that small grace.

Slipping out, she closed the door behind herself.

"I knew it," a voice greeted her. A voice she dreaded.

CHAPTER 24

Confrontation

Nick watched as Betsy emerged from the outhouse. "I knew it."

She startled, jerking away from him. "For the love of all, Nick!"

"You were trying to escape, weren't you?" The impulse to smirk almost tipped his lips upward, but his hurt underneath kept him from doing so.

"I..." She ran her hands down her skirt, fingers shaking as she gripped at the fabric.

But he refused to speak again until she said something that rang with a sense of honesty.

She looked at him as if expecting something from him. Was she so afraid to start? To speak into whatever this was between them? Whatever she felt?

"Nick," she said before her tongue darted across her lips. "I don't know what else there is to say." Her eyes took on a pained look. As if she hurt as greatly as he did. But that couldn't be.

Blast! He couldn't wait forever. "I spoke with my sister."

Her eyebrows lifted and the appearance of injury about her features deepened. "Oh?"

"Yes." He stepped forward.

At first, it seemed as if she would back away. Only, the privy was behind her. Did that prevent her? Or did some sense of respect or—dare he hope, care—for him still her movements?

He chanced another step.

"Please," she muttered. But it was half-hearted.

"Her redress may not have been merited, maybe it was. But it did accomplish something." His words were low. How much longer could they linger before someone from the house wondered after them?

She looked to the ground as her face colored. The rosiness only enhancing the fine beauty of her features. Was the blush from his nearness or from memory of Anya's words?

"I noticed, in her recounting, that you didn't deny anything."

Her head jerked up, her gaze on him. "What?"

"I told myself it was an oversight on your part." How could she not sense the heat between them? It drew him closer. He was magnetized by her very presence. But he paused. His heart could bear only so much. He dared not make an overture he would regret.

She looked to the side.

"Was it?"

She closed her eyes. Her face flushed anew.

"Betsy, look at me, and tell me you feel nothing for me." He swallowed. How had he ended up here—putting his heart out for her to deny once more?

She grimaced. But her affect remained downcast, her eyes fluttering open, but her gaze set on something in the distance.

"Look at me."

With painfully slow movements, she shifted her focus and then her gaze met his. "It was not an oversight."

He let out a long breath. Had he held it?

Though he had been the one to push, the fact remained that her admission changed nothing. He still wanted something beyond this town, and she wanted a security he couldn't offer. Yet it did change something...her heart had answered his. But what was he to do with that?

It was he who then broke eye contact. Too much swirled about him

—his father's arrest, the investigation, Denver. He could not allow himself to become caught up in this any longer.

"That distresses you?" Her words were soft with the hint of a tremor about them.

He glanced up at her. "Perhaps."

She let out a shaky breath. "I understand." Striding forward, she moved in the direction of the house.

But he caught her arm. "No, you don't."

Her gaze landed on the point of contact between them, then followed along his arm to his face. "Don't I? I am not the kind of woman that deserves you."

That surprised. "What?"

She looked away again. "I...have done great evil. In my heart and in this town. I don't deserve..." Her wavering voice broke off her words.

He gentled his hold, the desire to wrap her in his arms nearly overwhelmed him. "That's not true."

"Isn't it?" She stared at him, resigned.

"No. If you only knew how I..." He stopped himself.

She watched him.

This was torture. He released her. "There is so much more going on."

She sighed. "Your investigation takes priority over everything else."

What did that mean? He met her gaze and saw it—she was accustomed to being second. To being used for what could be gained through her. For what she could do, not who she was.

"Do you know how difficult it is to resist you?"

She dropped her regard once more. "That is kind." Stepping out of his soft grasp, she moved once more in the direction of the house. "I wish I might be able to offer you more than a broken spirit."

As her skirts swished, he clamped his eyes shut. "I helped arrest my father this afternoon."

The movement of fabric stilled. Was she so moved? "Your father?"

He let out another breath that caused his muscles to quake. "I had to follow where the investigation led. I had not dreamed it would lead there."

Gentle footfalls sounded from her direction. "Would you have still followed it if you had known?"

Would he have? He had asked himself the same question multiple times. "I don't know."

"I do." Her voice was nearer.

He turned.

She was little more than an arm's length away.

He wanted to question her statement, but he knew the answer. As well, he wagered she, in fact, did. Dropping his chin, he blinked back the sting in his eyes.

A moment later, her soft fingers touched his arm. "I'm so sorry."

He believed her. But could he look her in the eyes again? Dare he display such vulnerable emotions?

She set her other hand under his chin and drew his face up.

Then he saw...tears brimmed her eyes. Tears for him.

He leaned his forehead against hers, letting his hands grip her upper arms for support. Then he released a trembling breath and let his hurt soak into her for a moment.

And she bore it.

The door at the back of the homestead creaked.

He looked up and found Anya glaring at them.

His words were quick. "Anya, it's not what you think."

Betsy whirled, dropping her hands, shrinking back into herself.

Anya's eyes narrowed. "I warned you."

"Anya," Nick bit back. "This is not your concern."

His sister looked at him. "Isn't it? She makes of your heart something to entertain herself. As well, Karl's heart."

Nick swallowed again. How this would affect Karl had not escaped him...as if his brother needed any more reason to hate him.

His gaze remained steady on Anya, but hers flew to Betsy. "I warned you. It's time you got exactly what you deserved."

"Anya, don't—" Nick managed to get out before she called.

"Karl!"

Nick was torn between protecting Betsy and stopping his sister from summoning the man that could make this messier. But he held back. Did he, too, want Betsy to make a choice once and for all?

Anya spun toward the interior of the house. "Karl!"

The stomp of hurried boot steps thundered louder than was possible. There was no way to stop it now.

How did she get herself into these things?

Betsy glanced at Nick, hoping to communicate her regret. And helplessness. Would he be able to aid her?

When the stomping neared, she was not fully prepared for Karl's appearance. At first, he seemed rather concerned about Anya's yelling. But as he took in the scene, his features darkened.

"What is this?" He looked from Betsy to Nick and then back.

Nick had pulled away from her, but the places where their skin had connected still warmed her. She was glad for any solace from the bitter cold of reality.

Betsy couldn't think. She couldn't look at Nick. She couldn't respond. She couldn't do anything but stare at Karl's angry face.

"Someone answer me," Karl fumed.

Anya folded her arms over her chest. "It seems your darling Betsy is playing both sides of the fence."

"No," Betsy insisted, drawing Nick's regard. The weight of his regard didn't help.

Karl's eyebrow quirked. An odd gesture with his tight, reddened features.

"What would you call it?" Anya's face registered her own anger.

What had Betsy done to deserve this? But she knew...this, too, was her due. She had yet again done a terrible jig and it was time to pay the piper.

Summoning all the courage she had within her, she stepped forward. She wished she'd had time to think this through, to decide her best course of action. But a decision must be made. Now.

"Karl, I didn't mean to hurt you. I—"

"What are you saying?" he seethed as he came down the couple of steps and into the yard, his fists clenched. "What is this about?"

"Calm down." Nick stepped between Karl and Betsy.

"Stay out of this, traitor." Karl spat the words in Nick's direction without looking at him.

Betsy was thankful for Nick's impulse to protect her, but she couldn't hide behind him. "Karl, perhaps we should speak in private..."

Nick jerked around, curiosity and worry lined his eyes. "No."

She put a hand to his arm. "It will be all right."

"You're not going to hide behind your wiles and continue to manipulate my brothers." Anya clenched her jaw. "Best have it out here and be done with it once and for all. Who do you choose, Betsy?"

Betsy licked her lips, her mouth suddenly dry.

"That is..." Anya smirked. "If either of my brothers will have you."

That was a very real danger. And Betsy suddenly knew what she had to do. For one had her will, the other her heart. But only one might have her future.

"I—" Betsy started, but the door opened once more.

Mother and Mrs. Hammond stepped out of the house.

"What is going on out here?" Mother's clipped words were directed at Betsy.

Mrs. Hammond looked to each of her children, seemingly at a loss.

And, soon enough, every gaze was on Betsy—all but one held some amount of anger. But that one mattered most. And that one silently pled to be important. To be her first choice.

She took in a full breath. This was it.

"Spit it out," Mother insisted.

Betsy ignored her and looked at Karl. "I'm sorry, Karl. Truly I am, but I am in love with your brother."

Mother gasped and gripped for something, anything to steady herself.

Nick's exhale, nearest her, was likely not audible to the others.

Karl's features straightened until he had a blank look about him. It was the eeriest thing. "Please, give us a moment."

Nick stepped to Betsy, "I won't allow you to—"

Betsy held up a hand. "All will be well."

"Ungrateful child," Mother screeched. "Mr. Hammond," she said as she turned to Karl, "Give me a moment with my daughter. I will straighten this out."

"No." Betsy tensed under her scrutiny. "I have to speak what's in my heart."

"Heart? What kind of nonsense is that?" Mother scoffed. "You have just thrown away any hope of a secure future."

"I said, 'leave us,'" Karl ground out. His whole demeanor was as the calm before the storm. It unnerved Betsy.

Mother whirled and returned within the structure, followed closely by a slow-moving Mrs. Hammond.

Anya shot another hard glare in Betsy's direction. "Are you coming, Nick?"

He looked at Betsy, who nodded. As nervous as she was, she had to fight her own battles, and she had to face her own choices. It was time.

Anya waited.

As Nick passed Karl, he leaned toward him. "For what it's worth, I never intended for this to—"

"Silence!" Karl held up a hand. "The least you can do is allow me a few moments."

Nick nodded. Then he glanced back at Betsy, offering her a small smile. Then he joined Anya and they walked inside.

As soon as the door closed, Karl put a hand to his forehead. "I don't understand."

"I can't imagine how difficult this must be. Believe me, I never wanted to—"

Karl's hand shot up again. "Quiet." His voice was edged with danger.

It unsettled her. But she seamed her lips.

He stepped to her. "Let's get one thing straight."

His gaze lifted to hers and she prepared herself for his wrath.

"My wife will *not* be caught in such a compromising position."

"I understand. And I hope you—"

"So, you need to end this thing."

"What?"

He paced, his steps short. "I can be a very forgiving man, but this will not be tolerated."

"Did you not hear what I said?" Confusion swirled through her mind. What was this?

He paused and stepped toward her. There was little room between them now. "I did. And I am telling you it will not happen again."

"I don't understand, I just—"

He cut her off again with a gesture. "Know this, Miss Callaway," he said as he closed the distance between them and grabbed her arms, "You will *not* embarrass me."

This was crazy. Surely, he didn't think they had a future. Not after what she'd just said.

His grip tightened and he slammed her into his chest, his mouth crushing down on hers. The kiss was hard, demanding, possessive. It was nothing like the sweet press of Nick's mouth.

She tried to shrug him off.

He held her tighter.

She broke the kiss with a cry.

He put a finger to her lips, silencing her. Then his finger trailed the side of her face, as his other hand ran along her hair before cupping her face. "There now, darling, I'm glad we have that all sorted out."

"Karl, I don't understand."

He leaned forward.

She tried to shrink back, fearing another assault.

But he pressed a dead kiss to her forehead. "You will understand. And you will behave." His words were cold. "Or you will regret it."

He grabbed her hand but shifted so there was more space between them. "Mrs. Callaway," he called.

They waited. She feared saying anything. Perhaps she *did* need Nick's protection after all. But what would Karl do to Nick if she begged for his aid? No, she needed time to think.

After several moments, Mother came to the back door, handkerchief to her face.

"I think it's time you took your daughter home. She needs some rest after her trying day."

Mother looked at their hands, and her lips moved into a small smile. "Of course, Mr. Hammond."

She moved as Karl walked Betsy into the house and down the hall. Once they reached the great room, however, he simply continued on to the front door and out onto the porch.

"Betsy..." Nick was on his feet, following.

Anya tried to grab for his arm, but he pulled free.

Betsy looked at Nick, attempting to extricate her hand as tears streamed down her face. "Nikolai..."

Karl jerked her forward and to the surrey. He wouldn't so much as look at Nick. Would he hurt his brother? Surely not...

Now beside the carriage, Karl all but pushed and lifted her onto the bench.

Nick stood on the porch. "What is the meaning of this?"

Betsy wanted to respond, but the words became choked in her throat.

Almost immediately, Mother settled beside her, grabbed the reins, and clicked her tongue for the horse to move.

Now free of Karl's hold, Betsy struggled to her feet. She could slip down. Then, if she could make it to Nick...

Mother snapped the reins, and the horse increased its speed.

"Nikolai," Betsy called, turning in her seat to look back at the house.

He ran after them, but was helpless, unable to stop the horse or even to catch them.

What would happen to her? Even with her confession, if Karl and Mother used their power to tear them apart, was there hope for a future?

CHAPTER 25

Tension

Nick watched the Callaways' surrey carry Betsy away. It broke his heart to hear her calling for him. And he was absolutely helpless.

Not for long.

Shifting his focus, he moved toward the barn. He'd saddle a horse and intercept them. Then he would dare anyone to try and come between him and Betsy again.

But what if her mother tried to strong arm her? What could her mother do? What *would* she do in her desperation to control her daughter?

He sensed movement to the side before he was shoved.

Nearly losing his footing, he tried to maintain his balance, but Karl's assault kept coming, his fist swinging.

Nick ducked in time, but that did not to stop the attack.

"Karl!"

"It's not enough that you have Pa arrested. You have to take her from me too?" Karl swung again.

Karl's fist grazed Nick's shoulder that time.

As Nick straightened, he brought his arms up to defend himself.

Karl stepped into his path. Would he really try to prevent him from leaving?

"Out of my way, Karl," Nick warned. "You can't stop me."

"What did I ever do to you?" Karl's words shot out. "Why do you hate me so much?"

Nick backed up. "I could ask you the same question. You have been nothing but a thorn in my side—celebrating my estrangement, encouraging it even, and then threatening me when I returned."

Karl's face scrunched into a mixture of pain and anger. "Stay away from her." He jerked as if to lunge at Nick again.

Nick sidestepped him easily and he fell into the dirt. "Don't you see? I love her. I can't...I won't be kept from her."

Karl rolled over, his fine suit covered in dirt. As well, he had a scrape across his chin. Despite that, he laughed. "You don't know her. She won't give up a future for some fairytale. Love...*ha*! What is that to anyone?"

Nick stared at his brother. Was he truly so calloused? Would he marry a woman who loved his own brother?

Not this woman. Betsy wasn't who Karl thought she was. Not anymore.

Resuming his stride, Nick went into the barn and grabbed a saddle.

"You aren't thinking straight," Anya's voice filtered in from the barn entrance.

He afforded her a look. "Aren't I?"

"You know you can't trust her. Not with her history." Anya stepped closer.

He wouldn't listen to this.

"Nick." She set a hand to his arm, an attempt to still him.

He shook her off with a gentle movement.

"You know I'm right. I don't want to see you get hurt."

He set the saddle on a painted mare and paused. "That's the thing about love. You have to trust it. Have faith. Give it all you have."

Anya's features were stricken.

He gripped the reins and walked toward the wide opening, but he paused. "Or it's not worth anything."

He swung into the saddle and urged the horse onward as lightning split the sky.

As soon as the surrey came to a halt outside the Callaway home, Betsy climbed down and rushed in the opposite direction...then kept going.

"Stop this instant, young lady." Mother's voice was sharp but not rushed.

"You can't cage me in. Not anymore."

Silence fell between them. It was curious and disturbing at the same time.

Betsy looked over her shoulder.

Mother stood beside the buggy, watching. Nothing in Mother's features indicated that she was bothered in the least. "We shall see."

Betsy slowed, her mouth dropping.

Did Mother mean that? She wouldn't stop Betsy from going to Nick?

"Walk all the way to Timbuktu for all I care." Mother continued her casual stroll to the front door.

Betsy halted. Mother couldn't be serious. Looking to the ground, Betsy tried to make sense of Mother's manipulation.

"But..." Mother's voice rang out across the space. She had paused at the door.

Betsy looked up.

"You will not be welcome in this home. Ever. Again." The flash in Mother's eyes was enough to preach of her sincerity.

Betsy folded her arms. "It won't be soon enough." She resumed her way toward town, but her steps were more measured, and became slower.

Thunder clapped.

So, she would walk in the rain. What did that matter? A little water never hurt anyone. Except...it would make the journey infinitely more difficult. And dangerous.

Lightning flashed across the expanse of the sky.

"Come now, Betsy." Mother's voice sounded closer than she imagined it could from so far away. Had the woman stepped out into the yard? "You are not a stupid girl. Never were. You know what is best for you, what will give you a future."

Betsy slowed further, arms straight by her sides, fists clenched. She hated that she did so. Why did her mother have to know her so well? Why did her mother's voice drive her to such places?

The woman wasn't wrong. What kind of life could she and Nick have?

A good one.

God, if You're there, give me the strength to walk into a brighter tomorrow.

She picked up step again.

"Just imagine your father's poor heart when he finds you've run off."

That gave Betsy pause. Her father had always been a bright spot in her life. And meant everything to her. He doted on her and cherished her. She couldn't break his heart.

"Yes, your father will be so distressed." Mother's voice became softer, and her words slowed. Almost as if a dove cooed the sentences.

Betsy could not deny her mother had pulled the winning lever. Nick would understand. In fact, if Betsy could speak with her father, she could make him understand. And he would help her and Nick.

Yes, that was the answer.

But for now, she had to return home, play the part of the obedient daughter...and bide her time.

CHAPTER 26

Seeking

Betsy watched from her second story window as the rain poured. It was a dismal afternoon. Fitting...after the way her day had gone. Too much contained within one cycle of the sun.

Droplets made streaks down her window. It did nothing to abate her tears. In fact, this reflection of her mood only intensified her sadness. Had she given up Nick? Traded him for comfort? Maybe more so for her father's wellbeing. But traded him all the same. Would he understand?

She glanced at the sky. For a moment, it had almost felt as if she grasped heaven. Those glorious moments in Nick's arms, with his lips on hers. Could anything be so pure, so right?

Indeed, it may be the only touch of heaven she would ever have. For her sin surely would keep her from being acceptable to a holy God. Not that there was anything about herself that she believed was worthy of Him. Didn't He only want those who obeyed His commandments? She had given up on that years ago.

For what? The chance to grasp at a little bit of happiness on this dust ball called earth? Was it worth it?

Even should Nick look favorably on her again, with love in his eyes, would it secure her soul's eternity?

God...

This was nonsense. Or was it? Did she only think it was because her mother living out Christian virtues looked very different than Nick?

Are you there?

She wanted desperately for an answer. Maybe she couldn't expect one with her sin muddling everything in her life and heart.

But the reverend had said that God loved everyone. Could that be true?

What do You see when You look at me?

If only there was a way to see through His eyes. But would she like what she saw...what He saw...when He looked at her flawed heart?

A gentle knock drew her attention to the opposite side of the room where her door was.

Who would that be? Mother with another lecture? The woman had given Betsy an earful while accepting her back into the house.

Or perhaps Father? It was time for him to be home. Would Mother have gotten her claws into him?

Or would it be Maria with Betsy's dinner and a pronouncement from Mother for her to take supper alone in her bedroom?

Even with the risk that she may not like what whomever came to say, she was curious. What did it matter anyway?

"Come in," she called.

The door swung open far enough for Father to poke his head around.

"Mind if I come in?" His voice was gentle, but the hard undercurrent gave Betsy reason to believe that he and Mother had already had a long enough conversation.

Betsy relented. "What can I do for you?"

He stepped into her room, leaving the door ajar.

Was Mother listening from the hall? That would be just like her.

"Long day?" His tone was gentle.

As much as it was not typical of him to come to her room, it was less like him to ask after her day.

She would participate, but her gaze wandered back to the window. "Yes."

"Rain's coming down pretty hard."

She nodded. She could have been out in that. Could have almost been to Nick's by now. Why, oh why didn't she continue?

"Listen," he said as he eased farther into the room. "Your Mother tells me that there was some sort of confrontation today. With the Hammond brothers."

She jerked around. Why, she wasn't certain. Dare she feign surprise? She wasn't. "I suppose you could say that."

"I hope you know that your mother and I just want what's best for you."

Betsy fought down the urge to snort. Perhaps Father wanted what was best. Mother just wanted *her* way.

"But there are certain agreements you make when you accept a courtship."

Not this. How many courtships were broken off every day due to a lack of compatibility?

"And..." Father continued, "You must think of your future. I know you think you care for Nick. But you cannot turn a blind eye to Karl's offer. And that hope for a comfortable living. Your mother and I won't always be here to take care of you."

Betsy shrugged and shifted her focus back to the rain, which was now no more than a drizzle.

"I want you to think about that. Karl is a solid man, with a certain future. You have no idea what it is like to scrape by and have to work hard to make a way in life."

He wasn't wrong. Betsy knew. Just not in the same way he meant.

But she didn't know what of this was him talking...or Mother's manipulation. Was Father always bending to Mother's will? Did he have his own opinion?

She bit at her lip and nodded.

"I'll leave you. But I want you to think about what I said." The sound of his footfalls neared the wall with her door. Then paused. And came back toward her. The scent of tobacco smoke and mint surrounded her as he pressed a kiss to the top of her head.

Then he was gone.

And she was alone once more.

Nick pushed on through the rain, he cared not how it poured. He had but one thought—get to Betsy. She needed him. And that was all that mattered.

So, he trudged onward, urging the horse through the mud-packed pathways. The horse resisted at times, but he encouraged the animal forward. As he went, the rain let up and became little more than a heavy sprinkle, but the roadways were still mired and slowing his progress.

After what seemed a lifetime, the Callaway home stood before him.

This was it. What would he do if her mother answered the door and denied him access to Betsy? That was a real risk.

What if her mother had locked her in her room? If Betsy was trying to get to him and couldn't? That, too, was a real possibility. One he was prepared to face. He would not be turned away.

As he dismounted, he gave the horse a good pat. She had served him well. For that, he was grateful.

Taking a breath and steeling himself for the worst, he moved to the front door. It was now or never.

He lifted a hand and knocked.

Though he expected their servant to answer, when the door opened, that was not who he faced off with.

Mr. Callaway stood just inside, his features betraying nothing. How had he come to the door so quickly? The man must have been waiting.

"Mr. Hammond," was the only greeting given. Would he not invite Nick in out of the sputtering rain? At least the front porch was covered.

"Mr. Callaway," Nick started, a bit flustered already. "I would like to speak with you. But I must ask to see Betsy first."

Mr. Callaway stepped forward, now fully blocking the way into the house. His frame was not bulky, but Nick did not wish to force past him. It was not that drastic a situation...yet.

"*Miss* Callaway is not able to receive." His words were not harsh but decided all the same.

"Please, sir, I need to make sure she is well." Nick hoped his words did not reek of the desperation he felt.

"I can attest to her health. But she doesn't wish to see anyone. Especially you."

Again, though it was difficult for Nick to hear, Mr. Callaway's tone was straightforward.

Could that be true? That Betsy did not wish to see him?

Then he remembered his words to Anya. He had to trust Betsy, and trust in what they felt for each other.

"I beg your pardon, sir, but I don't believe that." Though the conversation remained civil, Nick's delivery became tight.

Mr. Callaway frowned. "I don't care what you believe. She will not be seen."

What could Nick's do? Press in, past Mr. Callaway? Risk engaging the man physically and injuring him?

"Respectfully, sir, you cannot keep us from each other forever. It won't work."

One of Mr. Callaway's eyebrows quirked. "And you are certain she feels the same?"

The hesitation in Nick hurt him more than the forced separation. Still, he answered with a firm, "Yes."

Mr. Callaway stepped onto the porch, the drizzle now having stopped. And he closed the door firmly.

Did he think he could block Nick? If Nick wanted to go in, he could and he would. But his sense of propriety held him in check. For now.

"I did want to speak with you," Mr. Callaway started. "Shall we sit?" He indicated a pair of rocking chairs to the right.

"Again, no disrespect, sir, but I'd rather stand." Nick's patience started to slip.

"Very well." Mr. Callaway's tone hardened. "Suit yourself."

The man stepped to the closest rocking chair, not bothering to look back. Did he trust Nick not to trespass into his home?

Nick hated that he was right. Such an egregious action would be a last resort.

Mr. Callaway sat and rocked.

"Sir, I don't mean to be rude...but I would like to know—"

"I have a proposition for you." The man did not look in Nick's direction but stared out at the yard.

Would he offer Nick money to go away and stay gone? Did he think so little of Nick's integrity?

"I'm not interested in your money, sir. Your daughter and I are not business transactions that come out to some tidy total."

Mr. Callaway jerked his regard to Nick. "Will you hear me out?"

Nick let out a long breath. It wouldn't serve him to anger Mr. Callaway. That would only make things more difficult for Betsy. Much less, for his efforts. So, he would listen.

At length, he nodded.

"I know of your aspirations."

Nick furrowed his brow. What was Mr. Callaway talking about?

"I have...connections higher up the chain. I could make an assignment as a U.S. Marshal a reality."

Nick paused. Was that true?

Mr. Callaway rose and stepped toward Nick. "I have the resources to set you up nicely with such a commission. And with comfort."

Nick couldn't imagine it. But it didn't matter. It tugged at his heart, but the beat of it was for Betsy. For a life with her. That was surely where God led. Not a pay-off with everything Nick had worked for and dreamed of.

"You don't want a wife to slow you down and hold you back. I don't want my daughter to spend her days alone, in a home that is not suited to her comfort." Mr. Callaway leaned forward. "It would serve us both."

Nick licked his lips. "I won't sell your daughter...and our future..."

Mr. Callaway held up his hands as if in surrender. "Do you really want that kind of life for Betsy? Lonely and far away from everyone and everything she's ever known? Would you do that to her, *Deputy*?"

Nick sucked in a breath as he tightened his features. "I want every good thing in the world for her, sir. You must know that."

"Then leave her be. She will get over this infatuation. As will you. Don't let some flitting feelings," he said with a wave of a hand, "...dictate the whole of your future. And hers."

"You are making a fine offer...more than I could hope for," Nick said, not wishing to deny how attractive it was. "But I cannot accept."

Mr. Callaway shrugged. "Have it your way, then. There will be nothing of the kind when Betsy tires of you."

The older man walked past Nick and to the front door.

"And she will. She'll come to her senses. The future you offer is no life for her. I know my daughter. It's only a matter of time. Then you will be broken-hearted and still a low-placed civil servant."

Nick's pride took a beating at that, but he held firm.

"Either way, you need to get off my property. Or I will send for the sheriff. And then you might not even have a hope of a future in the law." The man opened the door and stepped inside.

Nick's body tensed. But he must hold strong to his faith in God's plan, his faith in what he and Betsy had. What else did he have left?

CHAPTER 27

Decided

etsy looked at the dawn streaming sunlight into her room. The day was new and fresh, but not for her. She had been awake throughout the night. At first, waiting for Nick to come. Then wondering why he hadn't. Had she done something to anger him? Was he upset that she didn't come to him?

Still, the fact remained that he had not come for her.

Maybe she wanted too much. Maybe she looked for the fairytale—the prince riding to the aid of the princess.

One thing seemed certain—God either hadn't heard or hadn't cared. Could be both.

She sat up, pulling herself to the edge of the bed. What did the day hold? And after, what did the rest of her life hold?

Might she remain abed, ruminating in her disappointment? That may be best.

A solid knock landed on her door. Who dared disturb her?

"Who is it?" she called, not truly wishing to speak with anyone. Least of all her mother.

But that was who opened the door.

"Gracious, girl, do you intend to stay in bed all day?" The words held a hint of judgment. That was all she knew from her mother, though—judgment and manipulation.

"I may." She pulled her knees to her chest. Her hair, which she had not braided for bed as usual, cascaded down her back.

"I can't do anything with you." Mother groaned and turned.

"Why?" Betsy's voice shook.

Mother paused and looked over her shoulder. "Why what?"

Betsy glared at her mother as she fought tears. "Why do you hate Nick so? Why is he unfit in your eyes?"

Mother shifted to face Betsy fully, her hands clasped about her waist. "You are a beautiful girl."

In spite of herself, Betsy's lips tipped in a small smile.

"And as senseless as you can be."

Betsy balked. It wasn't as if she couldn't have guessed her mother felt that way, but the woman had never come right out with it.

"What future could you have with such a man?"

Betsy sucked in a breath, gathering what courage she could. "One filled with love."

"Love...indeed." Mother scoffed. "I had love once. Or so I believed."

Betsy arched a brow. Did she mean that she and Father no longer had caring feelings toward each other? That wasn't something that Betsy needed to hear.

Mother stepped within the room and sat on the opposite side of the bed. "He was a good man...tall, handsome, and the most shocking burst of red hair I'd ever seen."

So, not Father.

"You never told me about this." Betsy watched her mother as the woman gazed toward the ceiling, her mind in another time and place.

"Alas, one day he up and left town...without so much as a good-bye. Then your father came along and made an offer for my hand. He had good prospects and my own father was more attracted by his offer."

What was she saying? That Father was her consolation prize?

Mother came back to herself and pinned Betsy with a stare. "Love doesn't last. It doesn't provide. It is unreliable. And I don't want to see your heart broken." Mother reached out to touch Betsy's hair. "God did not make you so beautiful for nothing."

Betsy looked out the window.

"If only he'd give you better sense."

Snapping her gaze to her mother, she opened her mouth to naysay such a pronouncement.

But Mother stood and said, "That will be all. Stay in here for a day if you so choose, but you will make yourself presentable for Karl on the morrow."

"Mother, I'd rather not—"

"That is not up for discussion. You will not throw away all hope of a comfortable life for such a silly notion as love." With that, Mother whirled and left the room, slamming the door as she did so.

Betsy swallowed as she tried to absorb it all. Was it true? Would the strength of her feelings for Nick not hold up under the weight of their differences? Dare she put her life in something so flighty?

But could she deny her heart and how it ached...no, *yearned* for Nick and him alone? The future she thought she had seen ahead blurred in the light of day. Perhaps she had been wrong.

Nick struggled to make his feet move. The day had come in bright and warm...though he was not to embrace it. His heart ached, wounded by the things that had filled the day before. Could one bit of hope carry him through?

It had been a long night, a night of wondering and worrying. What if Betsy decided he wasn't worth the risk? Could he move forward? What if they did marry? Would having a wife affect his ability to chase after his dreams? Could he give up everything he had wanted?

Sacrificing for her was not the problem. But God had no doubt called him to be a lawman. And how much more could he affect change for the better as a U.S. Marshal? It was about more than his wants or desires.

But what Betsy's father had said rang in his mind—dare he consign Betsy to a lonely life, weeks and months at a time without anyone? Moving here and there, living on the trail...

She wasn't cut out for that life, not really fashioned to be the wife of a man such as that. Could he force something that wasn't part of God's plan? All for the sake of his heart? A heart he had dedicated to the Lord and to God's future for him.

How could he take it back now? As if that were possible. He had determined long ago that he would follow Christ to the end. It may be time to stop fighting the flow of the story God was telling in and through him, and surrender.

Only...he feared his heart might not bear it.

Coming to a stop, he looked at the sign hung above the entrance. The letters of the word 'JAIL' lay stark against the brightness of the day. Everything was a mess. Pa had been imprisoned. Because of Nick's doing?

That was where the evidence had led. But it didn't change that something about it nagged.

Pa had always been an upstanding citizen, a man of integrity. Though much could have changed in the time Nick had been away. This man, who had rescued his wife, an immigrant, from certain destitution and gave her a life beyond her dreams and had loved her and had raised his children with a fear of the Lord burning in him...it didn't seem to suit.

This level of greed did not fit.

Yet, for the sake of the man that had raised him and turned him toward the Lord's path, Nick owed him a conversation. One that would be difficult. How would Pa receive him? That mattered not. He would do what was right.

He pushed the door open and stepped within.

The sheriff's desk greeted him. Only, it was occupied by Deputy Gyles, who looked up from a novel.

"Deputy Hammond, how might I help you?" He placed a marker between the pages and set the book on the desk, then reached for a tin coffee mug that had no hint of steam about it.

"I came to see my fath—Mr. Hammond."

"Oh?" Deputy Gyles's eyebrows rose. "I don't know that I have leave to let you."

Nick stepped closer, keeping his focus forward and not on the movement in the cell to the right. "Harry, I am asking as a favor. He's not just a prisoner, he's my father. And I owe it to him to let him tell his side...if he will."

Deputy Gyles looked to the right, as if to examine the security of the space about the cell. But Nick knew better...the deputy needed a moment to consider his request. "I'd rather speak with the sheriff before I allow anyone to—"

Nick set a hand on the desk. "I'm saying please."

Gyles watched Nick, the deputy's gaze seemed rather conflicted.

"You know you can trust me. Besides, you'll be here the whole time."

Gyles watched him. "I do trust you. And I'll give you the respect of your privacy." He reached for his book. "I'll be right outside though if you need me."

Nick nodded, his throat tight. "I thank you."

Deputy Gyles moved around him and stepped outside, closing the front door behind himself.

Then Nick had no other distraction. He glanced in the direction of the cell in time to see his father's figure shift. The shadow he cast moved from nearer the bars to the cot within.

How should he approach? What would his father's mood be like? Would the man be angry? Injured by the part Nick played in his arrest? There was only one way to find out.

Forcing his feet toward the barred barrier, he paused and met his father's gaze.

Pa sat upon the thin mattress. His jacket had been removed as well as his necktie, but even so, he remained one of the more distinguished men about Cripple Creek. Always had been.

"Have you come to gloat?"

Pa's words surprised. Gloat? Why on earth would his father think this was something he relished?

"No, sir." Nick wanted to avert his gaze, look at the floor...look anywhere else. But his father deserved better.

"Then why are you here?" Pa folded arms in front of his chest. Maybe a bit standoffish, but what did Nick expect?

"I came to hear you out."

"Oh?" The man quirked a brow. An expression Nick knew well. Pa was intrigued.

Straightening his shoulders, Nick pressed into the difficulty. "I think I owe you that much."

Pa sighed, uncrossed his arms, and leaned forward on the edge of the small cot. "I don't know how this happened."

Nick grabbed a nearby rickety wooden chair, pulled it over, and sat. "What was your involvement?"

Pa's glare caught Nick's. "I know the trail points to me, but I would never disrespect the people of Cripple Creek in such a way. But I can't expect you to believe me after..."

Nick swallowed. "After what?"

"After the way I received you. I wouldn't blame you if you thought all manner of horrid things about me."

Nick let out a breath. "I don't." And he meant it.

The fault always seemed to fall on his shoulders. Hadn't Nick been the one to turn his back on his father, his family, the future Pa had built for him? He had been the one to walk, well...*run* away.

Pa seemed to relax. "I don't understand how it has come to this."

Then Nick cleared his throat. "There is no denying that it was an inside job."

Pa nodded. "It certainly seems that way."

"And there aren't many employees of the bank."

Again, Pa nodded. "That's true."

"Mrs. Iverson was quite clear that she had kept you in strictest confidence about her jewels." Nick had no choice but to lay it out. "Unless... did you tell any of the tellers or..." He let his words fall as he hesitated to continue. "...Karl?"

While Nick's interactions with Karl had been less than pleasant, he couldn't see that his brother would do such a thing to their father. Much less have opportunity.

Pa looked to the ground and shook his head. "No...I kept her confidence. I did not even share it with Karl."

"Did any of them have access to the safe in your office?"

Again, Pa shook his head slowly. "I don't think so. If anyone did, it would be your brother."

Did he refer to Karl as such on purpose? For it certainly hit the mark. And though there was a part of Nick that questioned Karl's involvement, he didn't truly think Karl would do something like that. Not at the risk of Pa's bank. That wouldn't make sense. It was Karl's future.

"Besides your brother generally steered clear of my office. He had his own, after all. There wasn't cause for him to suspect the safe had anything so valuable."

Nick nodded. Even with what Karl had said and done, Nick had no desire to see him blamed for something he didn't do. But there was a part of him that wanted to clear his father's name. Because, when it came right down to it...he didn't believe Pa was guilty.

It didn't change the fact that, as a man of law and justice, he had to follow the evidence.

"I appreciate your visit." Pa's sudden words surprised Nick.

He met his father's gaze but quickly looked to the side. How could he face the man when he was helpless to do anything about his situation?

"How is your mother?" Pa's words were soft.

Nick looked at him. "She is well enough, but certainly struggling with all of this. And with Karl."

"Oh?"

Nick hadn't meant to say that. If nothing else, he and his father had always been honest with each other. "Yes. He is rather upset about this. It's causing him to...act out."

"I see." Pa's nod brought his regard to the floorboards. "And your sister?"

"She is lashing out in her own way." Nick worked the muscles in his jaw as he clenched his teeth. How else could he explain Karl and Anya's actions?

"This must be incredibly difficult for them." Pa's voice was firmer than Nick could have expected. "And it's my fault."

Nick rubbed a hand along his stubbled chin. "Do you believe that?"

"It must be...not in the way I'm being accused, but I had a duty to protect Mrs. Iverson's property. And I failed. In that, I am guilty."

Nick seamed his lips, determined not to say things he would regret.

Pa's gaze settled on something in the distance. "It is a terrible thing indeed to leave an old man alone with his thoughts."

Nick dared not speak.

"He finds that there are a great many regrets in his life." Then he looked at Nick. "Things he can't undo, no matter how much he wishes he could."

Nick squirmed. The conversation had taken a turn. How could he face Pa and let the man see his hurt?

"I..." Pa took in a breath and let it out. "...think I am tired. Might you excuse me? I would like to take what rest I can."

Nick nodded. As he stood, he found that his chest was tight.

Pa didn't move. Had he only wanted to get rid of Nick? Perhaps. The space between them had become tense and strained.

Nick walked toward the door, but something held him back. He paused near the desk, fighting the impulse to promise things he couldn't be certain to perform.

But the words pressed out before he could stop them. "I will find the truth, Pa. For you. For all of us."

With that, Nick rushed to the door and stepped outside. How would he fulfill such a vow? Were there any pieces of the puzzle that were an ill fit for where they landed? And if so, what were they?

CHAPTER 28

Mercy

Mother had been rather difficult...and pushy. There was no leeway for Betsy to slink away from her responsibility. So here she stood, outside the bank, in her best dress with hair done up in a complicated, yet elegant design.

No need to put off 'til tomorrow what she might get out of the way today. She would see Karl today. But she still couldn't make herself go in.

With Mr. Hammond in jail, she was surprised to see the bank open. But, she supposed, business must go on. Besides, Karl had proven plenty capable of running the bank without his father present. If only it hadn't had to happen this way. Could it be that Karl's odd behavior yesterday was due to his father's arrest?

She could hope.

Still, the urge to move on and delay her confrontation with Karl filled her. Might she have reason to pick up something at the General Store to aid in quelling any remaining ire? That seemed sound enough.

She lifted her skirt in the front so the hem wouldn't drag quite so much and turned toward the General Store. It stood just down from the bank, just a short walk away.

Betsy had not quite forgotten that the last time she was in town, Anya had publicly shamed her.

Even had she neglected to recall it, the stares and whispers around her served as quite the reminder. It didn't matter. She would push through. After all, it wasn't the first time...

After what felt like hours, she made it to the entrance of Mr. Yerby's business. Catching her breath, she pressed in.

The couple of ladies chatting near the checkout counter fell silent and stared. Had they not expected Betsy to show her face in town ever again? What was that dramatic pause about? If they did it for effect, they'd best keep it moving. For it did nothing to injure Betsy. Or so she determined.

Mr. Yerby looked up from his ledger and, after a blank expression for a moment, he nodded in greeting.

She would not let their reactions define her. Lifting her chin, she marched farther into the store to the anonymity of the aisles of goods.

Glancing up and down, she searched for something that might suit Karl. But the items blurred.

No. She would not give these busybodies the satisfaction of her tears.

Shaking free of those confounded emotions, she refocused on the shelves. Only to find herself in an aisle of baking goods.

She frowned to herself. That would not do.

I will conquer this.

Strolling to the next aisle, she looked at carved figures and other trinkets. That seemed a waste, but what else might she purchase for him? Pickled peppers? Nonsense.

Although...he'd be hard-pressed to turn his nose up at a jar of Mrs. Yerby's strawberry jam. She often provided some to stock the shelves. Karl did have a taste for the fruit. Maybe she could find some. After all, strawberry season had passed.

Making her way to the aisle of canned goods, she hunted for the jams. Then for the strawberry jam. She spotted that there was only one jar left...and smiled. It was hers!

But as she reached for it, someone on the other side of the shelf in the next aisle grabbed for it as well. Their hands collided.

She looked up, determined to fight for the delectable sweet. And met Katherine Sullivan's gaze.

Betsy jerked her hand back.

Katherine, likewise, seemed surprised. After a span of seconds that passed incredibly slowly, Katherine waved and said in a soft voice, "You take it."

As if Betsy hadn't tried to take enough from the woman. Guilt slammed into her anew. "No, I insist. I'll...find something else."

With nothing further, she whirled toward the door and rushed off.

She couldn't do this. None of it. Facing the townsfolk, or Karl...or, least of all, Katherine. It was unthinkable.

A rush of movement behind her had her bemoaning what might be next.

Betsy refused to turn. She pushed on faster.

The footfalls picked up pace and a hand fell on her shoulder. "Betsy."

It was Katherine. And she was breathless.

Betsy owed it to the woman to at least let her speak. It was her due.

So, Betsy stopped and turned. "Katherine."

She wanted to look to the ground. Meeting Katherine's gaze seemed too bold. And too difficult. Still, her former schoolmate deserved Betsy's full attention. So, she looked Katherine in the eye. And waited.

Katherine put a hand to her stomach and sucked in several breaths. "You are quite difficult to catch."

There was a little movement toward a smile on Katherine's lips. That couldn't be. This would be nothing short of torture. But she would let Katherine have her moment, let her spill her frustration and deliver the words Betsy fully deserved.

"Sorry. I..." Then Betsy looked down. "I wasn't certain you wanted to see me." But she forced her chin back up. She would not rob Katherine of her moment.

Soon enough, Katherine caught her breath. "Can we talk?"

Betsy took a moment to steel herself. "Of course."

"Can we...go somewhere a little more private?"

Now that surprised. Did Katherine not want to take hold of the opportunity to do this where it could do the most damage? Betsy had not been so kind in her actions toward the Sullivans. In fact, she hadn't cared who saw or who knew.

Still, she nodded. Perhaps Katherine wanted to remain good and righteous in the eyes of the townsfolk...not let everyone hear what horrid words she would use.

Betsy could give her that.

Katherine held out a hand in the direction of the café. "Can we grab some coffee?"

That also surprised. Katherine gave every impression that this would be a kind, friendly chat.

Betsy waited for the slap of reality but couldn't find it in herself to deny Katherine what she was owed. So, she again nodded and followed Katherine to the town's favorite eatery. A place they would still have quite the audience.

Mrs. Abby greeted them, her eyes widening. "May I help you?"

"We'd like a table. And perhaps some coffee?" Katherine said. "Maybe some of your peach cobbler too?" She looked to Betsy.

"None for me, thank you. Just coffee." Betsy still couldn't figure out Katherine's plan here. She'd just have to wait to find out.

Mrs. Abby led them to a table near the window.

Great. More onlookers. Was this Katherine's plan? Wedge Betsy in and trap her in the café? Then lay into her for everyone around to hear?

But the café was largely empty. The breakfast hour had passed, and it wasn't yet time for lunch. More and more curious.

They settled into their seats and Katherine set her basket down, then adjusted the utensils at her setting. At last, she folded her hands on the table and looked at Betsy. "You look quite lovely today."

"I thank you. That is kind." Then Betsy pulled in an uneasy breath.

"It's been quite pleasant this morning. Especially since the heat has—"

Mrs. Abby brought their coffee mugs, a small pitcher of milk, and a bowl of sugar. "Your cobbler will be out shortly."

Katherine smiled and nodded. Then went about fixing her coffee.

Betsy didn't think she could stomach anything right now. But eyed Katherine's. Would she be wearing it soon?

Then Katherine paused. "Look, Betsy..."

Here it comes.

"...I don't want things to be awkward."

What?

"Haven't we struggled enough between us?"

Memories flooded Betsy's mind—of the schoolyard teasing and taunts she sent in Katherine's direction, of her unabashed pursuit of Wyatt, of her overtures after their wedding. But most of all, she thought of Katherine's best friend, Ellie Mae, whose death resulted from a dare Betsy issued. All for the sake of gaining Wyatt's attention. It was all her fault. And she'd never been able to bear it.

"Betsy?"

She shook her head. "Just...ah...remembering something."

Katherine's smile was kind and sympathetic.

Did she know what Betsy thought? What she felt? It seemed as if she empathized.

"That's what I wanted to talk about. Our past has not been pleasant. But I'd like that to change."

She couldn't mean that.

"I've seen...a change...in you. Nick certainly thinks so." Katherine took a sip of her steaming brew.

The mention of Nick's name drove the invisible dagger deeper into Betsy's heart. But she tried to stay present.

Katherine continued, "I...don't know if it's possible, but I'd like us to be friends."

This was unimaginable. "Why?"

"We've been through so much. More than many. And it seems time to bury whatever hatchet remains between us and move on. Don't you think?"

Betsy swallowed, not trusting her own voice, yet knowing she needed to say something. "But I...have sinned against you. Greatly."

Katherine set a hand over Betsy's. Her touch startled, yet soothed. It was a foreign feeling. "And I have been forgiven much in my own life. There is no sense in holding a grudge. None."

Betsy didn't know what to do with that. Spite she understood, hate she understood, manipulation she understood...but forgiveness? "I...don't deserve that. Least of all from you." She looked at their hands.

Katherine leaned down while peering over as if trying to catch Betsy's gaze. "None of us deserves grace. That's what it's all about."

Betsy swallowed against a rising thickness in her throat. Was this what God's grace was like? Was it possible He could forgive her? Wasn't He the judge of all mankind?

"I know this is a difficult conversation. But I really do want to ease the tension and bring some light back. I know Wyatt would like that too."

When Betsy spoke, her voice had more force than she'd thought possible. "I don't understand. I tried to steal your husband. I tried in every way I could. I was manipulative and underhanded...and you want to forgive me?"

"Yes." Katherine was serious. Everything in her affect spoke to such.

But Betsy looked into her eyes and saw how difficult it must be for Katherine to even have this conversation. Yet the gentle woman, her old schoolmate pushed through all that.

Perhaps honesty *was* the best response. "I...don't know what to say."

Katherine smiled and leaned back as Mrs. Abby strode to the table with a small dessert plate, piled with cobbler.

After the woman left, Katherine leaned in and said, "Just say you'll give it a chance."

"No."

Katherine's eyebrows arched and her eyes widened.

"I mean...not until I ask you for your forgiveness."

Katherine's lips curled upward. "A thousand times over, it is given."

Betsy wiped at the moisture that ran down her face. When had she teared up? There was nothing more to say.

Katherine's fingers fell on her hand again. "Please say yes."

The tightness in Betsy's chest eased. And she wept.

The sun beat down on Nick. For whatever reason, he had ridden out to Mrs. Abby's homestead. That was a lack of foresight. She was not there, of course, as the café would be open, but neither was Mrs. Iverson...as he should probably have guessed. It would have made more sense if he were to have looked about town first.

He returned to the center of Cripple Creek and found Mrs. Iverson

—and her eager claws—at the dress shop. But she had nothing further to contribute beyond that she never dealt or spoke with anyone at the bank except for Pa.

Something still nagged at Nick. So, he found himself looking to the café. Dare he disrupt Mrs. Abby this close to the lunch hour?

There was an antsyness within that would not settle. And he knew, it could not wait. Had his father not earned the chance to be freed? If he were innocent. And that was where the rub lay.

Nick wanted to believe that he was. In fact, there was a part of him that *needed* to believe that.

So he marched to the café, thanking the good Lord for a breeze. And extending that prayer to asking for favor in his endeavors.

He stepped within the dining area and was greeted by one of the ladies who worked for Mrs. Abby.

"May I help you, Deputy?" The young lady blinked rapidly at him. Was there something in her eye?

She wasn't in school the same years as Nick, so he wasn't certain about her name.

But she offered him a bit of a sly smile and he realized...she was flirting.

His face heated. It was no revelation that many of the ladies in town found him rather handsome. Still, he wasn't used to being an object of affection. The girls in his school days were always nice enough, but they'd been too caught up on the fact that his mother was a Russian immigrant to show any genuine interest.

By and large, they'd ignored him.

"Deputy?" the young woman's voice interrupted his wayward thoughts.

"Oh...my apologies. I am looking for Mrs. Abby."

The server frowned. "She is rather busy right now."

"I know. But I really need to speak with her if at all possible. It will only take a minute." He didn't often use interest in him to his advantage, but he did smile at the younger woman.

She grinned. "I'll see if I can get her." Then she moved off in the direction of the kitchen.

He scanned the dining room. What if Mrs. Abby spoke with a table of customers? Perhaps he might intercept her.

His gaze landed on a table by the window and his heart stopped. There was Betsy. Her features were worn, and her eyes reddened. As if she'd been crying. About him?

Now that was rather conceited. Hadn't her father dashed any hopes he'd had? Not entirely. Perhaps he should speak with her.

His heart raced as he took a step in that direction. But he noticed her companion—Katherine Sullivan. What would the two of them have to chat about?

As he watched, he noted that they were engaged with some amount of interest. That was new. Perhaps something had come from a random interaction. Maybe even...some healing?

He couldn't bring himself to interrupt, though it didn't stop his gaze from settling on Betsy. She was beautiful. Always had been. But in that moment, there was something different about her. Something lighter. Something new.

Perhaps he had been over-reaching, a fool to think she could really care for him. Their kisses had spoken volumes, especially her reaction to him. But that wasn't always a good indication of the future. Maybe...

Mrs. Abby scurried to him. "Deputy, I hope this is important. I have much to do before the crowd descends."

"It is, Mrs. Abby. Might I ask to speak with you somewhere more private?"

She folded her arms. "No. It's here now or somewhere else later. After the lunch rush."

Nick frowned, but there was no way he could wait. "Very well. I wondered if you had any recollection of your sister speaking with anyone else about her jewels."

Mrs. Abby's eyebrows furrowed. "No. She was very private about them. She only talked about them at the bank, with Mr. Hammond. Is that all?" She turned.

He reached for her arm. "Please, Mrs. Abby. It's important."

She looked down at his hand.

"Look, if my father is guilty, I need to know for certain. And if he isn't, I need to see him released. My mother is terribly upset, and my sister and brother are...well, my family is distraught."

The lines about Mrs. Abby's eyes softened. She set a hand to his. "I wish I could help. But that's all I know. She took the jewels to the bank on arrival for safekeeping and insisted on only speaking with Mr. Hammond. Alone. Then again when she took them out and returned them. That's all I..." Her eyes glazed over.

"Mrs. Abby? Did you remember something?"

She waved a hand. "Nothing important."

"Tell me. Any tiny detail, no matter how insignificant, may help my father." He heard the pleading in his voice and hated it. But, in for a penny, in for a pound. "Please?"

"Very well." She sighed and shifted to face him, directing him to the corner. She licked her lips and looked down.

Why? It almost looked as if she felt guilty.

"I...may have talked about the jewels."

That wasn't expected. "With who?"

She shoved a breath out and pinched the bridge of her nose. "Only with one person...at the bank. It was harmless. I didn't mean for—"

"Who was it, Mrs. Abby? Tell me..."

Her gaze jerked to his. "Is this all my fault?"

As much as he wanted to shake the woman, he forced himself to remain calm. "No one is blaming you. And no one will. It's the bandits who have broken the law." Though he held back from referencing the passage in James that called the tongue a restless evil and full of deadly poison.

"It was only with Karl. I promise. No one else."

Nick's pulse raced. Karl? But his brother had said he didn't know. Would he lie and point the investigation toward Pa? Would his brother do such a thing?

"Oh...I've messed up everything. Maybe I was jealous, maybe I was—"

Nick took hold of her shoulders. "You are certain. You told no one else? Maybe another bank employee was nearby..." He grasped at straws. But he couldn't bring himself to believe that his brother...his *brother* would lie and then stand by and let Pa be arrested.

"I don't know...maybe. I can't say that I remember anyone else lingering. We were in the hall outside the offices and the teller had been helping someone else. I just..."

Mrs. Abby droned on, but Nick didn't hear anything further. He had to tell Sheriff Jones. Would it be enough to set Pa free? Or would he be trading a father in prison for a brother behind bars?

Either way, he had to follow the evidence, and let the truth come out as it would. There was no stopping that.

He had to find Sheriff Jones.

"Mrs. Abby," he said, lowering his voice, "It is not your fault. Thank you for your honesty."

She sniffled. When had she started crying? "Of course. Do you think my sister will be angry with me?"

No more so than my brother with me. "I think you will work it out. Again, no one blames you."

She nodded.

"I have to take this information to the sheriff. And you probably should get back to your customers." He released his hold on her.

She tossed a glance at the dining area. "I suppose."

He smiled at her, forcing the gesture as he felt anything but. "Take a minute, get some breaths, and do what you do best."

She nodded. "All right." But there was no lightening to her affect. With her back now to him, she moved off toward the kitchen, a slowness about her steps.

He looked at Betsy once more. At least she wasn't at risk if Karl had done this awful thing. As long as she was thusly settled in conversation with Katherine, he had time to clear this up.

Betsy said a heartfelt farewell to Katherine with a promise to see her again soon. How did this happen? The interaction that should have left her dejected and her heart bruised...had instead given her a friend. Was that God? Could He be working these things out?

She didn't know, but she was grateful.

Turning in the direction of the bank, she paused. Did she truly want to see Karl? Could she withstand another emotionally draining interaction? Besides, she had no desire to encourage him or assuage his ego. Nor did she wish to deal with his proud and demanding nature. Could she skip it altogether?

But Mother would no doubt check on her activities. Ask her how it went. This whole situation was exhausting.

As she strolled toward the bank, she noticed that her steps were lighter than usual. Had the burden of Katherine's coming ire weighed so heavily on her? Perhaps so. And now that was gone. Completely gone. It was freeing.

Her steps slowed. Might she dash it all with a trying conversation with Karl?

She wanted to believe her mother cared and wanted the best for her. As well, Father surely only wanted for Betsy's life to be better. But these last forty-eight hours had left her thinking that might not be the situation at all.

A man caught her gaze. He also moved in the direction of the bank. She was struck by his pronounced limp. His appearance was rather rough, and his bandana caught her eye. It was the same blue that one of the bandits had worn. And his limp was of the kind that would result from a wound...such as a bruised shin.

She locked onto his face, her heart beating hard. Wouldn't her boot to his shin cause such an injury? Could her well-placed kick temporarily lame a man?

Glancing around, she looked for Sheriff Jones or a deputy. No lawmen were about. Could she chance making it to the jail? If she did, she might lose the man among the townsfolk. And he headed toward the bank. Would he and his remaining partner try to trespass again? Take the money they had left behind?

She slipped to the boardwalk and hugged the front walls of the businesses while she kept a keen watch on him and followed some distance behind.

Every now and again, he glanced about himself as if he worried someone followed. Though he didn't look in her direction. When he paused, she'd reach for an apple, a newspaper, or make as if she were quite interested in a window display. That was the best she could do. And it was working.

He neared the bank and stopped again at the north corner of the building, looking this way and that. What was he doing? Gauging the crowds and wondering if now was the time to strike? Or looking for his partner in crime?

Apparently decided, he moved into the alley between the bank and the haberdashery. Then he was gone.

She sidled along the buildings in that direction with some measure of caution. Soon enough, she was at that same corner, but shielded from the alleyway by the haberdashery. Leaning her back against the building, she tried to school her breathing, hoping that would slow her racing heart. It did not.

The very real fear that she might lose track of him filled her. Might he cause more mischief and mayhem, or worse, shoot someone? Maybe it would be Karl who suffered. Or an innocent teller.

She couldn't allow that. The memory would certainly haunt her for the rest of her life. And Nick would never forgive her if she let something like that happen. Especially if she might prevent it.

Taking a deep breath and steeling her nerves, she looked around the corner.

The man walked down the length of the bank and disappeared in the direction of the bank's back access.

She had to stop him.

Filled with a renewed sense of purpose, she sprinted as much as possible with her long skirt into the darkened passageway. Her breaths came in gasps. She bit at her lip and forced her inhales and exhales to even out and quiet while her lungs screamed for release. But she was almost there.

As she stepped to the back of the buildings and looked toward the bank's rear entrance, she found only the vacant stairway. Two horses were tethered farther away, tied to a post. Where had the man gone? Into the bank?

She pressed out a breath. Maybe it was best to go get the sheriff or one of his deputies. Or even Nick.

Turning, she rammed into a solid chest.

A sickening laugh filled her ears.

"Looking for something, deary?" The man had a grisly smile. Was this the other bandit? The bandana hanging around his neck was a dingy green.

Once more, Nick's instructions from weeks past revisited her. She struck out her knee and punched at his face.

He gripped her tighter as he hunched over.

She shoved at him. "Get away from me!"

He toppled over, still grabbing at his midsection...or perhaps a bit lower.

She spun toward the alley. She had to get help.

Something solid landed on the back of her head. And all was dark.

Nick had been trying to reason with Sheriff Jones for the longest time. He had shared what he discovered from Mrs. Abby. And, while the sheriff seemed concerned about this new information, he was not about to do anything rash. Least of all, release someone he had reason to suspect.

"I just can't, Deputy Hammond. Not based on this small piece of information."

Nick let out a breath and set his hands to his gun belt. "No? Can we at least question Karl?"

"Certainly. In fact, I think we should." The sheriff met Nick's hard gaze with a glare. "Let's go over there right now."

Nick nodded, but there was a hesitation in him. As much as he wanted to see his father released, he didn't wish to see his brother in a cell. Maybe more than that, he didn't want to discover Karl's duplicity.

As he turned in the direction of the bank, he spotted Katherine Sullivan rushing toward them.

"Sheriff Jones," she called as she ran. "Sheriff!"

The sheriff paused, as did Nick, and waited for Katherine to close the distance.

Sheriff Jones called into the jail for Deputy Gyles to grab a glass of water. Then shifted his focus back to the out of breath woman drawing near.

By the time she slowed to a stop, Deputy Gyles had stepped to the door and handed the sheriff the water. And now the older man extended the glass to Katherine.

She waved a hand. "I...have...to...tell...you." Her words came in pants.

"Slow down. You won't tell us anything if you collapse." Sheriff Jones held out the water again.

She took it as Nick set a hand to her elbow and steered her to a nearby bench.

Then she gulped the water, nearly spitting it back out. Then she slowed her sips.

"What happened?" Something foreboding tugged at Nick. Katherine had been with Betsy. Had something occurred between them? Where was Betsy?

Or, had Katherine discovered that Betsy was perhaps involved with the bandits? He chided himself. That was less likely. They had attacked Betsy. He'd seen it himself. They'd left her injured.

Besides, he had to put some faith in her. Regardless of how discouraged he'd become. Or how dejected.

Sheriff Jones held up a hand. "Give her a minute."

Katherine shook her head. "You don't have a minute. Betsy's been taken."

Everything in Nick's being froze.

"What do you mean?" The sheriff's voice rose.

"Betsy and I had coffee. But after we parted, I noticed her following a man." Katherine seemed sheepish as she shrugged. "I was curious."

"So, you followed Betsy as she was following this man?" Nick's words rushed out.

"Yes. She went into the alley behind the bank. I was worried, so I watched her discretely. Or at least I hope I wasn't spotted." Katherine scanned the street.

"I'm sure you weren't," Sheriff Jones soothed. "You did well."

"What happened in the alley?" Nick fought past the sick feeling welling in his stomach. It made his words harsher than he'd have liked.

But it didn't seem to faze Katherine. "She followed the one man, and another attacked her from behind."

All warmth drained from Nick's face and his head swirled. But he firmed his stance and pulled himself together. He wouldn't do anyone any good that way.

"She knocked him down, but the first man hit her in the head with the handle of his gun. Then the two carried her off behind the bank." Katherine's wide-eyed stare landed on Nick. "You have to help her. Now!"

Nick didn't need to think twice. He raced in that direction.

The calls of the Sheriff followed him, warning him about an ambush or some such nonsense.

But Nick ignored him. He had to get to Betsy. If he wasn't too late already. He rushed to the bank, cutting to the left as he approached. His feet pounded, echoing through the dark alley. Then he popped out behind the bank.

And found nothing.

Nothing but the signs of a scuffle.

But no one was there—not the bandits, not Betsy.

He wouldn't give up yet. Running to the far corner of the bank, he found evidence of horseshoe tracks. But nothing more.

She was gone.

He had to get to his horse. There had to be a trail. He would follow it and find her. And he had to do it now.

Nick made his way back to the front of the stores, intent on the jail where he had left his rented horse.

But as he stepped into the sunlight, the sheriff met him.

"Slow down." Sheriff Jones's voice was gruff. "You can't go off like that."

Nick wouldn't be delayed. He continued toward the jail, the sheriff trailing him.

"Stop," Sheriff Jones called. "Deputy!"

As much as his heart fought to keep going, Nick paused and turned. He leveled his gaze on the sheriff. "They have her. And Lord only knows what they are capable of. They might..." He couldn't finish the sentence, though he couldn't blind himself to the possibilities. "I just...I have to find her." He pressed on.

"I understand the urge to rush off half-cocked." Sheriff Jones moved into his path again. "But we have to think about this. Or else you and who knows how many others will be killed."

Nick flared his nostrils as he pushed out a breath that felt a bit too big for his body. "I can't just stand around and wait."

"Where will you go?" Sheriff Jones's tone sharpened. "Do you know where they took her? Do you even know who *they* are?"

Nick looked to the side. Sheriff Jones was right. And he hated that.

"I want to get these criminals every bit as much as you do. But we need a plan."

There was sense in the sheriff's words. Not that Nick had to heed it.

"I'm sorry, Sheriff. I have to take that chance." He pushed on toward his horse, loosening the reins from a post and pulling the animal around to mount.

"What if you get her killed?"

Nick halted. And looked over his shoulder.

"Hear him out, Nick." Katherine was suddenly next to the sheriff.

"Without a plan, you not only risk your life, but hers." The sheriff's features were set.

Nick let out a long breath. "I'm listening."

CHAPTER 30

Taken

Betsy's head hurt. That was inescapable. She shifted and it hurt all the more. What was this?

She opened her eyes but saw nothing. Total darkness.

Was she blind? What had happened?

Closing her eyes again, she searched her memory.

The alley...the bandit...and something had slammed into the back of her head.

Did that explain the blindness? And how she got here? She ran a mental inventory over her person, moving different parts of her body to test for any broken bones or bindings.

Nothing bound her, and no one inhibited her movements. She lay on a mattress that must be thin, as it offered little support. And it smelled. Goodness, it smelled. Reaching out, she felt beside the mattress and found what must be the floor. So, the mattress wasn't on a frame.

Her head hurt something fierce. And the smell that accosted her—earthy with an undercurrent of waste and urine—nearly had her gripping her stomach. The fact that she kept her last meal was nothing short of miraculous. However, the nausea may be more likely due to the headache or head injury.

It hurt her head to move anything, but she couldn't take a chance on staying put. Whomever had left her here would be back. She had to take the advantages she had.

Rolling over, she landed on the hard floor on her hands and knees. There was a scratching to her right, muffled though it was. She prayed it was a squirrel outside the room rather than a rat scurrying inside.

What did it matter? There was good enough reason to push on even without that added challenge.

Crawling forward, her shoulder hit something. She bit her lip to keep from crying out.

Feeling along the object, she decided it was a wooden stand of some sort, perhaps decent and sturdy enough to help her rise.

Leaning against it, she tried to maneuver her larger than necessary skirt. Why were women never dressed for these kinds of situations? The damsel in distress was always, like her, in a fine gown. Useless.

Finally, with only a bit of stumbling, she was on her feet. But where was the wall? The door?

She reached out. And banged her hand on the wall. Hard.

Shaking the offended extremity, she wanted to scream at her luck. Still, she managed to keep her mouth shut.

Then she moved to the wall, side-stepping around the space, keeping her hands on the flat surface.

As she walked, she let her mind wander. Fear about her vision swelled. But she bit that back too, she couldn't let that take over. She closed her eyes...or did she? Were they already closed? She wasn't certain.

Either way, she paused, setting her forehead to the wall and breathing desperate words.

God, help me. I don't know what to do. I don't know how to face this on my own. Be with me. Show me.

When she opened her eyes and started moving again, the smallest pinprick of light shone from off to the right.

She saw light? Holding back a shout of relief, she fought tears. Could it be that God *was* with her? That He had heard her? That He cared?

As she paused, a rumble of voices came from the other side of the wall. She couldn't discern the words, but there were men outside...wherever this place was.

She held her breath, hoping to catch something, anything that might give her a clue.

The scratching became louder and something furry brushed past her skirt.

A sharp inhale was all that kept her from screeching. Then she bit her fist. What was that creature?

Wait. Where were the voices? Had they stopped? Had they heard her?

Across the room, a creak sounded, and light flooded the space.

She shut her eyes against it, grimacing as it pierced her head. Slamming her back against the wall, she threw an arm up as if that might block the pain.

"Hey," a rough voice said. "Look who's awake."

She slid along the wall, trying to create more distance, but a hand gripped her forearm and jerked her forward.

"Imagine that," the other voice muttered. "And she's ruined that pretty dress."

"Sad thing," the first voice said on a laugh. "Let me help you with that." Hands gripped for her skirt and tugged as if to tear it. But the stitching held. Thank goodness for that.

Betsy slapped at the man, her vision slowly adjusting to the brightness.

He ducked. And his companion reached forward and grabbed her wrists. "Now, now, we'll not have that."

Hoofbeats thundered outside of wherever they were.

"It's the boss," the first man seethed.

"Bout time," the second ground out. "How long did he expect us to just sulk in this forsaken shack?

Betsy stilled, she would bide her time and choose her moment.

The two men looked at a door on the far side of this outer room. This room seemed perhaps bigger than what she could discern about the one she awoke in. That room had been little more than a dark hole, without windows or any other opening to the outside. Who would construct such a cave-like space? Had this been someone's house?

This space, however, had light pouring in through a window and a slim doorway. Taking in the poorly constructed walls and weathered doors, she decided this structure was a worn down home…it appeared almost as if it had been taken over by children. A smattering of cloths and dishes were scattered without rhyme or reason.

The one man jerked her to himself. "We'll let him decide her fate."

Unkept teeth appeared in the other man's smile as he waggled his eyebrows.

He would not trespass on her. Of that, she was determined. She would die first.

Whomever their leader was stopped a horse just beyond the door. Shadows and outlines were visible about the poorly sealed door. The person—a man it seemed—tied off the horse and stepped to the flimsy barrier.

Then it opened.

"What is she doing here?" came his exasperated words.

It took another several moments for her eyes to adjust to the direct sunlight now streaming in. But her mind screamed with recognition.

Boots clomped, stirring up more dust as he came closer.

Then she was looking directly at Karl Hammond.

"Turn her loose," came his insistent command.

"But, boss—" one man argued.

Boss? How was he involved in this?

"Let. Her. Go." Karl's voice held a threatening air.

The first bandit shoved her toward him.

She stumbled, but Karl caught her. This must be some mistake.

"Are you all right?" His words softened.

Yes, for certain this was a misunderstanding. He didn't lead this ragtag band of thieves.

Karl looked at the criminals. "Why did you bring her?" he demanded.

"She followed me," the one with the limp said.

"And she attacked me," the other added. "What would you have us do after she saw our faces?"

Karl pushed out a breath. "Go and gather the trunks. It's time you made yourselves scarce."

The men trudged out of the shack.

"Karl…" Betsy's voice shook as she spoke. "What is all this?"

He cupped her face. "It's nothing for you to worry yourself with. I'm just doing what I can to secure our future."

"Our future? What about your father? The bank?"

"Quiet!" His jaw muscles hardened. Then he set his other hand to the other side of her face. "I have to make sure my...brother...doesn't risk our happiness. Or our wealth."

"But...*this*? Why?"

"Nick was getting in the way...and would stop us. Eventually." Karl's eyes were darkened by the shadows of the dim interior, but they were wide. And wild.

"But your father was giving you the bank. Your future was secure."

"*Our* future," he yelled, gripping her hair and tugging her closer.

She whimpered.

"You don't understand. Nick was his favorite. Was *always* his favorite. The firstborn, the child of hope. I was second best. Always."

"But you don't think your father would have—"

"I said 'quiet'!" He growled. Then his grip eased, and he ran a hand down the side of her face. "Just trust me. I'm doing this for you."

Had he framed his father? Had he directed the bandits to attack the stagecoach...maybe stagecoaches? Risking the lives of innocents? "No. You've betrayed your father, your family, countless people..."

His brow furrowed. "An acceptable cost."

"You can't mean that." How was this happening?

The lines of his mouth tightened. "You *will* understand. In time."

Nick urged his horse onward. Was there any hope? Every second that passed put Betsy in greater danger. Of all manner of horrid outcomes.

But he wouldn't think that way...he couldn't. One thing was certain —he'd keep going until he found her. Come what may.

She needed him. And that became the heaviest driving force he had ever known.

"Let's rest the horses." It was Wyatt. He had been deputized for the manhunt. A few men in town had been called upon and encouraged to do so. Wyatt had been the first to volunteer. And had joined Nick's search.

Sheriff Jones led a small contingency, as did Deputy Gyles. The lawmen assured Nick that they wouldn't rest until Betsy was home safe.

Indeed, they did all they could. But the truth remained that she could be anywhere.

Nick gritted his teeth. The need to continue weighed on him, but Wyatt was right. The horses could only do so much without some manner of rest. Leading the way, he turned his horse to the right and down the hill to where a stream trickled by.

Wyatt dismounted and took off his hat, rubbing at his forehead with a cloth.

Frustrated by the delay, Nick wanted to remain astride. But it would be best if he refilled his canteen and refreshed himself in the few minutes they had.

If only their hopes of learning more from Karl hadn't been dashed. After the abduction, they found one of the tellers alone in the bank, the only person in charge. That wasn't how Pa did things. Nor did it sit well with Nick.

He still resisted the idea that his brother was somehow involved in this. Surely there was some sort of mistake, a misunderstanding perhaps.

Wyatt patted his horse's side and filled his own canteen. The two now crouched beside the small stream.

Nick kept his mind on their mission. His thoughts whirled with his knowledge of the area and where the band of miscreants might hole up.

Wyatt glanced across the seemingly never-ending wilderness. "I pray the others are having better luck."

Nick grunted. Why think on their failure thus far? It frustrated him.

Then the doctor's gaze was on him. "We've covered most of our assigned area. We need to check the cavern near Victor, but apart from that, I don't know what to tell you."

Nick's head dropped. Yes, he realized this too.

Come on...

He knew Karl better than anyone. If his brother was involved...*if*... where would they hole up?

A part of his mind bucked at the very notion. But if he were to get to Betsy, he must consider all possibilities.

"Nick?" Wyatt's tone was even.

Had the doctor entreated him multiple times?

Nick looked down, sealing his canteen after a swig. "Yeah?"

"We will find her."

Nick nodded. He wished he had Wyatt's faith in their ability. For every minute that passed, he became more dismayed. He stood and straightened his shoulders.

"We will," Wyatt insisted. "There is a real chance that one of the other groups has come upon them already."

Nick wanted that to be true, but he doubted.

Wyatt rose. "I've been thinking and praying..."

Nick watched the horizon. "Oh?"

"There's only so far they can go with a resistant, stubborn hostage such as Betsy."

That was a thought. After all, she was quite feisty. And he had no doubt she would fight with everything she had.

Wyatt eyed him. "And the bandits would want to be somewhere familiar."

Nick nodded. "You think they have a hideout they work from?"

A nod was Wyatt's only response.

Again, Nick didn't want to think of Karl being involved. He'd never seen those other men in Cripple Creek. Nor had the sheriff. They must be from elsewhere, likely hired guns. It made sense that Karl, if he were involved, would have a place that he felt safe. Felt in control. A base of operations...

Images flashed through Nick's mind. And he knew.

He grabbed for the horse's reins and put a foot in the stirrup, hoisting himself into the saddle.

Wyatt's arched brows and curious stare followed him. "Nick?"

"I know where they are." They had to go. *Now.*

If he were correct, if it was Karl, there was no time to waste. The band of miscreants may stay put for a time, but with the heat of the situation, they would move out as soon as possible. With or without their hostage. And if she became too much trouble, they might decide to just be rid of her.

Wyatt rushed around his horse and lifted himself into the saddle. "Where?"

Nick didn't want to take the time to explain. But he spat out some brief words. "Karl and I used to play in an abandoned shack some distance from town. Near the old Independence lode."

"That's a ways off the beaten path."

"Exactly...secluded and familiar."

Wyatt frowned. Did he resist the thought that a longtime friend could be so devious?

But, again, they had to explore all possibilities. Even the ones they didn't like.

Nick put his heels to the horse's flank, spurring the animal into a trot.

Lord, open the way and watch over us. Grant us success!

CHAPTER 31

Found Out

Nick and Wyatt dismounted and tied off their horses a distance from the shack. They crept closer, using the scant grasses and shrubs for cover. And they paused when they had a good sightline on the structure.

Two men stalked about, loading a wagon. That must be the hired help. Had they hurt Betsy? Was she bound inside the small building?

Nick's vision blurred as rage bubbled up. He would make them pay.

He spotted a familiar looking chestnut colored mare with a darker mane. Karl's horse? Many horses had that same coloring. It didn't mean anything. But they were here, at his and Karl's hideout. The chance that Karl was not involved slimmed.

Wyatt's hand fell on Nick's shoulder. The doctor signaled that they should slink back.

He shook his head. They were close. Too close to retreat.

But Wyatt's eyes narrowed and the muscles in his jaw firmed. He would not be dissuaded.

With hesitant movements, Nick followed.

Wyatt came to a stop a few feet shy of the horses. He turned on Nick. "We have to go for help."

"No." Nick's response was sudden, shooting out before he gave it a thought. "We can't abandon her."

"If she is there, they have secured her in that...whatever it is. And from what I can see, there are three of them. With her life on the line, I don't like those odds."

Nick ground his teeth. This couldn't be happening. "I won't leave without her."

Wyatt looked over Nick's shoulder in the direction they had come. "It's not a smart move, Nick. It's just not. Are you willing to risk her life?"

Nick closed his eyes. "No." Opening them once more, he glared at Wyatt. "I understand what you're saying, but you have to understand... what if they run off with her? To somewhere we can't track? What then?"

Wyatt's eyebrows met and lowered. He was silent for some time.

"Why don't you go for Sheriff Jones, or Deputy Gyles, or any able-bodied man that can aim a pistol. I'll hide and watch."

"I can't leave you here. You'll do something rash."

"I will wait for reinforcements." He was no idiot, but Wyatt was right. Could Nick reasonably trust himself to hold back if it appeared Betsy was in imminent danger?

Wyatt arched a brow. "You expect me to believe that?"

"That's what I'm offering. Go without me or stay and we'll make a go of it the best we can alone."

Wyatt shook his head as he looked to the ground. "You're putting me in an awful position."

"*I'm* in an awful position."

"I know that." Wyatt's words were even quieter. "But you're thinking with your heart, not your head."

Nick flared his nostrils and firmed his stance. "That's my offer. Take it or leave it."

Wyatt studied him for a long moment. Then shrugged. "All right. I'll go. But promise me you won't do anything rash until I get back."

Nick wasn't sure he could make such a promise. Would it be okay to lie to his friend? No, Nick was a man of his word. So, he held his tongue.

"Whatever," Wyatt threw up his hands. "I'll be back as quickly as I can."

Nick looked toward the shack.

The crunch of boots on dry grass told that Wyatt moved on to his horse.

"Keep your head on straight," Wyatt whispered harshly as he mounted.

Nick turned just as Wyatt steered his horse in the direction of town.

Then he was gone.

Stepping to his own horse, he patted the side of the animal's neck. He needed a minute.

God, don't let me be a fool here. Protect her. Guide me, guard me...be my way.

Shifting his focus to the shack, he crouched and moved toward it.

Betsy pulled her knees to her chest as she sat on the mattress once more. Only, the door to this smaller room remained open and so some light came in. Enough for her to see that Karl paced. He strode back and forth, unhurried, as he talked to himself. It was more of a mumbling. Such that she couldn't make out what he said. Would it worry her more if she could?

There was a real part of her that wondered if this was the end. The more time that passed and the longer she watched Karl...*really* watched him, the more concerned she became that he wasn't quite sane.

One of the bandits came back into the smallish structure. "We got everything loaded. What's the plan?"

Karl jerked toward him.

Silence.

Did Karl have a plan? Was he unsure about speaking it aloud?

Then she knew...this would be the end for her. These men would not permit Karl to keep her around. She would slow them down, in every way that she could. And Karl dared not release her if he thought he might return to Cripple Creek at some point.

What, indeed, was his long-term plan? He had spoken of his and her future together. But he couldn't realistically think that would be in

Cripple Creek. Too many people sought justice. And Nick drew closer to the truth.

Nikolai.

The worst part of facing her mortality was that she wouldn't see him again, wouldn't be able to tell him the things that were in her heart. She didn't want him to wonder if she had cared for him. She did. So much.

But after the last several days, how was he to believe that?

And there was little hope she might tell him now.

Lord, Touch his heart. Heal it. Help him find love.

These spurts of prayer had become more regular throughout this ordeal. And...more than that, she actually believed God heard. And cared.

That was new.

When did that begin? The day she nearly went into the church to find solace? When Katherine forgave her? Or had it happened incrementally since the day Nick saw something more in her?

She didn't know, but the tiniest seed of faith had grown into something she put hope in.

Boots stomped across the rotting floorboards.

Coming back to the present, she jerked her regard up to see Karl closing in.

Using the wall, she rose. "W-What is it?"

"You're coming with us." He held out a hand in her direction.

What? That didn't seem right. But what could she do? Let them take her away where her parents, and Nick, and anyone else who cared would never know what happened to her?

She was decided. "No."

"What did you say?" Karl approached her, stopping just inches shy of her. "Don't be obtuse. Come here." He held out his hand again.

She pushed it away. "I'm not going with you. We both know how this will end. You might as well kill me now. I won't go with you."

His features contorted into something menacing. Then he grabbed her arm and pulled her toward the door.

She fought. Hard. Scratching at him, clawing at his grip, hitting him.

He kept dragging her. How was he this strong?

Now that they were out in the open, he threw her to the ground.

Her hands stung from the contact they had made with him, her fingers were sore from effort, and her body ached from slamming into the hard earth. But she lifted her gaze to his.

"Do you want me to kill you?" He spat out as he drew his revolver. There was something uneven about the way he now moved back and forth rapidly. His eyes were wild, and his features were pinched.

"No, I don't," she said tightly. She wouldn't cower and she wouldn't beg for her life, but she wasn't about to play into his sick game either.

He put his hands to the sides of his head. "Stop it!"

She swallowed. Her whole body tensed, as if prepared to run. But that would be foolish. And unbecoming. If he was going to kill her, he would have to look her in the eye and do it.

Rising, she stood firm as her fingers curled into fists.

He stepped to her. "You want to live?"

"Of course, I do." As much as she tried to hold her voice steady, it wavered. "But I won't grovel."

He glared at her. It became clear that he didn't know what to do. His plan had fallen apart...what of a plan there had been.

The other two men stood near the wagon.

"We don't have time for this," one hollered. "Be done with it."

"Don't tell me what to do," Karl said as he spun and leveled the gun on the man.

The bandit stepped forward. "Don't you point that thing at me. Have you forgotten who you're dealing with?"

Karl's breathing became heavier.

The other man stepped forward too, elbowing the first man. "We got it all loaded. Let's cut our losses and get out of here."

They shifted their weight as if to turn back toward the wagon.

"Quiet! I told everyone to just be quiet!" Karl pulled another gun from its holster and held one on the grimy men and one on her. "Don't make me do this!"

"Karl, you're not thinking clearly." Betsy kept her voice gentle.

He turned both weapons on her. "Quiet!"

One of the bandits rushed Karl.

A gun fired.

Betsy ducked. Had she been hit?

Nothing hurt. She looked at the men, now locked in a tugging fight for the guns.

This was her chance. Now. She whirled and ran in the opposite direction.

Weeds grabbed for her voluminous skirt, tripping her here and there. Still, she ran.

The sounds from the scuffle became a little more distant. She wanted to breathe out relief, but the danger wasn't over. She had to keep pushing her legs onward.

Arms grabbed her around the waist.

She screamed as she was lifted from her feet. Clawing and kicking, she became desperate to free herself.

"Betsy," a voice near her ear yelled. "It's me."

Nikolai?

But dare she believe it? Could her mind play tricks on her?

Taking a chance, she stilled.

He turned her to him, arms still wrapped about her.

Thank You, Lord! She touched his face. "Nikolai..."

He grabbed her hand and pulled at her. "We have to go."

More shots fired in the direction of the shack.

Would the victor come after her? Or take their ill-gotten treasure and run?

It didn't matter. They had to create distance. And fast.

CHAPTER 32

Endgame

Nick's heart beat as if it would burst. He wanted to help his brother, but he ached to get Betsy to safety. There was still great danger.

They moved slower than he wanted, but with her impossibly full skirt, it couldn't be helped.

If only there was a moment to spare to tear off the bulk of the dress and make easier their escape.

No matter...they were nearly to the horse.

A shot rang out, pinging past his head and spooking the horse.

He halted, turning and pushing Betsy behind himself.

There stood Karl, a crazed look in his eyes, gun raised in their direction, with cuts and swelling about his face. He'd been beaten, but he'd come out the other side.

Part of Nick was relieved. He had been certain his brother could not stand against the two thugs. Yet the danger remained. No matter how he felt that he knew his brother. Perhaps there was still hope.

"Karl," Nick called. "Put that down."

"I won't." He stepped closer, a definite favoring to his left side. "You can't have her. You can't."

Betsy side stepped as if she would come from behind him.

Nick held his right arm back to stop her.

"Karl, please..." Betsy's voice had become desperate.

Where was the woman who had faced down the butt of a revolver and stood? But Nick now stood in the way. Did that mean she cared for him so deeply she would risk herself?

"I...will go with you." Her words held a tremor.

"Is that so?" Karl's eyebrows rose.

Nick would not have it. "There's only one way we're going to end this." As much as the possible outcomes tore at Nick's heart, he had to face it. There was a good chance one of them wasn't walking out of here. And he needed to make peace with that. Somehow.

Lord, guide my hand.

"Grab his guns, darling," Karl demanded. "Throw them over there." He waved the pistol off to Nick's left.

"Do it," Nick murmured.

Betsy grabbed for his guns with trembling hands, removing them, and then carefully tossing them as directed.

"There now," Karl said as he smiled. "Come to me, Betsy."

Nick held both arms back to hem her in. "No."

Karl's eyes widened and he cocked the gun.

"You know this won't work. The authorities will come after you. Do you really want that—the life of a fugitive?" Nick held firm.

Karl snarled. "What would you know about what I want?"

"We are *brothers*. Always will be. I know you, and you know me. Don't make this more difficult than it already is." Nick's throat became tight. "Think of Pa...and Ma. And Anya. They don't want anything bad to happen to you. *I* don't want to see you harmed either."

"But you've taken everything from me. *Everything*."

The words Karl had spewed hit Nick oddly. "What are you talking about?"

"Pa was never going to give me the bank." Karl's hand shook. Was his resolve melting?

"Of course, he was."

"He never trusted me. Not like he trusted you."

Nick wondered if Pa had seen something none of them had. "Why would you think I would take it from you?"

"Why not?" Karl shrugged. "Fine brother you turned out to be. You took Betsy from me."

Nick stepped forward. "This is about me. You need to let Betsy get on that horse and—"

"No, Nikolai..." Betsy murmured, setting her hands on his upper arms. "You can't..."

Karl smiled again. "I think we are done talking. Now," he said, retraining his gun on Nick. "Send Betsy to me."

Nick stood to his full height. "You'll have to shoot me first."

Karl watched him. With his affect flat, there was no way Nick could determine what he thought.

"That, I can arrange." Karl let out a laugh that sounded nothing like the brother he had known.

And the air split with a bang.

Betsy screamed as the gun went off.

Nick stumbled but maintained his footing. For a moment. Then he fell to his knees.

"Nikolai! No!" She looked at Karl, fear and anger in her heart.

But he was likewise slumped.

Then she spotted one of the bandits standing behind Karl with a gun in hand.

Had the man fired? Had there been more than one shot?

She leaned over Nick as he fell farther to the ground, now lying on his back.

"Nikolai?" She searched for the wound.

A dark red oddly shaped circle grew from the upper right of his chest.

"No," she cried.

Boots pounded the earth. Was the bandit coming after her?

She jerked her regard in that direction to find him running the other way. But it did not escape her notice that Karl was laid out on the ground as well, unmoving.

The ground rumbled. She looked the other way and saw a small contingency on horseback coming toward them. A sheriff's badge caught the sunlight.

Nick gathered her hand in his. "You have to go. Get help."

Betsy fought her tears as she squeezed his hand. "Help is here. Hold on."

He nodded, but his breathing was ragged.

"Nikolai," she said, running a now reddened hand over the side of his face. "I have to tell you. I need you to know that I..." She swallowed, emotions getting the better of her.

"Don't..." He murmured. "Don't say things you don't mean just because I got shot." His lips spread in a smile.

"Nikolai..." She pulled his hand to her heart. "You have to know. I can't live with myself if I didn't tell you the truth."

His gaze wavered.

"Stay with me," she pressed. And leaned over him, careful not to disturb his wound. "Nikolai!"

"It's getting difficult...to stay awake..."

"No," she pled. "You stay here."

The hoofbeats came closer. And slowed.

"Get the doc," someone yelled.

"Nikolai," she pushed out through tears. "I won't leave you. Don't you leave me either."

His eyes slid closed. "You're safe." Then his body went slack.

Wyatt knelt at Nick's other side and pushed her hands away. "I need to see."

She leaned in. "Nikolai..."

Wyatt motioned for someone.

Strong arms lifted her.

She fought them, but they held firm.

"You need to let the doctor work." It was Deputy Gyles.

"But...I told him. I said...I wouldn't leave him." She muttered through her sobs.

Sheriff Jones was instantly at her side. "Doc knows what he is doing. If there's hope, Dr. Sullivan will pull him through."

She couldn't respond, couldn't nod. Couldn't do anything but resist as they tugged her farther away. "I have to stay."

Sheriff Jones looked to his deputy. "Take her back to town."

"I won't go," she insisted.

"Think about Nick." Sheriff Jones leveled his gaze on her. "He needs space. And he would want us to get you to safety."

Nick's words to her echoed in her mind. The sheriff was right.

She stopped fighting and allowed them to put her astride a horse.

Then Deputy Gyles mounted behind her. "He's tough. A fighter."

She nodded but stared after the place where Nick lay as the deputy spurred his horse onward.

Outcomes

The world was hazy...and had been for who knew how long. Nick wasn't certain he could discern where he was or who stood over him. He prayed it wasn't someone with nefarious intentions. For he had no way to defend himself. Or Betsy...

Betsy!

He struggled against the hold sleep had on him. It wooed him, but he resisted. He had to get to Betsy. Had to ensure she was well and safe.

A vague memory claimed him as his mind joined his body in coming to life.

Then he hurt. God help him, he hurt.

He couldn't move his arm or his shoulder. And the ache in his body kept him still.

A figure leaned closer. "Nick?" The voice was comforting in its familiarity—Wyatt.

Was he in the clinic? Was he well? He certainly shouldn't be with the level of pain he was in.

"Nick, you awake?" the voice entreated again.

He moaned. It seemed the only sound he could emit.

Hands gripped his wrist. "Pulse is nice and strong."

Nick opened his eyes. While his vision was somewhat blurred, he took in the world around him. He lay on a bed in a small room. Was it perhaps one of the rooms in the clinic?

Wyatt watched as Nick became increasingly aware.

"You there?" Wyatt continued to try to engage him.

"Yeah..." Nick heard the muffled, groggy word. Had it come from him? His throat was raw from the effort.

"You sure did give us a scare." Wyatt's face came into focus. He smiled down at Nick. "I told you I couldn't trust you."

Nick tried to return the smile, but his parched mouth longed for liquid. "Water."

"Of course." Wyatt lifted Nick's head and pressed a cup to his lower lip. "Slowly."

Nick obeyed, though everything in him wanted to gulp.

As his dry mouth and throat were soothed, he tipped his head away.

A *clunk* nearby led Nick to believe the glass was set on a bedside table.

But he had to know what happened. There were only images in his mind, disjointed as they may be. The one thing he did remember was the search for Betsy.

He lifted a sluggish arm and motioned Wyatt closer.

The man came a bit nearer. "What is it?"

"Betsy." Nick coughed, trying to clear his throat. "Where is she?"

Did Wyatt read the fear in his eyes? For the doctor laid a hand on his shoulder. "She is fine. Worried about you...though we all are."

"What...happened?"

Wyatt sat on the edge of the bed. "You saved her."

"I did?"

"You sure did."

Nick concentrated and some of the images coalesced into reality. Yes, he had gotten to her. They ran. And he stood between her and danger. Then...

He widened his eyes. "Karl? What happened to my brother?"

The darkness set in his mind could not be. He refused to accept what it told.

Wyatt shook his head. "He didn't make it. I'm sorry."

Nick shut his eyes, fighting the burn of tears.

"I would have done everything in my power to save him. But...he was gone the instant the bullet hit him." Wyatt's tone was solemn. And Nick believed him.

The next question was the hardest to ask. "Did I...?"

"No. One of the bandits survived their physical exchange. And even though that man had been shot, he managed to fire off a round."

Nick frowned.

"The hit probably deflected Karl's aim. Or else your Ma would be burying two sons."

The pain of his physical wounds paled in comparison to how his heart rent in two. His brother...it wasn't possible.

"I might as well tell you the rest. The injured bandit didn't make it far before the Sheriff and his men caught him. The jewels were returned, and any other identifiable valuables were passed on to the stage office. So, you did it. You're the hero of this story."

Why did he feel like anything but the hero? He couldn't save his own brother. But...maybe Karl had been too far gone to begin with. How long had he been unstable? How had they all missed it?

"There is someone who has been anxious to see you." Wyatt smiled. "Actually, she's been a downright nuisance."

Nick looked to his friend. "Betsy?"

Wyatt nodded. "Let me fetch her. You grab what rest you can. It will be a bit of a recovery."

Nick nodded. Or as much of a nod as he could manage.

And as much as his heart was torn, as much as his body screamed in pain, there was a light in that darkness. Betsy would be here soon.

He wanted to see with his own eyes that she was well and whole. That was all that mattered in that moment. That...and a prayer of gratitude.

"Betsy, please stop. You're going to wear a rut in the floorboards." Katherine's voice soothed.

But Betsy only paused. "What else am I supposed to do, Katherine? I can't do this anymore."

"I think it's about time you call me 'Katie.'"

Besty offered a small smile, but soon enough her smile fell as she twisted her lower lip with her teeth.

"He is through the worst. If there were cause for concern, Wyatt would tell us."

"But Wyatt said there is still risk of infection and further damage and..."

"Would you stop it?" her friend gently chided. "And be thankful he is alive?"

"What if he doesn't wake up?"

Katie frowned. "That is always a risk. But Wyatt is very careful with the medicine."

Betsy nodded but chewed on her lip.

Katie patted the bench beside her. "Please, sit."

Betsy looked from Katie to the bench and back. Could she still her movements and her worry for a moment? She could certainly try. This wasn't serving anyone.

Shrugging, she stepped to the wooden seat and settled on it. "There. Happy?"

Katie smiled. "Very."

"I just..." Betsy started, her emotions rising to the surface again. Had she not shed enough tears? "I..."

"What?"

"I'm trying to find my way. But my faith is so small."

"Is it?" Katie said easily.

Was that not a problem? Nick's fate hung in the balance and Betsy didn't think she had the faith to sit here one more minute, much less to pray big prayers. "Katie, I...don't know that I'm cut out for this whole trusting God thing."

Katie's soft smile didn't falter. "You're not?" There was something of a twinkle in her eyes. What was that about?

Betsy let out a breath. "No. I'm new at it, but I wonder...maybe I'm not cut out for it at all."

Katie took Betsy's hand. "The truth is, friend, that none of us is."

Betsy furrowed her brow. "What?"

Katie nodded. "Faith and trust are difficult. Especially in hard times."

"Then how do I...that is, what am I supposed to do when things get tough?"

"Surrender."

"Excuse me?"

"It's perfectly acceptable...better, even, to come to God with your mess and your small faith. You can be honest with Him about that. And ask Him to grow your ability to trust."

"It can't be that easy."

"Then how come it is?"

Betsy let out a loud sigh, wishing her frustration could be expelled so easily.

"I will pray with you, if you'd like."

"Right now?"

"Especially now."

Betsy closed her eyes and let Katie's simple words rush over her. As her prayer came to a close, Betsy felt the urge to add her own words.

"God, I am just now learning what it means to trust You. To really believe in You. It's not easy. And I have things in my past that make me doubt. But I want to believe. Help me."

Katie was quiet for a long moment.

Had Betsy said something wrong? Or maybe she should have said something different?

Then Katie squeezed her hand and whispered, "Amen."

As Betsy lifted her gaze, the door behind her creaked open. She wiped the few trickling tears away as she rose and stepped around to the clinic door.

Wyatt had emerged. "He is awake."

"Thank heavens!" Betsy couldn't help the urge to hug Wyatt, but she turned to Katie and embraced her instead. Then she shifted her focus back to Wyatt. "May I...? May I see him?"

"Of course." Wyatt smiled. "He's in the recovery room."

She waited for him to lead the way, but he moved to Katie and took her hand.

"Aren't you going?" Wyatt asked, his features lined. "Don't wait for me. I'll give you two some time."

She nodded and slipped within.

In moments, she opened the door to the recovery room.

Nikolai lay still. More so than she expected. Was he really awake? Had he gone back to sleep perhaps? Or maybe...?

He sucked in a deep breath and grimaced.

"You *are* awake." Her words rushed out. She closed the distance to the bed.

His eyes opened and he met her gaze. There was a relief in them that stole her breath.

"Nikolai," she breathed as she sat on the bed opposite his wound and took his hand. "Do you hurt?" A tear fell. She did nothing to stop it.

He reached their clasped hands up to catch it. "Not now."

She pressed his fingers to her lips. "I was so worried. So...scared."

"So was I." His voice warmed her. Inside and out.

"Nikolai, I..." How to say it? Her heart burst for her to give him the words. But it almost seemed as if they should come with pomp and fanfare. Not in a quiet room, spoken into the desperation in her soul.

"What, sweetheart?"

Sweetheart. The word was indeed as a balm over her healing heart.

"I love you." It was no great overture, but the words were real, and they were honest.

His eyes glistened and he grasped her hand. "Good."

Had she heard that correctly?

"Because I am so in love with you, Miss Callaway."

And for that moment, everything felt right and whole in the world. But just for that moment.

Then reality came screeching in.

"Nikolai?" Her mind said it wasn't the time, but her heart needed to know. "What will we do? How will we make a future for us to be together?"

He tugged her closer.

She leaned over him.

"Let's worry about that tomorrow." Then he pulled her nearer, such that their lips were but an inch apart. "Are you going to kiss me?" His voice rumbled in his chest...a pleasant feeling under her hand.

She pressed into him with care and let this moment be enough.

CHAPTER 34

Resolutions

Nick sat in a chair in his old room at the Hammond homestead while his mother busied herself about the room. The woman had not stopped moving since he'd been brought here several days past. How did she have the energy? For his part, he spent more time sleeping than he cared. 'Recovery' was how Wyatt phrased it. And he'd said it was necessary. So, Ma insisted upon it.

A knock on the already opened door startled him. He looked up from watching his mother fuss with the sheets.

Anya stood just outside. "May I come in?"

He waved her in. "Of course."

The last few days had been difficult for him and Anya. She seemed to carry some guilt about all the happenings between him and Betsy and Karl. Pair that with the grief over Karl's death, and that left a long road ahead.

But Nick was determined to not be a stumbling block on that path. "How was town?"

"Hot. And busy." She rolled her eyes. "But a telegram came for you. I promised I'd deliver it safely." She strode forward and set the paper in his hands.

"Thank you." He focused on her instead of the paper. That could wait.

Anya shifted from one foot to the other. Then looked toward Ma. "Let me help with that."

Ma and Anya worked together to settle the linens in place. They were quite the duet.

And he was grateful for them. He would be sad to go back to Denver.

But he hoped to take a piece of Cripple Creek with him—Betsy. Though he had yet to broach the subject with her father. Would he consent to giving Nick her hand? Did it matter? Betsy had already said that she wanted there to be a future for them. And that was regardless of what anyone else thought.

Anya took the discarded linens out of the room, and Ma went to fluffing the pillows. Hadn't she already done that?

He looked down at the paper. Might as well.

Opening the fold, he read the contents. It was from Sheriff Brandt. He sent his regards and was glad of Nick's recovery. However, he'd had to replace Nick's position as a deputy due to the extent of his absence.

Nick dropped the paper. That wasn't expected.

Perhaps he hadn't communicated as adequately as he could have with Sheriff Brandt. And, true, Nick had been determined to stay and see the robbery solved no matter what. That wasn't exactly how one spoke to their employer.

Either way, there was no job for him in Denver. No livelihood. No way for him to support himself, much less a family. What would he tell Betsy?

Ma continued to scuttle about here and there.

"Ma, you don't have to—"

Another knock sounded at the door, which remained open.

Though as Nick glanced up, he met Pa's gaze.

The man had not been to see Nick since he got settled. What had made him keep his distance? Grief over Karl? Anger at Nick? What?

"Might I come in?" Pa asked, the lines of his face all the more prominent.

"Of course."

Pa smiled at Ma. "I would like a word with Nikolai."

She gave him a stern look but nodded and stepped from the room.

Nick would wager she wasn't far away, though. Just around the now-partially closed door perhaps?

Pa stood just within the room.

Nick shifted in his seat. Being in bed or in this blasted chair all day wore thin long ago. "What can I help you with, Pa?"

"I...hoped to apologize."

"Apologize?"

"For the way I have treated you."

Nick frowned. Now this was uncomfortable.

"I wanted to decide your future. And I see now that I shouldn't have. It's important that you make your own way."

"Thank you. That means a lot." Nick sighed. "Just as well, I have received word from the sheriff in Denver. I don't have a job to go back to."

Pa's eyebrows arched. "Oh?"

"That's what the sheriff says."

Pa looked down for a moment. "You know, I still need someone to take over the bank."

It was Nick's turn to be surprised. "You mean that?"

"Yeah. I have...worried for some time that Karl was not as...together as he could be. I just didn't want to face it." The last words were choked out. "Maybe if I had..."

"You can't think like that. We were all a bit blind to the extent of his...paranoia."

"Regardless, I won't be around forever. Much as I'd like to be. And I would like to leave the bank in your hands. If you'll have it." Pa's features scrunched in a hopeful cautiousness.

That would solve many problems. It would provide a good living for him and Betsy. She would have all the luxury she'd been accustomed to. He could give her that.

It was very tempting.

"Pa...we're right back where we started."

Pa frowned. "I suppose. But maybe...this is a chance to get it right this time."

Nick sighed. "I am no more built to run the bank now than I was those years ago. It would kill something inside me."

Pa nodded. "I guess I knew that."

"I will pray for direction for you with the bank. The people of Cripple Creek have a lot of respect for the Hammond name."

There was a space between them where Karl's deeds echoed. But neither spoke of it.

Finally, Pa spoke. "Speaking of the bank, I'd best get back." He turned toward the door.

Nick was relieved he'd have some moments to think...about this telegram, about the implications...

Pa halted at the threshold. "You know, son..."

That had Nick's attention. Pa hadn't called him that in a long time. "Yes, Pa?"

"I understood that Sheriff Jones is set to retire. Something about joining Mrs. Abby's endeavors at the café. Less dangerous and all that..."

"You getting at something?" Goodness, how Pa could rant.

"Well, Cripple Creek will need a new sheriff."

Nick's eyes widened. Could that be the open door he needed?

"Just a thought." Pa winked. "But I can't think of anyone I'd rather vote for."

Betsy tried to keep her knees from shaking. This was a big day...for the town and for her and Nikolai. The outcome of the race for sheriff would be announced soon.

She and Nikolai had decided to take a walk to pass the time. Even now, she waited for him to collect her.

Things had been...strained at her house. Her mother refused to speak to her, and her father walked around sheepishly. And she didn't blame him. How could he offer the man she loved a bribe to just go away?

But her mother's tongue had been restrained. That, she guessed, was due to Father's insistence that it be so.

It didn't matter. Lord willing, she and Nikolai could move into their own home soon.

Betsy settled into a rocking chair on the porch to give her legs, and knees, a break. Of course, as soon as she settled, the dirt stirred on the horizon from an incoming rider.

She rose and stepped to the edge of the porch.

Nikolai brought the horse to a halt just short of the raised area. As he dismounted, she rushed to him, throwing her arms around his shoulders as soon as his feet hit the earth.

"You all right?" he asked, a bit of a laugh about his words.

"No...are you?" She pulled back to look at his smile. "How are you not worried?"

"What do you mean?" There was a twinkle in his eyes.

She slipped free of his arms and swatted at him. "Nikolai Hammond, don't tease me. How could you not be more worried about the decision to..." She paused. "Do you know something?"

He laughed outright then. "No, I promise." He held up his hands in surrender. "I just have too many reasons to be happy is all."

She arched a brow in question.

He set an arm around her shoulders. "Shall we take that walk?"

Part of her wanted to resist, to punish him for his obvious glee in the face of their yet unknown future...but she couldn't. "Very well."

He steered her toward the side of the house and the meadow just beyond.

They walked for some moments in silence. Until she couldn't stand it anymore.

"What has you so giddy?" Her voice was more accusing than she'd like. But there was a lot at stake in this sheriff poll.

"I have the prettiest girl in the whole of the territory on my arm. Why wouldn't I be giddy?"

"You charmer. Don't forget 'the feistiest.'" She grinned. Her stubbornness might be a bit much for people at times, but channeled into resolve, it served her well as her faith grew.

"Of course." He pressed a kiss to the side of her head, bringing their stroll to a stop. Then he turned her to face him.

She gazed into adoring eyes and felt...whole. God had brought them together and she would cherish that. Though, how He would prepare the way for their future remained to be seen.

Leaning into his embrace, she murmured. "What will we do if Mr. Yerby's son wins the election?"

He tightened his hold, squeezing her gently. "It doesn't matter."

She jerked back. "What?"

"It doesn't matter. It won't change anything."

"You've become addled." She let out a nervous laugh. "It makes the difference between us marrying this spring. Or waiting for another year."

"Or does it?" he said matter-of-factly.

She set a wide-eyed gaze on him. "What are you saying?"

He took her hands. "I'm saying that I am ready to trust that God will guide us and provide for us no matter what. No matter the results of this race. I am ready to take that leap with you...are you?"

She looked to the ground. "I don't want to stand in the way of you realizing your dreams. It will be so much harder for you to make your way with a wife in tow."

He pulled her closer. "I know I'm the one who said that." He sighed and ran the back of his hand down the side of her face. "But I realized something."

She licked her lips. "What's that?"

"*You* are my dream now. A life with you. A family with you. It doesn't matter if I am Sheriff of Cripple Creek or a hired hand at a ranch or a stage driver or wherever else God leads. I need you in my life."

"You mean that?"

"I do." He tipped his head toward her and set his forehead against hers. "So how about it? Will you be my wife? No matter what?"

She tilted her chin and kissed him. Fully, recklessly, deeply.

When they broke apart, she whispered. "No matter what."

Pounding hoofbeats came nearer.

Nikolai turned, setting a cautious hand to hover over his sidearm.

"Nick," the rider called as he neared. It was Wyatt. He spurred the horse to where she and Nikolai stood.

"This best be good," Nikolai said. "I was about to tell the world this woman here is soon to be my wife."

"That's fantastic news," Wyatt said, a broad smile on his face.

"So, what's the point in you rushing over here?"

"The results are in...*Sheriff*." If possible, Wyatt's grin widened.

Betsy threw her arms around her Nikolai. "God is so good."

Ignoring the fact that the doctor stood by, Nikolai claimed her lips once more. "Always."

Epilogue

Katie put the last of the yellow and white daisies in Betsy's hair then stepped back to examine her work.

This had been the most wonderful day. Friends, old and new, came around Betsy. Loving on her and helping prepare her for this most anticipated day.

Now, with every single piece of her in place, she was ready. Stepping out of the clinic, she found her father waiting for her. She took his arm, basking in his smile.

Would her face crack from the all the beaming? It would be well worth it.

"You ready?" Father patted her hand.

Her father had not only consented to her joining her life with Nikolai's, but he had also blessed the marriage. Mother had not come around, but Betsy had every hope she would...eventually.

She nodded, letting the fabric of her light green dress drag just a bit. "I am. More ready than ever."

He escorted her to the church.

She stopped him just before they reached the door.

"Everything okay?" Father asked, his features drawn with concern.

She set a hand to her midsection. "Just need a minute to catch my breath."

"Take all the time you need." He squeezed her hand. "Just remember, Sheriff Hammond is waiting."

That brought another smile to her face. Could she collapse from happiness? God had brought everything together for them—their lives intertwined, their hopes rebirthed, and their future a road they would travel side-by-side.

Father opened the door to the church and the congregation rose.

Reverend Timothy Johnson stood at the ready by the altar.

Though Reverend Dawson was the town's current preacher, and had been eager to marry the pair, she and Nikolai decided that having their schoolmate and friend perform the ceremony made it all the more special.

As well, Wyatt stood up with Nikolai, and Katie had preceded Betsy down the aisle.

But once her gaze landed on Nikolai, all else faded.

He was her once in a lifetime. The grace of God manifest in her life. Evidence of her redemption in His eyes. And she would cherish it. For as long as they both should live.

Keep reading for a sneak peek of the first book in the Convenient Risk Series!

Thank you, dear reader, for for reading along with me! If you enjoyed this story, I would sincerely appreciate if you would submit a review. It would mean so much to me!

To read more about these characters, follow along with the Cripple Creek Series. Find it at:

https://saraturnquist.com/cripple-creek-series/

Amanda stared at the blood on her hands. Her husband's blood. She was numb. Cried out. She shoved the door open with her hip and stepped into the fading day. Her focus was on the water pump across the yard. The few steps stretched out before her. Holding her hands away from her body, she moved toward it, not caring that she stirred the dust of the dry earth beneath her feet.

The pump's handle was solid and cold. She yanked her hand back. Jed's blood now stained the metal. It couldn't be helped. Grasping the handle once more, she pulled it up then pressed down. Her long blonde hair fell into her face. Amanda fought the urge to push it to the side. Again and again she pumped, until water began to flow from the spout. Thrusting her hands underneath, she rubbed at the dark red covering her skin.

Once all traces were gone, she tugged at her apron, wrapping her hands in the thin fabric. When she looked at them again, they shook. And she could still see the deep crimson upon them.

She blinked. The red vanished.

Spinning on the balls of her feet, she turned back toward the house. The clicking of her shoes alerted her that she was once again inside.

And the smell.

"Where were you?" A gruff voice greeted her.

She jerked in that direction.

The tall frame of the doctor filled the doorway to her bedroom. His scowl accused her.

"I needed some fresh air."

He shook his head. Had she disappointed him? "You were needed in here."

She nodded, lowering her gaze to the floor as she stepped toward him.

He held up his hands. "There's no point now. He's passed."

"What?" It wasn't possible.

The doctor moved past her, his shoulder grazing hers. "It was only a matter of time."

Amanda's heart stopped. Cold surrounded and pervaded her being. Her breath rushed out of her. Would she be able to draw in another?

In time, it did come, but with it came the tears. There were more. After all.

To read more, find *A Convenient Risk* here:

https://saraturnquist.com/convenient-risk/

Hope in Cripple Creek (Book 1)

Tragedy strikes Katherine Matthews and the small town of Cripple Creek, Colorado. An epidemic teams her with an old enemy, Wyatt Sullivan, the town's doctor. In the midst of desperation and death, Katherine has decisions to make. But she has no idea to what extent they will affect her daily life and livelihood.

Katherine faces a crisis of faith and hard choices. Will life ever be normal again?

Christmas in Cripple Creek (Book 2)

Katherine and Wyatt have settled into a well-earned, comfortable life together. Until an unexpected attack threatens to bring an end to their happily-ever-after. And on the cusp of the town's yuletide merriment.

As they come to grips with their new circumstances, they begin to realize the difficulty is far from over. And new challenges arise.

What will become of their family? Of their Christmas?

Faith in Cripple Creek (Book 3)

Jane Millington has come to Cripple Creek to visit her friend. But a few bumps along the way land her face to face with a man who would rather not become entangled. Not that Jane is looking for a relationship.

Saddened to find her friend struggling after the birth of her child, can Jane offer the hope that she needs?

Timothy Johnson still lives with the sting of betrayal. And he is determined to never risk his heart again. But a chance encounter with a woman who is only passing through leaves him curious.

Can Jane and Timothy offer healing the other so desperately needs? Will they be able to see beyond past hurts, lean into faith, and find love?

And the prequels...

Lauren Crawford is nothing she should be. Put off by the War between the States and her own experience on her father's plantation, she longs for something more. Under the control of her parents, there is not much room for anything but submission. Still, she dares to defy them...

The war changed Tom Matthews. And he has plans of going beyond his father's humble farm. He will do whatever it takes to make those dreams come true. Until he finds himself drawn to a southern belle he would rather despise. He is soon caught up in a situation not of his own making.

How much is too much for the one he loves?
Dare he sacrifice his dream?

In the rugged terrains of Cripple Creek, David Matthews' world has always been overshadowed by his father. Each sunrise over Stoneybrook Ranch reminds him of the path laid out before him—a life scripted by expectations he isn't sure he can live up to.

Mary Foster has held a silent affection for David since their youth. And while her mother suffers the ravages of a disease they fight to contain, Mary's heart patiently beats in the hope that when David finds his place in the world, there might be room in it for her.

Will their paths diverge in the vast expanse of the frontier?
Or perhaps love can guide them to find in each other the very thing they are lacking in themselves—home.

Acknowledgments

This is absolutely a book of my heart. Redemption for Betsy was not something I set out to do when I wrote *Hope in Cripple Creek*. In fact, that was intended to be a standalone. However, things happen and the characters continued to speak to me...so we saw more from Timothy in *Faith in Cripple Creek* and found out what happened to the Betsy—a character you kind of enjoyed hating in the first book—here.

I want to thank my critique group for reading scenes and giving me feedback. You are each so valuable to me! As well, to Cindy Smith and Kelly Hollman who read the scenes as I finish them...you are priceless and so necessary to keep me going and keep me honest.

Julie Sherwood, my editor, you continue to keep my stories solid and my work looking more polished. You always push me to make the book all it can be.

Cora, you impress me over and over with your cover designs. These covers for my Cripple Creek Series are no exception.

To the photographer who makes me look good, VerBull Photography, I know I'm taking full advantage of your skills.

For my husband and number one fan, Greg Turnquist, who urged me out on this writing journey to begin with, I could not be more thankful that you saw the potential and have believed in me every step of the way.

For my sister, you make me want to be better. For my dad, you make me feel so good to have achieved this dream of writing. For my mom, I will love you forever. And for my kids, you give me every reason to smile.

Last, but certainly not least, my readers, you give me a reason to keep writing.

About the Author

Sara is a coffee lovin', word slinging, Historical Romance author whose super power is converting caffeine into novels. She loves those odd little tidbits of history that are stranger than fiction. That's what inspires her. Well, that and a good love story.

But of all the love stories she knows, hers is her favorite. She lives happily with her own Prince Charming and their gaggle of minions. Three to be exact. They sure know how to distract a writer! But, alas, the stories must be written, even if it must happen in the wee hours of the morning.

Sara is an avid reader and enjoys reading and writing clean Historical Romance when she's not traveling.

Please follow along with her journey through her newsletter at: http://saraturnquist.com/list

Happy Reading!

facebook.com/AuthorSaraRTurnquist

instagram.com/sararturnquist

x.com/sararturnquist

youtube.com/@SaraRTurnquist

pinterest.com/sararturnquist

Also by Sara Turnquist

CONVENIENT RISK SERIES

A Convenient Risk

An Inconvenient Christmas

A Less Convenient Path

A Convenient Escape

An Inconvenient Acquaintance

These Golden Years

A Less Convenient Arrangement

Ranch Hands Collection (ebook only)

LADY OF BOHEMIA SERIES

The Lady Bornekova

The Lady and the Hussites

The Lady and Her Champion

The Lady and Her Secret

RAILWAY ROMANCE SERIES

Laura, The Tycoon's Daughter

ACROSS THE YEARS SERIES

Among the Pages

Between the Lines

STANDALONE NOVELS

The General's Wife

Trail of Fears

Off to War